CW00384011

*"BANG-UP FOR MEN has got to be one of the funniest and poignant narratives on prison life ever. It captures the absurdity and banality of prison like no book I've ever read. Congratulations on a very fine piece of work."*

Erwin James
of the *Guardian*
Author of *A Life Inside*

*" There are few subjects about which people are more ignorant, or hold deeper prejudice, than imprisonment. Prisoners are a complex mixture of the bad, the mad and the sad, all of whom need help to enable them to live useful and law-abiding lives. Over the years, the arts have proved themselves to be an invaluable entry point for many who could not see how to turn their lives around. However, the process of turning presents many challenges to teachers and taught alike, as Adrian Rudesind brings out vividly in his novel about an art teacher who goes to work in a prison. The author spares the reader no detail of what goes on in the hearts and minds of prisoners. The result is not for the faint-hearted, but not to use their language to describe their feelings, would be not to present the challenge as it is."*

Sir David Ramsbotham GCB, CBE
Chairman Koestler Awards Trust
Former Chief Inspector of Prisons (1995-2002)

*"BANG-UP FOR MEN is the book I wished I had been able to write about my experiences as an art teacher in prison. It is a wonderful account of a journey into a part of society that most people prefer not to think too much about. Adrian Rudesind's first impressions of this world*

*are - like most people's would be - filled with a sense of innocent curiosity mixed with a strong desire to leave. But gradually he reveals to us, through sensitive observations and hilarious commentary, that actually this world is rich with absurd, tragic and highly amusing characters. And that for him, meeting and working with these characters has made his life infinitely more interesting and rewarding than he could have imagined. I really have laughed out loud in recognition of some of the stories, characters and thoughts he writes about!"*

Angela Findlay
Arts Co-ordinator, Arts in Prison Projects
Koestler Trust

*"This book is written with such vivid description that the characters are genuine throughout. It portrays the stark reality and at times, the frustrations of prison life. Adrian Rudesind presents us with a gritty and at times, sad, emotional account that leaves one feeling touched."*

Susan Ashmore
Chief Executive Officer
Anne Peaker Centre for Arts in Criminal Justice

*~Well hello! You out there. I read Bang-Up for Men as a man actually banged up in prison. It was like reading a travel book about the place where you live - you already know it. Ade's book captures the atmosphere of this place perfectly. It's not all stripy pyjamas and razor wire, you know, but daily pain, anger and frustration all interlaced with lashings of twisted humour. This is the bread and butter of prison life.*

*When I get to Fiji and I want to remind myself what this place is like (as if!), I'll pick up the boss's book.*

*PS Where's the chapter about me, then?*

Gareth Thomas, HMP Feldon Park

# BANG-UP FOR MEN

## THE SMELL OF PRISON

Adrian Rudesind
April 2006

Adrian Rudesind

with original drawings
by J.M. Walsh
and
an Afterword by
Angela Neustatter

Starborn

BANG-UP FOR MEN
The smell of prison
by
Adrian Rudesind

First published in 2006
by Starborn Books

e-mail: sales@starbornbooks.co.uk
website: www.starbornbooks.co.uk



The author acknowledges references to the work and ideas of Angela Neustatter as expressed in her book *Locked in Locked out* (Calouste Gulbenkian Foundation, London 2002)

The author and publishers gratefully acknowledge the support of the Welsh Books Council in the publication of this book



ISBN 1 899530 22 3

# CONTENTS

*All names of both characters and places in Bang-Up For Men are fictitious. Adrian Roe, Frosty, Star, Dunaway, Billy, Insect, Jabba, Nigel, Mr Nash etc. are all invented characters. Feldon Park is fictional too. However, there is one exception, and that is Fiji, which really does exist, in more ways than one.*

# PROLOGUE

The smell of prison is a rather pungent cocktail of sweat, roll-up tobacco and disinfectant that pervades the entire gaol known as HMP Feldon Park. It hits you like halitosis as soon as you pass through that big mouth of a door. The fragrance belches itself through the airways of the entire building. Once inside you are immersed, you enter it and it enters you, you become one of the ingredients and can never escape from its grip. This earthy mustiness concentrates in places where men are together for any length of time, places like the gym or the association areas (the shower rooms are particularly bad, so I've been told), but you can smell it no matter where you are. It's borne homoeopathically, wafting along the corridors, through the air vents, into the unlikeliest corners and recesses, seeping into bags, into briefcases and clinging to clothing. It lurks like a stowaway, only to reveal itself, weeks later, when you least expect it. You can be miles away, at home, minding your own business, when *pow!* - one sniff and you're back, as quick as lightning, to the shiny scrubbed walls and floors of Feldon Park.

I often thought of marketing this very male fragrance as 'Bang Up For Men'. A raw, tough scent for gangster wannabes. Once sprayed, you are enveloped in a mist of raw criminality, an aura of incarceration that is completely captivating.

*'The scent you can't escape'...* Like other well known brands already marketed, it evokes attitude and credibility, but surprisingly, this one also has traces of fear and hopelessness that are quite depressing, and take it to an altogether different level of appeal. The smell of fallen angels. Who can resist it?

*'It's tough, it's rough and it's injured...'*

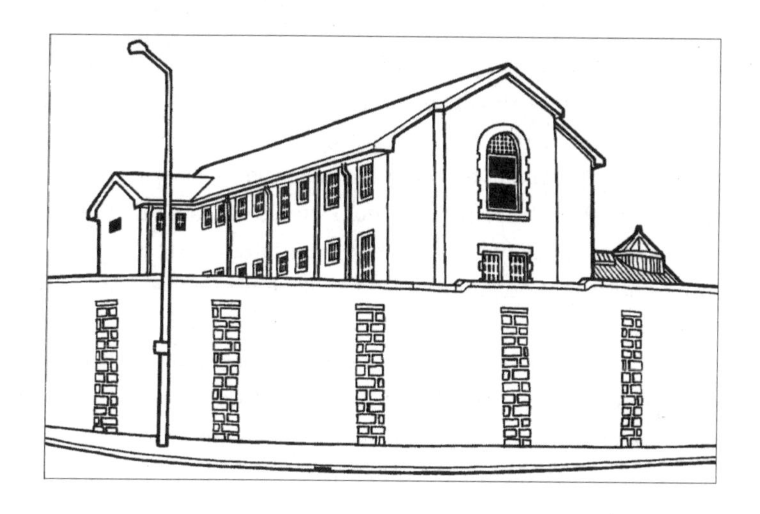

# 1 BIG MOUTH SETS THE SCENE

***Paradise*** *(F. Paradis, L. paradisus, G. paradeisos.), noun. The Garden of Eden, a place or state of bliss; heaven; a park or pleasure ground. The unobtainable. That which is always out of reach.*

Adrian Roe believed in fate, and that if he let it, it would not only shape future events in his life but could also open doors to higher realms, enabling angelic beings to get a foot on the ground and do what they have to do. It only took a short while and the whole course of his life might be redirected as a result. Fate played a part in how this story began, if not completely then at least ninety-nine per cent. There was only one requirement needed to instigate the process: he had to let go of his thoughts, he needed to take a back seat. If fate had something it wished to bring (and it usually did), it would climb into the driving seat and take over, setting the controls to 'whatever'. Some people can do this letting-go consciously - if they are enlightened - but most mere mortals do it unconsciously. One only has to lower the threshold for a few nano-seconds and become vacant, and in steps fate when least expected. You find yourself no longer in control, and the scary thing about it all is that you don't know it's happening until afterwards, and then it's too late. It can leave you open: what will be, will be, and the start of this story finds him at one of those times in his life.

Adrian Roe was a teacher. He taught Art in a private school and it had been going on for too long. He felt unfulfilled, it was all going nowhere rapidly. He had begun to lose his edge, and he needed a change from silver-spooned kids and their silver-spooned parents. Whilst it went against his social upbringing to teach in such a privileged establishment, at the same time, it also was the very reason he was working there. Wasn't his own experience of school awful? Bad? Shit in fact? The bullying, the lack of inspiration, the I-don't-care attitude; and we're talking both staff and pupils here. But it seemed the world was divided into camps, with little middle ground.

Adrian had always had a dream - one of many - that one day he would leave all this behind him and find himself in some tropical paradise teaching adoring native students who would clamour for knowledge that only he could bring them. There would be no social division, no fee paying distinctions. He would live a Gauguin-like, missionary-like existence - without the syphilis, of course - where life's biggest task was 'could he endure any more pleasure and would he ever tire of it?' Come on! It was only a dream, and dreams are unreal by nature. But when a close friend of his landed herself a position overseeing the placement of students in their gap year in Fiji, and had to go there regularly to settle them in, it was as near as dammit the fulfilment of a dream. The problem was that it was not him. Close, but not close enough. 'Hey, I'm over here!' his brain was shouting hysterically, but his face just smiled amiably.

One lunchtime, while poring over photographs of endless white beaches, palm trees and turquoise seas and listening to the tales of islands that were so remote that maybe the placement of some teenage student there was not a good idea, he half-consciously muttered something like:

'I wish I'd done voluntary service when I was young...' To which his friend replied: 'Why don't you do it now? Many organizations prefer "older" volunteers: they're more *mature*, more *reliable*, more *financially stable*...' - and, with a snigger - '...less likely to run off with the chief's daughter.'

Obviously he was not any of these things except the older bit, so was probably less suited to it now than he ever was before. To maintain some sort of inner dignity he said - and this is where his consciousness descended to an all time low and fate stepped in:

'Well, you don't have to go traipsing round the world to find people who need help. They're right here on our doorstep.'

'Oh, and where exactly are you thinking of?'

'Here in South Wales,' he replied. 'All about us are people who have slipped through the net. Look at our prisons for instance, full of youngsters who have never had a chance, full of youngsters who have had the odds stacked against them ever since they were born. These are the people we should be helping. You know, the ones that never had an education. '

'Yes, but they need at least A-levels to do a gap year.'

'Most of those guys would probably have degrees if they were taught properly.' Adrian spoke with a nervous wobble. It had something to do with the fact that he didn't have a degree himself.

A wonderful speech, that. Trouble was, it wasn't him speaking. He hadn't said anything. Fate was talking. He was somewhere on that island, the one that was too far away, rearranging the palm leaf mats on the beach for his next lesson. The closest he'd got to the terrible deprived estates of South Wales was various news reports on TV, and occasionally rushing through them on the train heading for somewhere else.

He went home feeling, 'Ah well, it could be worse,' which really meant 'I'm feeling OK,' which alternated periodically with 'it could be better,' which really meant 'I'm not OK.' What he hadn't realised was that the wheels were setting themselves in motion, and fate was prearranging the next part of his life.

I have forgotten to mention that his friend, when not risk-assessing desert islands in the South Pacific, was a magistrate on the local bench in South Wales. Wearing that hat, she was, unbeknown to Adrian Roe, in earnest conversation with his future paradise atoll.

When they next met up, she presented him with a list of telephone numbers and names.

'These,' she said, 'are the phone numbers of the education departments of all the custodial institutes in Wales. You should follow them up. You never know - they might stop being prisons and become universities.'

He thanked her and scanned the names and numbers in front of him. His eyes lingered just a little longer on the name HMP Feldon Park than they did on the others and, as is the way with such things, his fate was sealed.

# 2 BREAKING IN

*'And God placed at the east of Eden an angel with flaming sword in hand, to prevent Man's entry to paradise...'* Genesis Ch 3 v 24

When Adrian arrived at HMP Feldon Park the funny thing was that he wasn't sure whether he had arrived or not. The entrance was not grand or imposing, but more like a farm gateway than anything 'prisony'. It even had a cattle grid. He drove past it twice, thinking this must be the back way in, but when he realised this was actually it, he entered. Inside was prisonland. The heavens were throwing everything they possibly could at his arrival. Rain lashed all around. (He was later told that this particular part of the country always had weather like this when just up the road 'it's lovely like'.) He knew straight away that this was due to the vibration emanating from the prison and all the men in it. Their collective thunderstorm. Although everything he could see through the whipping windscreen wipers was blurred, he could make out three things: the grey concrete perimeter fence, the sprawling car park, and the hospital-like entrance buildings. He sensed the buzz of a thousand incarcerated inmates all crammed together, all calling for education, for their various degrees, and here he was ready to deliver them. 'Hang on, boys, get the coconut mats out, I'll be there in a minute.' he thought to himself. He made his way to 'Reception', to a sign that shouted out above the only door he could see, and towards what he thought was an awaiting sunshine welcome.

As he swung the double doors open, he was confronted by a row of prison officers all wearing their best spiky haircuts, best frowns and best beer-bellies, standing behind a line of tables. The guardians of paradise. He put on his interview smile and went to introduce himself, surely they would be delighted to meet him? However, they got there first, and cut him dead in mid-sentence.

'Over here, please,' shouted the first, in such a way that it sounded like, 'Shift your arse here, scumbag'. Welcome to the world of Feldon Park etiquette..

'No doubt,' thought Adrian, 'they have made a mistake. They'll soon realise who I am and what I'm here to do.'

'Name?'

'Adrian R…'

'Empty your pockets...'

'Sorry...?'

'Put your arms out. Body search...'

You *what*...?'

'Legs...' The officer frisked him. 'You can't take that in...'

'My wallet...'

'...Put it in that locker and sit over there. Got any ID?'

'Driving licence...'

'Let's have it.'

'It's in my wallet...'

'Why did you leave it there? You knew you'd need it. 'Who are you here to see?'

'Mr Nash, I have an interview with him at ten.'

'Oh... you're not on a visit then?'

This should have been telling him something by now but, as is the way in such cases, he didn't hear it at the time. Although the penny had dropped, his Guardian Angel was looking over the perimeter fence and not paying attention. He found it hard to concentrate with so much going on. The officers continued their interrogation.

'Why didn't you tell us? What's in that folder?'

'Artwork...'

'Put it through the X-ray machine. You'll need to sign in.'

He was given a mountain of paper and no time to read any of it:

'Fill in here, please, and here, and here, and I'll phone someone to escort you over.'

The second officer walked over and, completely ignoring Adrian, asked:

'Is he on a visit?'

After a few minutes all the officers were of one accord: he was not on a visit. However, it didn't stop them giving him their prize frowns and icy stares as he took a seat. He picked up a magazine from the coffee table in front of him, not that he could read any of it, he was far too edgy for that. Why did these guys not admit they'd made a mistake. It seemed it was definitely Adrian's fault. 'Is he taking the piss or what?' Wanting to educate inmates was obviously highly suspicious and not to be encouraged.

After an interminable wait, Adrian took his leave of the un-welcoming committee. It was not a moment too soon, their attitude had made him nervous. His escort was a small, bespectacled, buck-toothed girl who silently led him through the now gaping-wide doors into...the prison. There was something not quite right about her, but he couldn't put his finger on it.

His head was racing with images of countless TV dramas, none of them pleasant. His whole body began to speed up. The adrenaline was pumping.

Jeez, this was only a job interview, but already it felt like he was starting a life sentence. *Help, I'm innocent. I only wanted to go to Fiji. Is there anything wrong with that?*

His escort hardly said a word, except 'Alright, butt?' to everyone she saw. 'Alright but what?' thought Adrian They passed many grids and doors, behind which there were, he guessed, unseen figures lurking. Eventually she received an enormous bunch of keys that almost dislocated her hip to which they were clipped. Adrian listened to them jingle, they sounded just like the ones in *The Shawshank Redemption*. They set off into the unknown

'It's called a campus,' she told him as they went through yet another set of gates. Adrian tried to make conversation.

'Funny, I'd have called it a prison.' Though funny it was not. Maybe she'd heard this many times before. Adrian thought he'd better change the subject. He was coming across as frivolous. He got the feeling she didn't rate him much, maybe she'd seen it all before; man comes in with head full of ideals and leaves after five minutes. Another *Guardian*-reading liberal.

'Have you worked here long?' he enquired. 'It's interesting what makes one decide to work in a prison?'

'I've done three years...' she said in such a way that he later noticed was identical to inmates describing their sentences. '...When I applied for the job of administrator I didn't realise it was here. I thought it was the college'.

Adrian already knew that is was all due to a lowered consciousness. That's how it works. It sounded perfectly logical to him. A horrible silence accompanied them that made Adrian want to talk more but all he could say was, 'Oh,' and then quickly followed it with, 'Do you believe in fate?'

Adrian didn't hear her reply which was a good job probably as he wasn't really listening anymore. He was stunned by the sight of row upon row of bars confronting him, like lots of toothy grins, and by the realisation that each set had someone locked up behind it. His head and heart began pounding in unison. They had entered prisonland proper, and Adrian was overwhelmed.

# 3 MEET THE BOYS

*'Paradise is the most sought after and yet the most elusive place in the world. Many seek it but very few find it. Men search the entire planet looking for bliss. They do not realise it is within each one of us, just beyond our daily existence, just behind everything we do. Just sit very still and empty your mind then it will reveal itself. If you keep asking questions and become restless you will scare it away.' - 'Opening with the Lotus',* Sri Ram Baba Das

The interview was held in a nondescript office by Mr Nash and his deputy, Nigel. They quickly looked through Adrian's work and then began telling him about all the wonderful things that happened in the education department. Adrian found himself asking them more about their work than they did about his, to which they answered very positively. Overall, Adrian assumed that they were employing some new interviewing technique that he was unfamiliar with so he just tried to go along with it, trusting his Guardian Angel. It felt unchallenging to him, and when he was offered a position, it was no surprise, he thought he would be. Maybe these guys were enlightened and could perceive the workings of karma. They didn't need him to explain anything, they could see everything in his aura. It would have been more dramatic and more in keeping had they just said 'Welcome, my son, your destiny awaits.' But no, instead they invited Adrian to have a cup of tea in the staff-room. Adrian wanted to ask them one final question. 'What degrees do the men do here?' but he didn't get a chance to ask because one of them suddenly had an idea.

'Hang on, though! This may be a good time to show you round first, as it's tea break and the rooms will be empty.' (Don't want any prisoners complicating matters). 'We have three art rooms.'

Adrian was taken past several empty classrooms, sterile and institutional, down some stairs to where there was a droning noise like a far-off football match. As they walked along, Adrian noticed an all-pervading smell that seemed to come and go but never completely disappear. Welcome to the world of bang-up. He noticed it was not that dissimilar to the changing rooms at his old school, but more grown-up, somehow. It was a smell that he didn't like, it filled him with dread, though having not smelt it for so long, it also had a nostalgic quality about it. Adrian summed it up as *comprehensive*. They stopped at some heavy automatic double doors. Nigel, the ideas man, pressed an intercom button.

'I see the boys are out. It's still their tea break too.'

The use of the word 'boys', to describe the men, reinforced the word *comprehensive* in Adrian's brain.

Before Adrian had a chance to say anything, the intercom spoke a strange language that was definitely not English but a mixture of crackles, clicks and 'Alright mate'. Adrian craned his neck to look inside but the first door began to open as he did so. They stepped inside and once over the threshold, the heavy door shut again behind them as, simultaneously, the next one began to open.

The far-off football match was now not far off at all, in fact, it was so close that they were in it, but why did he feel he had come in at the wrong end of the pitch? The smell reached gagging proportions. Just in case there was anybody in there who hadn't noticed their arrival, a loud security alarm heralded their approach as they stepped through a metal detector doorway. 'Wally Alert, Wally Alert', it shrieked. Adrian winced.

Someone abruptly pulled the plug on the match and all became deathly quiet. Crammed into a breeze-blocked room were forty or so inmates who all seemed to be cloned from the same prototype. An angry sea of bald heads, sports-wear and tattoos. 160 eyes turned and burned. The 'boys', having stared at Adrian for two second, watched him flinch uncomfortably, and subsequently judged him for the rest of his life, then directed their attention to his escort. It was time to run the gauntlet.

'Nigel, I need to change my timetable... Nigel, I've got a visit... Nigel, I need a pass...'

'Nigel... Nigel*!... NIGEL!!...'*

Nigel swiftly dodged through the boys (biggest 'boys' Adrian had ever seen) with a 'Yes - no - don't know - next week - fuck off...,' each question deflected with the dexterity of a Chinese ping pong player. Nigel had obviously developed advanced people skills.

After a lightning tour of the art rooms, the smell of which again reminded Adrian of his school, they were joined in Room 14 by the 'class'. The room consisted of two large tables surrounded by an array of plastic chairs. The walls were covered in shelves with messy piles of God knows what on them which were all covered in a thin film of clay dust. They hadn't been moved for awhile. Once again, the thing that most left an impression on Adrian were the grinning bars at the window. White, round and fat, more like pillars than bars. Before Adrian could take in anything else, Nigel and he were joined by the eight men returning from their tea break. None of them looked at Adrian, though he knew they were all very aware of his presence. They sat down and began work on their various projects in silence.

'This is Adrian. He is going to be joining us,' announced Nigel. He waved his arm at Adrian to get him involved. Adrian was acutely aware that he was grinning a lot, and then overcompensated by frowning too much. Ignoring his self-consciousness, he began to walk around the room at arm's length, looking over the inmates' shoulders until he saw an opportunity to contribute. He then homed in.

Sitting on their own were two men. They were laughing and joking together and seemed to be enjoying themselves. One was drawing a pit bull terrier.

'Hi,' said Adrian. 'Nice dog!' (Not!) 'Can I join you?'

The men stopped laughing but made a space for him to sit down. Whatever he drew next was probably going to be the most important thing he'd ever do. He could feel himself about to shake.

The next five minutes were spent helping to make the saliva drool realistically out of the dog's mouth over its oversized fangs. The globs of gob glistened. The 'students' were suitably impressed by Adrian's light dispersal technique.

'Wow! That looks real. It's fucking brilliant. Thanks, boss.' Then, turning to the others, 'Hey! Look at this. The new teacher did it, over there.' Adrian felt a warm glow fill his chest. The second student then piped up:

'Can you help me draw a car, boss?'

It was easy. Adrian latched on to them and began drawing a Ford Capri with every imaginable accessory attached. He chose to ignore the fact that nearly everyone else in the room had blanked him. Must be a sign of respect, he told himself. He could almost hear the breaking surf on the coral. The whole morning passed with the tropical sun shining from his arse. He had caught a glimpse of Fiji.

# 4 FUN WITH A RADIO, A NAZI AND MOFTY

*There is an island in the South Pacific that is perpetually sunny and warm. It has many beaches and palm trees, and everything grows in abundance. The people who live there believe that their island fell from the skies, and was a gift from the gods. It was perfect. They called it Paradise Island, which in their own language was 'Fiji'.*

By lunchtime Adrian Roe was surfing along the azure corridors, over the tables covered in graffiti, through the locks, bolts and beeping keyholes of his new-found home. However, he was about to hit a rock as a submerged reef headed his way in the form of Mr Nash, who was smiling - though it would have been less disturbing had he not been.

'How did it go?' he asked. Adrian wanted to be positive. It had been good, but he did wish to point out some reservations he had about blanking and how one kept discipline and the like. Unfortunately his reply came out as: 'Fine, really interesting, but...' Instead of being perceived as a generally good session with a few uncertainties, it was heard as 'Really interesting, butt!'

'Good, good' replied Mr Nash. 'As we are very short-staffed at present we were wondering, since you made such a positive impression this morning, whether we could timetable you for a class this afternoon.'

'There are only six in the group and they are no trouble,' threw in Nigel reassuringly.

'Great,' replied Adrian. 'I can try one of my portrait lessons. They always go down well at school'.

'Excellent' said Mr Nash, 'The Y.O.s will enjoy that.'

Adrian looked puzzled and wondered whether he had left out the letter 'B'. He mouthed the letters to himself. 'WHY OH!'

'It stands for Young Offender, prisoners between 17 and 21 years of age.' said Mr Nash as if reading his mind.

* * *

Adrian went to the classroom and began setting up for the lesson. It was smaller than the messy clay one. It had one large table, the obligatory plastic chairs, graffiti instead of clay on the walls and the same fascinating grinning bars. He was told the session would last three hours with one fifteen minute break and was given three keys for two cupboards and a drawer. He was also handed a register with the six names of the students on it. It was a combination of several Joneses and Evanses. And that was it. This was his big chance to make a change in some poor unfortunate's life. He waited.

The room was unkempt and disorderly. To avoid the creeping sensations that maybe he shouldn't be doing this which had started to flutter around in his stomach, he spent his last few minutes trying to tidy up. (Ah, hello consciousness, back again?) There was a distant noise as the Y.O.s began arriving. His heart pounded. In walked the first, a large bald 'boy' all in red. He didn't seem to have a neck. The most arresting thing about him, apart from his sheer bulk, was the numerous tattoos all over his body. It wasn't so much the swastikas on either forearm that worried Adrian as the word 'skin' engraved across his forehead. Again, distant memories of his school days began to re-surface, bringing with them unpleasant associations.

'Where's Megan?' said Swastika. There was no need for introductions.

'She's sick, I'm afraid. My name's Adrian, I'm teaching you art today instead.'

'God! I hate fuckin' art.'

'Well, you're in the right place: this is a place where you could learn to love it.'

This poor young man obviously had not been introduced to the Fijian delights of education.

' Oh yeah? I want to go back to the wing.'

Meanwhile several other young men had arrived. They all managed to get into the room without acknowledging Adrian's existence.

'Megan's not here today, she's sick,' said Swastika,

'Say that again!' said a tall spotty youngster. 'Did you bring my tape with you?'

'No. We'll just have the radio'. He went over to the corner of the room and plugged in a radio and switched it on. It was incredibly loud. Adrian turned it down.

It was at this point that they all noticed his presence.

'Hi! My name is Adrian and I'm teaching you today. We are going to do a drawing lesson and I'm going to show you, step by step, how to do a basic portrait.'

'What? We don't work like that. We get on with our own stuff.'

'Well, today, for a change, I'm going to show you how to draw. But first I need you to sign the register.'

It was here that he noticed that there were six names and seven students. By reduction, he singled out the interloper.

'Who are you? I don't seem to have you on my list.'

'Smith. I always come in here on a Monday. That list is always wrong,' he said, tapping the paper. 'Just write my name down there.'

The others all echoed in agreement. They had psychically perceived that Adrian didn't know the rules and were now all preparing to exploit this to the hilt. The radio had been turned up to maximum volume once again.

Accordingly, Adrian turned it down, to lots of disapproval.

'If it stays that loud you won't be able to hear what I have to say,' he reasoned.

'Well, hurry up and say it and then we can turn it up. How long will you take?' Adrian didn't answer and continued:

'Today I'm going to show you how to draw a face. You will also learn how to use a pencil for shading. Did you know there are many different types of pencil? Some are hard and some are black and soft.'

'Like Mofty,' said Swastika pointing to Mofty, a sensitive looking Afro-Caribbean boy who hadn't said anything so far. Adrian ignored the interruption and carried on. Smith put his hand up. Adrian was pleased that someone was taking an interest.

'How do they get the leads inside the pencils then?'

Adrian stared at him. This wasn't what he was expecting.

'I've no idea. Good question...' - though slightly weird - 'I'll try and find out for next time. If you can all put your paper this way...'

'Do they drill holes and force it in?' interrupted Smith, who wasn't going to let an unanswered question go that easily.

'I'll try and find out for you, but let's carry on. I want you to start by marking where the top of the head should go and then mark the bottom of the chin.'

A large freckly lad who laughed a lot at all kinds of inappropriate places in the conversation suddenly burst out with a critique of staggering insight.

'This is shit. I can't do it,' and then he scribbled on his paper and pushed his chair backwards across the room.

'Here, let me help you. We can soon sort this out'. Adrian went over and began rubbing out what he'd done. In the meantime, the radio reached maximum volume again. Adrian got up, went over and turned it off.

'Hey! You'd finished talking, so now it's our turn. You said we could have it on when you'd finished talking.'

The tall skinny lad switched it on yet again and turned, laughing sideways at the others. Adrian switched it off yet again. This was heading for a showdown. The Y.O. in question was called Mark Jones.

'I didn't say any such thing. It's to stay off until I say it can go on, OK?' Meanwhile, Smith seemed to have got stuck on a loop of thinking.

'Do you think they make the pencil in two halves and stick them together around the lead?'

'This is doing my fucking head in,' said Mark Jones. ' I want to go to the toilet. Give me a pass, guv.'

Adrian had no idea what he meant. Mark Jones indicated the drawer in the desk.

'They're in there.'

Adrian began fumbling with the keys, none of which seemed to fit. He was looking ridiculous.

'Here, let me. You're not very good at this, are you?' said a boy who hadn't spoken yet called Dean Griffiths.

'I can't give you the keys.'

'He don't need keys, guv,' grinned Mark Jones. 'He's da shoplifter.' Dean grabbed either side of the drawer and began to shuffle it from left to right, then with a flip upwards something clicked and he pulled it open. The others cheered with delight and began chanting:

'Shoplifter, e's da shop liftaaar.'

Adrian wrote out the pass for Mark Jones.

'I want to go to the toilet, too,' said Swastika.

'You'll have to wait till he comes back.'

'But I needs to go now or I'll piss myself.'

'Yeah and I needs to go as well,' adds Dean Griffiths.

'Sit down and wait till Mark comes back.'

The firing line took aim.

'Do you think they make huge pencils and then cut them up to regulation length?'

'I don't want to stay here. I want to go back to my cell,' said Swastika.

'Then go and tell the officer outside that you want to go back.' Getting rid of one didn't seem such a bad thing. If only it could be that simple. Swastika went out. Smith was about to say something else about pencils but Adrian pre-empted him with 'Next week,' and carried on the lesson. Surprisingly, the other half of the class were quietly getting on. He went to work with them.

After a brief while, the door opened and in walked the officer on duty with Swastika and Mark Jones in tow. He spoke to Adrian as if he was some sort of idiot, abruptly, in front of the class. Thanks a lot, Adrian thought angrily. Later Adrian realised that a number of the officers had a particular mental affliction that made it difficult to tell the difference between inmates and staff.

'I found these two walking round the corridors. Keep them in the room. Prisoners are not allowed to wander wherever they like. This is a prison.' (Funny, I thought it was a Fijian campus, thought Adrian.)

Mark Jones walked over and put the radio on again. Loud.

'If you do that once more I will give you a written warning.' (Whatever that was. Nigel had mentioned them earlier.)

'Can't we just have it on quiet like? It helps me work. It helps me to forget I'm in prison.'

'Different tack,' Adrian thought. Ever the optimist, he relented.

'Well, as long as it is quiet.' They turned it on again really loud.

'Turn it down!' Adrian said as forcibly as he could.

'I have,' said Jones. 'But the dial's broken.'

'Really!' Adrian said as Jones turned the dial. But the volume stayed the same. Adrian went over and flicked the dial: it was either really loud or really quiet, so he pulled the plug out.

'Is it off now? Cos I can't hear a fucking thing.'

'Will you just sit down and get on with your work.' Surprisingly, without further complaint, he did. Suddenly, Swastika, who had actually been quiet for a few moments, spoke. He too contributed a well-thought-out critical analysis of his work.

'This is shit, really!'

Adrian went over and sorted him out. (His drawing, that is.)

'I'm going to throw this in the bin when I'm finished. It's like a kid's drawing. The other teachers let us do our own stuff,' he shouted for everyone to hear.

Adrian started to draw the missing bits in for Swastika so that he could catch up; eyes, ears and the like. Swastika seemed pleased with the result, because he stopped speaking and began watching intently. Adrian suddenly found himself sitting very close to him. He was within his aura. (And his B.O.) There was a kind of communion. Something which can only be described as quite religious began to bind them. Worryingly, this was happening with, for all he knew, some neo-Nazi.

As the lesson progressed, the faces began to emerge from the papers, staring up from the desks at the sealed-in strip-lighting of the ceiling. Their gazes projected a sense of achievement into the air. The portraits, as they developed, showed that they all had been following Adrian's instructions, even though they had told him otherwise, and were quite accomplished, though somewhat scary. They had a rawness about them... *similar to African masks which Picasso would describe as the theatre-world, where image and form portray the less tangible and more elusive facets of the inner soul in turmoil...* Oh - and they looked like crappy cartoons too.

'Look at mine!' shouted Mark Jones (they all seemed incapable of ordinary speech). 'Looks like that ugly screw who was on yesterday.' He held it up and everyone burst into laughter. Now that they were working, the radio was forgotten and banished into the periphery. A solitary voice piped up again in earnest.

'Do you think they inject molten lead into the wood?'

'Next time. Remember?'

Adrian was beginning to think maybe Mr Smith had been banished from the other art room rather than run away from it. To avoid further questioning, he took the opportunity to go over and talk with Mofty, who was obviously the most talented of the group but also the one who was most excluded. Whether this was because he was black or because he was clever or for some other reason, he didn't as yet know. Adrian looked at his picture.

'That's wonderful. It looks good, doesn't it. Have you done a lot of drawing?'

'Yeah, a bit. I've done a lot better than this crap though'. He paused just long enough for Adrian to ask if he could see what he'd done, and then went over to the 'locked' cupboard and took out a folder. Inside were several obviously copied drawings of monsters and demons. Cleverly executed but with no quality of beauty, but then why should they?

'These are cool, not like this kid's stuff.' He was pointing to the picture he'd just completed with Adrian. Mofty then, with incredible reverence, showed each of his pieces of demonic art, and carefully drew Adrian's attention to every little detail in case he happened to overlook anything. Mofty was proud of his work.

When the class had all their finished pieces of work in front of them and they were waiting for the 'screw' to let them out, Adrian told them an interesting anecdote that he'd picked up.

'Well, did you know that many psychologists believe that when you draw your first portrait, you actually draw your own inner self? It's what lives inside you. So what you have in front of you is *you*.' Everyone looked at their work with new meaning. This new insight pleased them. Adrian couldn't help noticing that Dean Griffith's picture did look especially manic.

Mark Jones suddenly bellowed, 'Look, Mofty you've drawn a white man. There's a white bloke inside you trying to get out.' He stuck his fists up his shirt and imitated a man giving birth through his stomach. Everyone laughed, including Mofty who replied:

'Well, at least I don't have that ugly screw inside me like you do.'

It was a great relief when the end of the lesson came. The last few minutes were spent watching the clock, until eventually the officer came to check out the inmates. Adrian was surprised to see Swastika carefully trimming the edges of his drawing and then put it neatly in his folder. Adrian didn't tempt fate and ask him why it wasn't in the bin. As they left, Smith paused in the doorway and stared pencils at Adrian.

'But what if you ain't in next week. Then what?'

He left before Adrian could answer.

* * *

When asked by Mr Nash how it had been, Adrian told him that each had finished a portrait. He replied, with considerable surprise:

'Well done! I'm impressed that you got everyone to complete a piece of work. Well done indeed!'

As Adrian drove home that evening these words played on his mind, and he realised that to get the whole class to finish a piece of work was unusual. He also realised that before he could reach these poor unfortunates and change their lives forever, he'd first have to learn to survive. He hadn't realised how difficult life on Fiji could be. His hands slipped loosely over the steering wheel as he broke out into a sweat.

# 5 TATTOO

*Tradition dictated, on Fiji, that when a boy reached the age of fourteen, he began a series of trials to prove his manhood. Each task needed courage and was rewarded with a tattoo. The bravest men had the most tattoos. To have none was a sign of great weakness.*

When education resumed after the Christmas break, Adrian was asked to take on Room Fifteen on Mondays in addition to Room Fourteen on Tuesdays. As a new face on the block, he was being deliberately excluded by all the men, and he realised that, to get anywhere at all, he would have to overcome this 'blanking'. He needed to break the ice, and find some common ground over which he could amble, with the men, through the world of art and find Fiji. It required something personal and yet indirect. Over the holiday, Adrian had spent many hours trying to concoct various lesson plans, but when he arrived on the very first day, it was obvious that none of them were going to work. They were too abstract. They were from the 'out'. As he stepped into the classroom, he left all theory at the door and abandoned his plans. He started living in the moment. This was probably the best thing he could have done. He was stepping into their boat, which was drifting aimlessly about. He could now take control and set course to Fiji - except he didn't have a paddle yet. The men were 'now' people, so why shouldn't he be? Once he had made this mental quantum leap, the subject material for his next lesson was clearly staring him in the face. Tattooing. He was walking into a sea of tattoos with thc odd person attached to them - and he really did mean odd. Having none himself, he felt like he was entering the room decidedly naked. It seems if you have some empty skin, you may as well use it. Therefore, Adrian's new, live-in-the-moment chat-up line became: 'Nice tatts, can I see?'

Adrian eventually became an expert on tattoos. He could read them as a kind of secret language, identifying age, likes, and even where they came from. He could also tell how old a tattoo was by the degree of fadedness it had. (Black and blue being the most enduring. It didn't seem to matter where they were placed, they all faded at the same rate. Exposure to air didn't seem to affect them. The most unusual one that Adrian ever encountered was engraved on the inside of a Y.O.'s lower lip: it was the word 'Rowan'. Its owner told him it was the name of his girl friend and furthermore, it was secret. Adrian thought of him as the boy who constantly had true love on his lips. Aah! (When Adrian recalled this story later, it came out as AARGH!)

Looking afresh at his new class, through tattooed spectacles, Adrian could see a fantastic array of inspiration right in front of his face. He had to look no further. His students were a walking art gallery with loads of attitude. Living, breathing, perspiring art. Over time, he eventually got to recognise certain studios on the local boys, but he found the most intriguing patterns, and definitely most revealing, were the hundreds of home-mades done in a moment of impulse, possibly under the influence of something or other, only to be regretted later. The 'infills'.

Adrian threw his lesson plan out of the window along with all the other rubbish and began the day by walking, unarmed, over to Tony B., who was quietly working on a project from his previous lesson. He had no plans, no agenda other than to be one hundred percent there. Tony was painting a silhouette of a lion against a savannah sunset. The vermilion red was running amok. The fiery background was approaching Armageddon. The lion was probably being roasted alive. They spoke, briefly, about what he was doing and Adrian made a few suggestions. Although they were talking, the conversation didn't really go anywhere, it stayed firmly rooted in the banal. There was no meeting of souls. Tony B. remained distant. He was internally blanking Adrian. As he leaned forward to paint even more red onto the fiery sunset, Adrian noticed the end of a tattoo poking from under his shirt sleeve, so he tried his new chat- up line.

'Nice tatts...'

'Oh, that...' Tony pulled up his sleeve, and it was only then that Adrian realised he might have said the wrong thing. Almost the entire top of his arm, up to his shoulder, was covered by a big black blob, a nondescript mess, as if someone had made a monster-sized mistake. 'Nice' it definitely was not, but on closer inspection it was still possible to make out a rose with a jumble of letters in it. Adrian tried to say something positive, but it came out as 'Oh...'

'I know it's crap,' Tony said dejectedly. 'It used to be really cool. Can you see that red rose?' He pointed to the main part of the blotch. 'Can you see it? It used to be in a circle of flames with Lisa written across it. When we split up I just left it there. Then, I met Vicky and she didn't like it and told me to get rid of it, so I covered it up. I had Vicky written on top of Lisa. See - you can just make out the V. But we only lasted three months anyway and then I moved in with Becky and she wanted her name on there, so to cover up the others, the letters had to be even bigger and blacker. See - there's the Y.'

Adrian was getting the picture. Every time Tony entered a new life relationship, he superimposed the flavour of the month's name over the top of the existing ones. He had documented his love life on his skin. He was living art. He was a walking art form. Tracy Emin would have been proud.

'Why didn't you have the old names removed? With a laser?' Adrian naively enquired.

'God no! Do you know how much that costs? It's really expensive and also it leaves marks... and besides it *hurts like fuck,'* he hissed, ' so I just covers them up like. It's easier.'

'Never mind,' Adrian said. 'It's a bit like a record of all the relationships in life that you've had. It's a picture of your love life.'

'Yeah, I suppose so. But it's a fucking mess, ain't it.'

'Big Ron's got wicked tatts, guv',' shouted Jabba from the next table, 'ain't you, Ron?'

Ronald Pritchard looked up and grinned. Big Ron was big, really big. His size was impressive: he wasn't fat, he was just *big*. His head was shaved into a bullet-like shape. His hair had once been fair. He had light blue eyes and he wore sports trousers and a vest. Looking for an escape route from Tony, Adrian moved over to where Big Ron, Jabba, Thomas and Jim Jones sat.

'Show him your tatts, Ron,' insisted Jabba. 'Go on.' Big Ron's grin got even bigger.

Adrian could see that Big Ron had a line of Chinese characters across the back of his neck.

'What's that read?' Adrian asked innocently.

'Sweet and sour pork, guv',' Ron replied. Adrian laughed hollowly. This old joke had long since passed its sell-by date. He wasn't impressed by the tatts either.

'Show him properly,' chipped in Jabba.

Obligingly, Ron stood up. What happened next was completely unexpected and in-the-moment. Adrian's jaw dropped open as Big Ron dropped his trousers (and boxers) and stood there exposed to all. This was greeted by a huge roar of approval from the other inmates who all got up and gathered round. It seemed to be the cue for all sorts of mayhem. Jabba, in true Jabba fashion, took this opportunity to stand on the table and do a weird, jerky sort of dance. Tattooed across Big Ron's stomach was the head of a huge Chinese dragon. On its chin was a long, obviously masculine tentacle which fitted exactly with Ron's physical anatomy. 'Ow! I bet that hurt,' thought Adrian when he'd got over the initial shock. Further panic ensued when Adrian suddenly realised how easy it would be to misinterpret this situation, should an officer - or worse, the head of department - now walk in. It had all the appearances of some sort of gay, erotic ritual.

'Put it away, NOW!' Adrian found himself grinning. 'I've seen enough.' These blokes were crazy! What were they like?

Big Ron unashamedly pulled up his pants.

'My middle name's Dick.' He laughed.

'Wicked, innit?' laughed Jabba.

'Yeah, wicked,' Adrian agreed. He now also knew why he was called Big Ron.

* * *

Several weeks later, over lunch with Nigel, the subject of Big Ron came up, and Adrian told him, somewhat nervously, what had happened. However, Nigel laughed and laughed, and then told him a few more funny stories about Big Ron which dwarfed Adrian's encounter with Puff the Magic Dragon into insignificance. Big Ron had let Adrian off lightly, it seemed - or was he saving the worst for later? Apparently, Ron had several party pieces, all of which involved his manhood, and one of which was particularly dodgy. Adrian listened in disbelief, while downing his regulation canteen dinner. It was good to be distracted whilst eating in the staff canteen, as that way you didn't think too much about what was going in your mouth. Nigel told his tale.

'Ron's always been a bit strange. He used to walk around with his dick hanging out all the time. He would just get on with whatever needed doing with his flies wide open. He used to think it was funny. You'd be talking to him, all normal like, then look down and WHOA! He used to get a buzz out of shocking people.'

They both laughed aloud - in fact Nigel was laughing so much he couldn't speak for a while. Adrian wondered if he was having a heart attack, but he soon recovered and continued:

'It gets worse. He would creep up and stand really close, behind people, in a queue for example, with everything hanging out, talking and carrying on as if there was nothing weird going on. He would then manoeuvre the offensive member towards his victim's hand without them suspecting anything untoward. They naturally thought someone was trying to pass them something discreetly, which happens a lot in prisonland. Something was being pushed into their hand. Having been totally set up, they would then look down to see what it was they were holding. Jesus, it was so funny.' Nigel started laughing and stopped breathing again.

'It always happened at the end of the lessons,' he gasped. 'And was always done very publicly. An audience gave the situation a degree of respectability, I suppose. The subsequent shrieks of horror and delight could reduce any victim to complete embarrassment.'

'Don't any of the men think it a bit odd? That he wants to expose himself all the time. He just seems to be a glorified flasher,' Adrian said soberly.

'No. None of the inmates would ever dare question his sexuality, at least not to his face. He's a big bloke, and he has a bit of a reputation for being violent when provoked.' Adrian shuddered, remembering he had him again that afternoon. Sometimes it was better not to know things.

Nigel went on to tell how the 'joke' had become, at one point, almost a daily ritual that targeted the most reactive people. If any victim wished to get his own back, he would have to do it in such a way as to appear completely innocent, to avoid confrontation.

'The last laugh was on him, though. Big Ron eventually met his match when Withers, a serious Young Offender, joined the class. He didn't find many things in life funny. He had a very vulnerable exterior with a rather dark centre. He loved reading Stephen King.

'Three times, Withers had ended up holding the dragon's chin and three times he had been the butt of a bad joke which only exacerbated his displeasure. He was fed up with being picked on, so he worked out a plan to get even.'

The Feldon Park dragon met his Saint George.

Nigel again picked up the threads as Adrian downed his apple crumble which lay submerged in a sea of what looked like pus.

'Withers always worked on his own. I don't think anybody had ever heard him speak to anyone else, come to think of it. He was making a collage from old magazines for his art project. All the while, he must have been scheming as he stuck little bits of paper into a cityscape. He was so bloody clever. He worked, convincingly innocent, all morning, until it was time to leave and the men lined up to be searched. Predictably, up behind Withers came Big Ron. The expectant crowd were all watching with baited breath, as the feeler plopped out and was pushed into the waiting, floppy palm. Withers didn't pull away immediately. Had the others not been so intent on laughing, they might have noticed that his hand was absolutely covered in copious amounts of clear, sticky stuff. When Withers came to be searched by the officer who was frisking that day, Ron whipped himself back into his pants. The officer suddenly noticed

Withers' hands and said: 'What's all this stuff on your hands?' He didn't suspect anything.

Nigel had now turned a violent red and he shook with hysteria.

' Oh, it's just varnish,' replied Withers. 'I didn't have time to clean up.'

'God! You can't leave that on your skin. Go back and get it off. It's already beginning to set,' said the officer. 'You'll have to scrub really hard with white spirit to get that stuff off. *Next...!"*

'Ron's face dropped. It was hilarious. He rushed over to the paints shelf, soaked a paper towel in white spirit and began to rub himself furiously. The officer looked on in disbelief.'

'Oi! Ron! What do you think you're doing? Hey! You can't do that in here. Oi! STOP THAT NOW!'

By now Nigel was choking with laughter. It was a miracle he'd managed to get this far into the story without gagging to death, and desperately in need of a drink he rushed from the table. Adrian sat on his own and thought about his group. Was there *anyone* he could help send on their way to Fiji? Although he hoped they all would get there eventually, he thought it probably best that Big Ron found his own paradise island somewhere else. 'The Shetlands are very nice in June,' thought Adrian.

# 6 CARDS 'R' US

*When the King of Fiji had his birthday, his subjects presented him with trinkets of gold. The king was in his fifties and had more jewellery than he could possibly ever wear. One year, a young warrior who was poor and had no gold, gave the king a poem written on parchment instead. Everyone was shocked. He began to read. 'More precious than gold, more precious than pearls, it is the most treasured thing in the world, it is life itself, it is Fiji and I give it to you.*

*The king was pleased and from that day on it became a tradition to give cards on birthdays.*

Once on a Saturday night, over dinner, Adrian was asked by his friends, what was the worst thing about a spell in nick?

'I hear that it's all very easy nowadays, televisions and the like?' Quite different from the old days of military drill and slopping out,' said his guest, who'd obviously never been anywhere near a gaol.

Adrian thought carefully. It was hard to give a single answer, so many things were unpleasant at the same time: the indifferent officers, the harsh regime. It didn't feel like a holiday camp to him, and he didn't live there permanently like the lads did. He'd been teaching there now for three weeks, and that seemed a miraculous achievement.

'I think the worst thing is probably having to live, locked up, with the other inmates. It must be a terrible thing if you find yourself on the wrong side of "the law of the jungle" found on some of the wings.'

'Surely the officers keep control? That's what they're there for, isn't it?' said his guest. Adrian felt himself reliving a similar conversation his parents had had when he was a lad at school.

'Surely the teachers keep control? That's what they're there for isn't it?' It wasn't the case then and a recently overheard conversation between an officer and his new assistant didn't give much hope now.

'It's alright in there during the day, a lot of them are at work or in education but it becomes like Beirut in there after six,' he pointed his thumb to B block. Finding yourself at the bottom of the pile in 'Beirut' couldn't be very nice. Adrian turned to his guest.

'It can be pretty rough at times, you don't often see anything but you can actually feel the depression and fear in the air.'

Adrian's guest raised his eyebrows and began on his dessert.

Since he had started working inside, Adrian had already heard that one young man had committed suicide. Tragically, in the future, he was to hear of others, especially among the Y.O.s, on whose blocks the pecking order was more rigidly enforced than elsewhere. However, there were things prisoners could do to avoid rock bottom. For instance, if you have some useful skill, it could become your saving grace.

Mark Williams and Steve Hewitt were two such fortunate beings who had been rescued from what would otherwise have been the unenviable position of 'muppet' on the wing. They had gifts which on one's first meeting were not immediately obvious. Their skills reflected a current high-street shopping trend. They met the inexhaustible and inexplicable need to have a greeting card for every occasion. Mark and Steve were 'Cards 'r' us'. Their repertoire was considerably limited, but if it's cartoons you're into, then they're your men. Mark could draw any character that took your fancy, Pooh bear, the Simpsons, the South Park boys, Scooby Doo, Tom and Jerry, to name a few. Steve, on the other hand, could reproduce any football insignia, albeit preferably a Liverpool one, to help aid your celebration. So, what ever your occasion, between them they could meet your needs. Happy Birthday, I Love You, Merry Christmas were all readily available, as long as you didn't mind sweet little cartoons singing, 'You'll never walk alone,' thrown in as well.

Having set up this business enterprise, where better to ply your trade than the art rooms where materials are free and you can even get education certificates into the bargain. Adrian first came across them when he took on Room Fifteen, they were both on the register. They sat on the same table with the day's orders piled up in front of them. Life seemed sweet. Adrian was convinced that had they not had their speciality, it would have been hell for both of them, as they were so annoying.

Steve hardly spoke at all but when he did, there was one very, obvious thread of thinking that permeated everything: Liverpool FC. No matter what Adrian said to him, about art, television, politics, quantum physics, it was only a few seconds before he was back at Anfield Road. Once, for example, when the subject of his nine-month-old child cropped up, he managed to get in, within about three seconds, that 'he was the youngest member ever of the Liverpool Supporters club in Britain.'

Mark made up for Steve's reluctance to speak by talking as if there was no tomorrow. Unfortunately, everything he said was absolute crap. The only person who could bear him for any length of time was Steve, and one wonders whether he was really listening or attending some away game in his head.

Steve was in full swing when Adrian got to their table on his round of the room. Steve had just finished making a card for Darren. It had better be good as it was a birthday card for his kid. It lay on the table in front of him. He was folding some more paper for the next one, which he was doing for himself. Everyone knew this because he made regular 30-second public announcements. They were monologues, which was how he always talked. Mark never spoke to you directly, but aimed his monologue at you. He needed you as an anchor before he could launch off. He was on his pet subject, 'why am I in prison'. Being relatively new and not having heard this story before, Adrian got his full attention. It became immediately obvious to Adrian that here was one of those people who, as soon as they opened their mouths, made him go brain-dead. Something inside him turned off and he just glazed over while the rest of his body just wanted to run away.

'So I comes home early and she's gone out. She's supposed to be staying in, she said so earlier. So why was she out if she says she was staying in?' Adrian tried to say that he had no idea, but he wasn't participating in this one-man show. He wasn't expected to give answers. 'So I waited to see what lies she was going to come out with this time cos I knows she's sleeping round. Yeah. I could just tell. And she definitely said she wasn't going out. So I just sits in the chair and waits until I hears her come in. I shouts at her, 'Who is it this time? Who you seeing now? She was really surprised that I knew, and then plays the old innocent with me. She tells me she's been out "just to get some fags".'

Whenever Mark reported her bits of speech he did so in a high falsetto voice which was very scary. It reminded Adrian immediately of Norman Bates in *Psycho.*

'God, it doesn't take that long to get to the shop and back. She's lying to me. She's seeing someone. She then starts screaming at me and tries to turn the whole thing round like I'm the one who's done something wrong. Tells me I've got the problem. It was laughable. I'm not a violent man, it takes quite a lot to get me worked up, but when she realises I'm seething and I'm not having any of it she turns and walks out. The bitch. You can't run away from me, I shouts after her. You'll be back, begging - go on, go, whore!

'This time I'm not taking her back. I'll show her. I takes out all her CDs and puts 'em in a bag along with her make up and her porcelain dog collection and chucks them out the front door after her. I knows she'll be back soon and when she does, she needs to realise I means it, I'm serious.

'I then goes upstairs to the bedroom and I'm actually really worked up, so I takes out all her clothes from the dresser, and I rips them up. I don't do her leather coat because it won't tear. It's made of high quality leather. I nicked it for her, on her twenty-first, from Miss Selfridges. It had a price tag of £120 on it. She's probably gone to the shops to get some fags for real this time but after half an hour she still hasn't come home. I'm really getting fed up now, so I goes to this photo on the mantelpiece, it's of us on holiday last year in Mallorca. I smashes the frame and glass and then tears the picture in half and throws it on the floor. She still don't come back. I realises she's probably gone to stay with her mother and I remembers that she has taken her mobile phone with her, so I decides to give her a ring. Blah, blah, yeah, yeah.'

The story was following a well-worn path. Adrian could tell this had been delivered many times before, either in his head or literally. It had that totally flat quality. Oops! Sorry, I didn't mean to interrupt, you carry on, but...

'She answers. I tells her that I'm really pissed off but if she comes home now and says she's sorry, I might take her back. I thought I'd give her another chance like. But she tells me she ain't ever coming home, *ever*. So, I says you can't do that but she just says, just watch me, and hangs up. WHAT? I'll teach her to hurt me, the ungrateful bitch, after all I's done for her. I picks up this shard of glass from the floor and puts it on my wrist and pushes it in. Fuck! it hurt. See how you feel when they tell you that I've died...'

'How could she hear you? I thought you said she'd hung up,' said Steve in a dead-pan voice.

'She had, she had! I hate being hung up on (and interrupted). I think it's so rude. I lost it then and set upon that leather coat again. It's like the one thing that's left that reminds me of her. God, it's stubborn. It stood up defiantly to all my anger and wouldn't allow me to damage it. Then I has a good idea. I knows, I'll set it on fire and destroy it that way. She can burn in Hell. I didn't put that much petrol on it, but fuck, the whole thing went up in flames, big time. I tried to stamp it out but that only made it worse. I must have got some petrol on my leg. I also now realised that we had been ripped off. The leather coat wasn't leather but plastic, and once ignited it melted into a smelly, gooey mass that all of a sudden erupted into flames. I tried to stamp it out but the sticky plastic stuff stuck to my shoe and I couldn't get it off. Wherever I trod I left little footprints of fire.'

Mark was becoming increasingly animated as he relived it all. He got louder and louder, craning his neck this way and that, making sure everyone had heard him.

Steve suddenly spoke again. This time he managed to get Liverpool FC in. 'You was like a proper Red Devil.'

'Yeah,' said Mark with no acknowledgment at all.

'Yeah well, I showed her. I walked all over the house leaving little fires everywhere, soon the whole fucking place was ablaze. When I finally got outside the police arrested me. I got four years,' he said proudly. 'Arson.'

This was definitely time for Adrian to leave. He used the pause for breath to turn to Steve, who was painting 'Three Feathers' on a mug.

'What about you, Steve? What are you in for?' Adrian fumbled, trying to change the subject.

'The same,' he replied flatly, 'cept I burned down someone else's house, not my own.' Then looking over to Mark who was still all puffed up with pride. 'Wanker!'

From the far corner of the room a voice, remarkably like Jabba's, called: 'He put the "arse" back into arson, guv. Fuckin' twat!'

The final twist came at the end of the day when Mark finished his card. It had two hearts held up by Pooh and Piglet with the words 'I Love You. Always.'

'That's a nice card, Mark,' Adrian said.

'Yeah,' he replied, 'she'll come back, she's just waiting for me to get out.'

'Stupid fucker,' replied Steve dryly, 'she hasn't answered any card you've ever sent, yet you sends them every other day. Waste of time and paint if you ask me. She's most likely not living there anymore anyway. She's probably moved, and if she hasn't, she should do herself a favour before you gets out.'

With that chilling thought they left. Getting these two to Fiji was going to be hard. Maybe they could set up a post-card business. Adrian wondered what was being done to help Mark come to terms with his paranoid, obsessive relationship. Both these guys had big problems and needed a lot more than just a three hour art lesson making cards to solve them.

On the way home Adrian tried to think of ways of laterally introducing new elements into the 'Cards' business. Mark didn't listen well, and for him to accept anything he would have to think he'd discovered it for himself. Adrian later realised that this method was a valuable key to teaching in prison and he hung it securely on his imaginary key chain.

Mark and Steve's position was more complex than first met the eye, and to go in and upset the apple-cart and insist on change could be potentially dangerous for them. Adrian would have to work with and not against them. He decided to bring in, casually, some books of calligraphy and leave them on Mark's table and see if he'd take them up. If that failed maybe Adrian himself should do a few cards showing a different approach, just to sow a few seeds and let Mark grow them. As he neared home, all those cheesy cards were still flying around in Adrian's head. He wondered whether getting Steve to make a card that said, 'I'm sorry,' would have any therapeutic value. Whatever, the way forward seemed to lie in reading the situation first and then working with it.

# 7 DING BONG MERRILY WE'RE HIGH

*Marijuana is a native flora of Fiji and was traditionally regarded as a sacred plant to be used only by the elders and the shaman. In its leaves dwelt spirits and ghosts waiting to enter anyone who smoked it. To unlawfully commune with these spirits was a punishable offence, even though the plant grew everywhere. Trespassers would be set adrift on the ocean on tiny rafts and left to fend for themselves. Such were the laws in Paradise.*

Having decided to adopt the policy of 'reading' the men and then building on their existing interests and skills, Adrian found his teaching methods were far more popular than the cold, more formal approaches to art. He found himself teaching things like graffiti and tattoo design and lots of stuff that sailed pretty close to the wind. All went well until one day his lesson fell under the eye of the prison authorities. The man who pushed it over the limit was known as Spacey.

One morning, the television had been left on in the reception area, so, while Adrian and the boys were waiting, they sat and watched for a few moments, before going into the art room.

It was the morning news. There was something on about prisons, which was always good for a laugh.

'The Home Secretary said today in parliament that the widespread use of illegal drugs has reached epidemic proportions over recent years, and is a major contribution to the overcrowding of our prisons. Many new admissions, on arrival, need detoxing from Class A drugs.' (In here, son, see you in a week.) 'It's a growing problem that's pushing the system to breaking point and undermining our society. It's a problem that this Government is prepared to tackle.'

'*Bollocks*! Our society, my arse,' Jabba had suddenly gone serious. 'Whose society, did you say? You just pick which bits you want to fucking see, so just fuck off, you fucking poncy prat!'

'He can't hear you, Jabba, he's on television.' Adrian pointed out.

An officer came over and turned off Jack Straw, just as he was about to prove them wrong and answer: 'Shut up, Jabba! I am the Home Secretary. I know what I'm talking about.' This would have been even more entertaining if accompanied by an interactive, press-the-red-button slap in the mouth.

As they walked to the classroom, Adrian spoke with Jabba.

'I didn't know you were political.'

'I'm not, though me and Tony Blair are sort of fucking identical. Ain't we, Spacey?'

Spacey turned round and spoke to Adrian.

'It's the ears,' he grinned.

Adrian thought about what Jabba had said. He obviously didn't feel part of the same society as Jack Straw. Although Jabba and others had to deal with the drug addiction, the rest of society has to deal with it indirectly, so, in that sense, it is everyone's problem.

But Adrian couldn't think further because, having had it pointed out, he now couldn't stop looking at Jabba's ears. They really did look like the Prime Minister's.

Adrian didn't need to listen to the Home Secretary speeches. All about him were the results of drug abuse. A lot of the adults, and nearly every Y.O. he met, seemed to have had a drug problem. He recognised a set pattern. On the one hand, there is what addiction does to the individual, both physically and mentally, and on the other, there is the social factor, the use of crime to maintain an unrelenting habit. Addiction to drugs can turn anyone to crime. Prostitution, robbery, drug dealing. Whatever. All is valid as a means to an end. Addiction is ugly. The problems of the individual and those of society are intertwined. Many addicts have gone through every other means to support their habit before they hit rock bottom. Having lost everything, not only their possessions, their job if they had one, their family and friends but subsequently their self-respect too, there is still the need to find daily money with an increasing urgency that won't go away, and this is where it becomes society's problem. It's a no-win situation, and outside help is required if there's to be any escape from this downhill spiral. Prison can be that place; however, when the emphasis seems to be more on punishment and security than on dealing with the issues, help is quite often reduced to a well-intentioned afterthought. Most fall through the net. True, they come off the heroin while inside, but many return to it immediately, which questions whether the addiction itself has been cured.

There is also a distinction between drug-induced and other forms of crime. Once Adrian overheard one inmate say to a rather over-zealous officer: 'Don't talk to me like that, I'm a drug addict, not a criminal.' This left the officer perplexed and bemused, although everyone else around at the time seemed capable of grasping it.

That day, in class, the men were surprisingly quiet. Maybe they were deep in thought, or maybe they were just vacant smackheads (Joke, joke, back off, only joking!)

'It's like I said, it's your fucking problem as much as ours,' said Jabba again, though he wasn't talking to Adrian. He was still engrossed in some kind of psychic conversation with the Home Secretary.

Faced with such huge problems, Adrian thought it seemed kind of stupid that the prison had also to deal with more petty, soft-drug related crimes that clogged up the system even further.

'It's not all doom and gloom, is it, Ade?' said Jabba, alarmingly displaying some sort of atavistic clairvoyance again. Maybe, reading people's minds was a side-effect of being a life-long smackhead. (Joke! But perhaps he'd better watch what he was thinking.)

What Adrian was thinking about were the many cannabis-related offences. *Skin us up another spliff, butt.* Compared with the tragic effects of heroin and crack, it seemed slightly absurd to put them all in the same boat - and definitely not the one going to Fiji, either.

Admittedly, the number of cannabis prosecutions did seem to be decreasing over the years, either as society's attitude changed or because there was a necessity to prioritise what was criminal. Nevertheless, it is still illegal to smoke, buy or possess cannabis in Britain, let alone in prison. Which leads on to the next story.

In order of popularity, the things Adrian got asked to draw most frequently in prison were guns, assorted vicious dog breeds, cars, bits of female anatomy and Bob Marley. But ahead by far was the cannabis leaf. It has become a symbol for everything 'druggy'. The main champion of the five pointed, serrated leaf in Adrian's Thursday afternoon group was Ricky Evans, commonly known as 'Spacey'. No matter what Spacey drew, made, sculpted, it would always be adorned with his beloved ganja trademark. It became his tag. On this particular morning, Spacey was going to try his hand at throwing a pot on the wheel. This was promising and a welcome departure from the Rastafarian flag he was executing (literally).

'It's good to see you doing something new at last. Break out of the old mould,' said Adrian. 'Do you have anything particular in mind?'

'Yeah... well, I've got a few ideas like. I thought I'd make some presents for my family and pass them out on my next visit. I've been watching Lee throwing pots for weeks now and I think I can do it.'

'Well, have a go. Make sure the clay is in the middle and your hands are steady.'

Adrian showed him the basics and Spacey worked with surprising determination. By the end of the morning session, he had produced some rather fine vases which were left to dry before firing in the kiln. They were elegant, delicate flutes that could tastefully hold a single rose, or something similar. When the boys had gone, Adrian examined the pieces and found that the best one, for some inexplicable reason, had some holes in it. What was this? Adrian could only assume that someone was trying to sabotage his work. He made a guess as to who would do such a thing and could only conclude it was Lee, who had had to give up the wheel. With every good intention, Adrian carefully plugged the holes with clay and repaired them before loading them into the kiln. At a glance, you would never know they had ever been damaged. To avoid a load of aggro, Adrian decided it was probably best not to say anything and just let this one pass. Spacey had worked so hard this morning, it was a shame to see his work ruined. The kiln was fired that night.

When Spacey came back, two days later, he rushed straight to the racks to pick up his work. Adrian was pleased how the pieces had fired and was confident Spacey would be delighted. He couldn't wait for him to see his work. How wrong can you be? Spacey suddenly let out a shout.

'What the fuck? Who's done this? Someone's messed up my work!'

Adrian went over, thinking someone must have made more holes in his pots. However, the vases looked fine. Adrian picked one up and examined it.

'What's up? Hey! These have turned out well. This particular glaze is gorgeous.' However, Spacey was not a happy bunny.

'My best one's fucking ruined.'

'It's not. It looks really good. I know someone holed your vase, but don't worry, I've fixed it. Do you know who might have done it? I could have a quiet word...'

'*What!* You've ruined it! It's meant to have holes in it. It's not a vase, it's a bong. It's for smoking the weed.'

Feeling that this might not be legal in prisonland, and feeling rather stupid and definitely un-cred, Adrian questioned its existence, in a sheepish sort of way.

'I'm not sure you should be making one of those?'

'Course man, what's the problem? It's only a vase with holes in it. You said so yourself.'

'Yeah' piped in Jabba, 'Anyway, you can buys them anywhere on the out.'

'Funny, I don't remember seeing them last time I went to Tesco's. Maybe I wasn't looking in the right place. Maybe I should look for the section marked 'drug paraphernalia', between 'home baking' and 'pet food'.'

'Not Tesco's, man, you know, anywhere else.'

'WH Smith's? Homebase? Boots?'

'I'll pass it out this afternoon, boss? Will you help me draw the leaf on a card to go with it? I'm going to have to make another one this morning. A proper one, and this time don't interfere.'

Spacey went to the wheel and began to throw himself another one. It was actually very well made and Adrian began to think, well, if he's learning new skills, and they're not being used...This could actually be his saving grace, if the difference between a bong and a vase were just a few holes. Adrian thought that he must discuss this later with Nigel.

The thrown piece was put on the shelf to be fired later. It was fine to develop projects out of students' likes, as long as they were legal.

There seemed to be an attitude among the staff in Feldon Park that pervaded all corridors of authority. If something needs implementing do so with all your might. This can be paraphrased as: if you can use a sledgehammer, why use a nutcracker?

*Non useable potentia minimus, quan implemente destructio maximus* - this should have been taken up as Feldon Park's motto for it was enforced with a vengeance with regards to 'illegals'. 'Illegals' are everything on the out that is criminal, plus a whole bunch of other stuff as well.

When all the prisoners were gone, the officer on duty came to the room to check that the door to the kiln was locked, and his eye caught the *bong*.

'What the fuck's that?

'Oh, that,' Adrian said innocently. 'I think it's called a *bang* or something.'

'I can see that. What's it doing there?'

Adrian had to bite his tongue as he gave the obvious answer.

'Drying,' he replied. The officer went over to the shelf to pick it up and look at it.

'Whose is it?'

'Spacey's.'

'Well, he's not having it.' And without further ado, the officer broke it into pieces, before Adrian could say anything in its defence. It was judged, sentenced and condemned to death in two words:

'It's illegal.'

The next morning, Adrian was the one who had to face Spacey and explain what had happened. He was furious; the officer responsible was not on duty that day. Surprise, surprise.

After a near riot, threats of written warnings and a recitation of the 'Oxford Dictionary of Abusive Language', Spacey settled down. After a long sulky silence, he began to throw instead of a tantrum another pot, identical to yesterday's, with the determination of a wronged bonger.

'That'd better not be what I think it is.'

Spacey had a twinkle in his eye that conveyed far more than anything his mouth could say.

'I'm not making a bong, it's a vase. I want to make another one to make a set, like.'

The unseen sniggers around the room left Adrian unconvinced.

'You better not be taking the piss.'

By the end of the session, the 'vase' was put on the shelf to dry. It looked very respectable. Adrian checked it for holes. There were none, though he couldn't help thinking that something was amiss.

The following week, when Adrian again took that class, he asked Spacey how his vase turned out.

'Fine. It's gone out. I'm making another one today.'

Once again, the classroom sniggers made Adrian feel uncomfortable, but on a positive note, Spacey was actually beginning to throw some very nice work. Adrian wondered if Spacey could get an OCN certificate: 'Introduction to Bong Construction.' Each piece he threw surpassed the last. When finally completed, the vases were put on the drying shelf. Halfway through the morning Spacey asked to take a particular one down again to do some final work on it.

The unseen sniggers alerted Adrian to pay particular attention to these 'finishing touches'. One of the handiest things to develop in prison, for staff and inmates alike, is peripheral vision. It enables everyone in the room to be aware of everyone else without the embarrassment of face-to-face contact. It's what Adrian had earlier misinterpreted as blanking. (I spy with my little eye something beginning with 'I'... Err - illegal? Yes, that's it, well done.) He caught a glimpse of Spacey carefully doing something to his bong/vase. He positioned himself to maximise his view from the corner of his eye. Spacey had made several holes in it and was stuffing chewed-up paper mixed with PVA glue into the holes and then smoothing them over. Making temporary plugs. So that was his game. Adrian watched for a few seconds as after a while, Spacey painted over them so carefully with slip (liquid clay) that at first glance you would never know the holes were there. Adrian had seen enough and decided to pounce.

'So that's how you did it. You used paper.'

Spacey didn't get angry. He just grinned instead.

'Clever, ain't I. There's nothing wrong with it.'

'Yeah,' added Jabba, 'it's just a vase.' Jabba had the irritating habit of poking his nose into everything. He just had to be involved.

'You know, this is probably the best thing I've ever made,' said Spacey, momentarily forgetting who Adrian was.

'You won't be able to keep it,' Adrian replied. 'You'll never get it out of this room.'

'I don't wants to,' added Spacey, 'I wants it to go out on the next visit I has.' Prisoners were allowed to hand out things they'd made to folks visiting them.

'The officer will destroy it at the end of the lesson.'

Suddenly the bubble burst and Adrian had crossed back over the divide again. He felt like that slave messenger in ancient Greece who was murdered for bringing bad news. Adrianocoles.

There followed a lot of complaints and pleading that, overall, amounted to quite a convincing argument for the 'Legalise Cannabis Campaign'. Adrian felt that this, if badly handled, could go unnecessarily wrong and undermine a lot of the goodwill and trust he'd built up in this class. He didn't want to lose it all over a bong - or a vase with holes in. He needed to bide his time, and he was really glad he did because fate yet again played its hand and intervened. About time too, since it was fate had got him into this mess in the first place. Spacey was carrying his bong over to the corner where he was going to wrap it up to be handed out on the visit, when he slipped and dropped it. It smashed into lots of pieces. Hooray! It was the end of the day too and definitely no time left for anymore throwing. Adrian started herding them towards the door.

'Goodbye, you can go now, fuck off, see you next week...'

By the time the next session came round, the clay had thankfully run out, and they were back to drawing Bob Marley with a ridiculous-size spliff in his mouth. However, that's another story.

# 8 LOOK INTO MY EYES

*When Captain Cook first arrived on Fiji he was surprised to be met by a solitary man carrying a parchment and some charcoal. This man was the shaman and had been sent by the King of Fiji to draw the white warrior, who, as legend would have it, was to bring disaster to the island. Cook, being rather vain, thought it all very quaint and posed for the artist on the beach. Unbeknown to him, the shaman was casting strong magic and ensnaring Cook's soul as he drew. Once the likeness had been passed to the king, the islanders felt they had nothing to fear as they had tricked their adversary into giving away his spirit. Cook was in their power.*

*Shortly after, Cook left the island, wracked with dysentery which he attributed to the bad water. The king kept the drawing locked in a chest wrapped in chains at the bottom of a cess-pit.*

Adrian was in Room Fifteen and it was getting towards the end of a morning when an unusual phenomenon occurred. All the men were engrossed in their work and he was temporarily left redundant. Having spent forever that day showing other people how to draw, he thought he'd take the opportunity to do some drawing himself, so he took up a pencil and a piece of paper and positioned his chair in the corner of the room. He was immediately noticed and, unable to endure seeing him so relaxed, someone had to come over to see what he was doing. It was Ricardo.

'Are you going to draw something?' he asked. To which Adrian replied testily,

'No, of course not. I always have a pencil and a sketchbook in my hand. They're the symbols of my trade, I carry them everywhere.' The wit sailed over Ricardo's head.

'Are you any good at drawing people, like? Could you draw me? We're not allowed photos in here and I want to send a picture out to my kids.'

Adrian realised this was the only way he was ever going to get some drawing done, so he agreed.

'Before I start, though, there's a couple of things you need to agree to...' Adrian had to think quickly here, and get himself into the moment... 'First, I can only do my best and if it doesn't turn out very well you will just have to accept it. OK? No good getting mad at the bloke who pushes the pen.'

'Yeah, sure, no problem, but isn't that a pencil?' he asked.

'And, secondly, I shall be staring at you, and you've got to feel comfortable with that.'

'Sure. Shall I sit here, boss?'

Ricardo sat directly in front of Adrian, who started to work, looking first at the overall shape of Ricardo's head. Within about five seconds, the whole class had noticed something was going on and got out of their seats to join the party. Naturally, they ended up standing behind Adrian, looking first at his drawing, then at Ricardo. Talk about off-putting. Adrian sent them away and said they could come back and look later. (Or words to that effect.)

Once everyone had gone, something very special happened, something that was often to repeat itself in the future. A unique kind of magic descended upon them. A special relationship grew between Adrian and Ricardo. Adrian felt like he had stepped into a very private space, as if he had entered right into Ricardo's head, just behind the bone of his skull. It was just deep enough inside to see the person living behind the eyes.

There were probably several reasons why this happened. The prolonged eye contact was the most obvious, but the fact that Adrian was taking an interest in Ricardo, possibly the first time that anyone ever had, certainly was another factor. A mutual trust was set up between them. Adrian had stuck out his neck by actually taking on the task and putting his skills on the line, while Ricardo had to allow Adrian to scrutinize his face and look him in the eyes. It was all very powerful stuff.

An intimate little world was established between them, which enabled Ricardo to feel secure enough to talk to Adrian, whom he now thought of as 'safe'. However, having become close brought an intimacy that Adrian wasn't sure how to handle.

'How long's this going to take?'

'How long you in for?' Adrian asked.

'Not long now. I'm out in four months. I'm in for buggery, you know.' Adrian momentarily froze, thinking he'd misheard.

'Oh! Don't you mean burglary? Thieving and stuff like that?'

'No. I mean buggery. Arse-raiding and stuff like that.' He was serious. Knowing the absolute contempt and hatred held by most inmates for 'nonces' (any form of sex offender), Adrian was surprised he was being so open. Adrian was drawing his eyes at the time.

'Shouldn't you be on a protected wing? I wouldn't go around saying that too loud in here if I were you.'

'Yeah, but that's what I'm in for, I didn't say I'd actually done it. It's a wrongful conviction, all these lads in here know that.' Adrian was now on his nose.

'Oh...' he said rather uncomfortably. It was getting a little more difficult to concentrate on the drawing.

'I did do it like, but it was with consent.' Adrian was at this point drawing his mouth. His pencil flinched and he messed up.

'Oops, sorry. I've just buggered up your mouth. Got a rubber?'

*God - what was he saying!?* Adrian felt himself turning red. It was definitely time to change the subject.

They began talking about Ricardo's background and what he was going to do when he got out, and where did he come from, things like that. All of which Ricardo answered in his incredibly relaxed, casual way. Adrian sat there incredibly tense throughout, dreading his answers.

When he had eventually finished the drawing, he gave it to Ricardo to look at, and reminded him of his agreement. It was a reasonable likeness, considering the conversation and the intimacy of the situation.

Ricardo smiled, then said: 'This is great. It looks like me.' He took it to show everyone in the room. Not wanting to lose the drawing for ever, Adrian suggested that he went to the photocopier to make three copies: one for the artist, one to send out to his kids, and one to keep for himself. This was a good idea, so off he went to the photocopier boys who operated on the next floor. Five minutes later, he was back carrying his copies. He gave Adrian his but Adrian got the feeling that there was something missing.

'Where's the original?'

'Oh shit, I've left it up there in the machine. I'll have to go back and get it.' But it wasn't that easy - there were too many inmates walking around outside, and only a limited number of men were allowed to leave the classrooms at any one time. Ricardo was told by the officers on duty to wait.

His turn never came round and he ended up waiting until the end of the lesson. When, eventually, they were let out, *Horror!* All along the corridor, up the stairs and along the top floor were countless photocopies of Adrian's drawing stuck to the walls. Each one had been amended. Written above it was the word WANTED in large capital letters, and underneath FOR BUGGERY. In smaller script was: 'Check his dick for sh—'

Oh God! This was not looking good. Adrian thought Ricardo was going to go ballistic and at least disembowel him. Obviously, their mutual understanding of non-critical assessment didn't extend to the rest of the wing. The other classes had all been released before Adrian's and rather than immediately leaving were gathering around in increasing crowds, laughing furiously. Adrian tried to take the nearest poster down, but before he could get rid of it, out stepped Ricardo. He saw Adrian standing there with the offending poster in his hand. This was really not looking good. He came straight over to Adrian, who flinched. Instead of going nuts, however, Ricardo just smiled and said calmly:

'It's good to have a joke. It doesn't bother me. It would if it was true, but I knows I'm innocent so it doesn't matter.' Adrian explained this was a dreadful mistake and that he hadn't been involved. God! He sounded so pathetic.

Within seconds, the officers on duty appeared and came over to see what all the fuss was about. The crowds parted to allow their collective uniforms through. Adrian awaited their prescribed disapproval and half expected to get a lecture on keeping discipline or something. Instead they roared.

'Great joke! This is brilliant. Here give me one, I can put it up on the wing,' he heard one of them say. Jeez!

By the next day Adrian's ability as a portrait artist had spread throughout the prison and a sea of potential clients was seeking him out. Within five minutes of his class arriving, he was asked by several of them whether he was 'the boss who drew people.'

'Will you draw me?' was the request of the day. Adrian agreed, though it would have to be on a first come first served basis, providing he could find time at the end of the lesson. The man who asked him first that morning was called Robbie. The most notable thing about him was a string of tattooed bullet holes across his neck. He was a very twitchy sort of person. Someone who, you imagined, lived on the edge. When it came to Adrian drawing him, fidgeting was a problem.

'You're going to have to be still. I can't draw you jumping all over the place. Just look at me.'

This proved to be deadly. Any trace of normality went out of the window. He sat there with this ridiculous cheesy grin on his face, staring at Adrian's eyes.

'Like this, guv?'

They both burst out laughing. It took several attempts before they could resume.

'Try to be natural. Just relax!'

Natural for Robbie was being unnatural. Natural was fidgeting, twitching, talking non-stop, walking around, but Adrian needed him to be out of character and sit still. Eventually time kicked in, and the laughing and shuffling began to lessen as he settled down and felt more at ease. Adrian, eventually, began to set about his work. The movement hadn't completely disappeared but had metamorphosed into speech. All that peripheral activity was drawn in and condensed into words. He talked for England.

'What you in for?' Adrian asked.

'Well, it's a long story, but in a nutshell, it's murder.'

Adrian didn't believe this, but thought it better to let it go for the sake of art. He continued.

'I was in Paris on holiday with my girlfriend. You ever been there? I was sitting in this outside café sort of place drinking a beer, minding my own like, when this bloke comes up to me and asks me if I wants my picture drawn. He was a portrait artist, a bit like you really. So I says I do, cos my girlfriend would like it and wants to have it framed like. So to please her I agrees to pay him ten pounds for it. I sits there and he draws me like, it takes him about ten minutes. He then gives me this drawing that's supposed to be me, and it's fucking horrible. It don't look anything like me. So I says to him, 'Are you taking the piss or what?' I was so mad. 'You got to do it again,' I says, 'I'm not having that.' But he says that I'm trying to cheat him in order to get another drawing free and that I has to pay again if I wants another. He then gets up to go away. Well, I'm not just letting him get away like that, so I jumps up and blocks him, to stop him leaving. He then tries to push me backwards. So I grabs hold of him and hits him over the head with a bottle and I kills him like.'

There was a twinkle in his eye.

'How's the picture coming along, boss? Crap, is it?'

'Yeah, totally.' Then as an afterthought, 'It's a brilliant likeness of you, though.'

'Funny.'

'Good story that,' said Adrian. 'Strange how they put you in the wrong prison, though. This is a B Cat, you know. Anyway, I've nearly finished. I want to keep a copy of this, so I'll get it photocopied at break.'

'Why? Do you fancy me or what? I do look like David Beckham, don't you think?'

'No and no, in that order. And by the way I forgot to tell you I actually work for *Crimewatch* on TV when I'm not in here. I try to draw as many cons as poss, for future reference like.'

Robbie grinned as Adrian gave him the drawing.

'I've been on *Crimewatch* twice. Their drawings didn't look anything like me, but they were better than this.' There was laughter all round, and a good feeling in the air. Though totally different from the experience with Ricardo, Adrian, once again, recognised the now familiar closeness that had developed between him and the sitter. This was possibly the best way he had discovered to break the ice with individuals. He put portrait drawing next to non-confrontational teaching on his imaginary chain.

'I'm only joking. Thanks boss, it's cool.'

'If I'm your boss, you must be my slave,' answered Adrian, who was getting fed up with being called either 'boss' or 'guv' all the time.

'Piss off, boss...'

'Did you just tell me to piss off, slave?'

# 9 BILLY

*The story-tellers on Fiji were always regarded with respect and awe, for they were the custodians of the history. They were the ones who gave power to the deeds of the ancestors. Their sagas were re-enacted in the souls of all those who listened and were given life. To repeat these tales frivolously was an insult to the gods.*

One morning, on arrival at work, Adrian was taken aside and asked to teach, not in his usual art room, but in a classroom on the wing. This came to him as a complete shock, not only was he losing one of his groups but also he was unaware that education took place anywhere else in the prison other than in the Amenities Building.

'We need Room Fifteen for ceramics now. It is actually a ceramics room,' said Nigel.

Adrian was well aware that it was a ceramics room. Why else were there three bloody great wheels and a kiln in there. He'd never been told his group was to be temporary and no mention of the change had been made before this. There wasn't even time allowed to say goodbye, There wasn't time allowed to do anything at all. Before he could think properly he was being escorted by Nigel along more strip lit corridors to what was to become his new home, Delta Block. Adrian's hopes sank when they arrived, It was even more soul-less than the art rooms in the Amenities building. Its multi-functional use left it bereft of any character whatsoever. 'You'll have to carry any materials you need, back and forth. You can't leave stuff over here, you know, security!' That magic word that excused everything. Strangely, there seemed to be more officers in this part of the prison, but like the room, they too were multi-functional and although physically present, their minds were often elsewhere. Adrian looked around him, so this was it, a classroom attached to a wing, the setting for the next phase of his life. It would be here, in this cubicle like room that Adrian would instruct, listen, be confronted, laugh, sympathise, agonise, be amazed and of course... teach, and always laden down by tons of bags, paints, paper and countless folders that all needed to be accounted for at any moment.. It was also in this room that Adrian would meet so many enigmatic and extraordinary people, and of these, Billy Bates was probably the one whom Adrian respected the most.

Billy started on that first day in the new room. He walked in with the others but for some reason he stood out, not that he said very much, other than 'I'm not going to be here long, I'm out in a couple of weeks.' Adrian interpreted this as 'don't bother trying'. But amidst the layers of mindless sportswear that he wore, he carried a dignified quality Adrian hadn't expected. His whole persona seemed non-confrontational and distant. He did what was expected of him yet also made it quite clear there was a limit to what he would do. There were certain things he would try and others he would not. He conveyed all this without saying a word. Adrian felt secure, the boundaries displayed were obvious.

As time passed, Adrian got to know Billy increasingly well. It seemed Billy's life so far, all twenty-six years of it, was packed from the word go with more 'issues' than most people would ever have to deal with in a full long life. From the moment he had entered this world it appeared the odds were stacked against him. Adrian often wrestled with the question of why it was like that for some people. He found some of the answers when studying reincarnation, and the rest he found in Angela Neustatter's book *Locked In, Locked Out,* where she points out seven conditions or events which could, if in one's biography, increase the chances of ending up behind bars. The more of these you had experienced the greater the chances. They were:

1) Coming from a dysfunctional family
2) Coming from a family where there is a history of crime
3) Poverty
4) A history of drug abuse
5) Low attendance and achievement at school
6) A history of abuse
7) Mental health problems

When Adrian looked back at his own childhood he saw several of these things to some extent, but then not enough to warrant ending up inside. Each one was just above the cut-off line, just above the 'you'll make it all right' point. Perhaps that's why he was *just* all right.

Billy, on the other hand, had all of these and not surprisingly had spent most of his adult life incarcerated. A very sad waste of a life, and yet he seemed, on a certain level, to ride through it all and remain intact. He had qualities sadly lacking in many people that are more fortunate, including, Adrian felt, himself. He had what could only be described, badly, as an illogical wisdom interlaced with an even more illogical humour, which meant that he laughed a lot at things that weren't funny.

It helped Billy that he joined the class with another, more extrovert man who took centre stage, allowing Billy to come in less noticed. Feeling the need for a supportive friend in this empty new classroom, Adrian found himself giving Billy a lot of quiet attention. This was something Billy was not used to but he responded positively. Billy and Adrian became good friends almost instantly, they just seemed inexplicably to click. Over the next couple of weeks, Billy taught Adrian many things about prison and about himself.

One day, over tea-break, Billy told Adrian his story. Adrian wasn't sure why he chose that moment or why he needed to, but he did. It was very private and very difficult for him to talk so personally. Adrian realised that something significant was about to happen and felt privileged but also felt a great sense of responsibility descend upon him. There was a definite struggle in Billy's demeanour when he told this story, his dignity wrestled with pain.. Billy was standing on thin ice. He began by talking about his parents...

'They both were heroin addicts.' He said this as if it was the most normal thing in the world to be. 'My father was a dealer, but I don't remember him much. He was a bastard. I hated him. He used to beat me all the time,' he stared at Adrian and then lowering his voice '...and other things.' Billy maintained his stare with difficulty, he needed to make sure Adrian understood the *other things*. 'He got shot when I was seven. Whoever did it, did me a favour! If they hadn't done it, I would have had to do it myself! The only bad thing about him dying was that my mum had to get her own smack from then on. She couldn't find money to score, so she started house-breaking, I used to go with her. The first time I went, I was shit-scared. She pushed me through a sky-light into this posh bungalow so I could open the door for her, I nearly pissed myself with fear. But I soon got used to it.'

'Did you ever think that what you were doing might be wrong?' asked Adrian.

'They put my mum in prison and put me in foster care, that was wrong. I hated being with those people. I gave them hell. There wasn't any one of them who could manage me.'

Adrian noticed Billy was putting on a brave face. It was obvious he had been really hurt, and still was. He then told Adrian, with a twinkle in his eye as if to change the subject, how none of them *lasted*.

'I was too difficult for them, little sod I was.' Then his face once again blackened, 'Eventually I got put in a "home". Those bastards actually abused me there. Those stinking bastards. *They abused me!*

Billy was reliving it. His face became sweaty and contorted Adrian felt so sorry for him. He wanted to hug and comfort him but thought better of it.

'That is so terrible!'

'I got them though, later on, I gave evidence against them. They're now in nick. If ever I should meet one of them I'd kill them.' Adrian believed him. Billy's story was so painful. Had he opened up Pandora's Box to find himself in danger of not being able to deal with all this stuff? Deciding it was too late to shut the lid, he thought the best thing to do was to move the story on.

'What happened next?' asked Adrian.

'I started taking drugs. Anything to escape. It did help for a while and things didn't seem so bad for a bit. But they wouldn't leave me alone, they had to interfere, eventually they detoxed me.'

'How old were you when that happened?'

'Eleven, I'd taken a load of amphetamines.'

The next part of the story was all about drugs and detoxes. Adrian was speechless. They seemed to happen with alarming regularity and somewhere along the line the amphetamines had become heroin. When Adrian asked him how old he was when he first was sent to prison, Billy replied that he didn't really know, as it was a gradual progression, which had begun with children's homes, secure units, Young Offender Institutes and eventually led to prison. There wasn't an exact beginning.

'Are you going to keep clean when you get out?' Adrian asked.

'I dunno. I'd like to stay clean. I always say that I will but then don't, I'm beginning not to believe myself anymore.'

It seemed to Adrian that Billy's life consisted of stretches of time in prison interspersed by the odd spell outside where his uncontrollable need for heroin led him to commit crimes of alarming severity. Adrian and Billy stared at each other. Here was a registered drug addict with a criminal record as long as his tram-lined arm. Despite having no education at all, a string of relationships behind him that corresponded to every release, and two children somewhere who he was not allowed to see...despite all this, he was optimistic about the future.

'Not to worry, hey? It could be worse.'

But for the first time ever, Adrian doubted it.

But worse it did appear to get, however, when several weeks later Billy, without warning, disappeared. He had been taken to the Health Care wing after discovering a large lump on his testicle. Even the gods thought this was too much and granted mercy and spared him. It turned out to be a cyst.

. Knowing Billy's story, made Adrian's working relationship with him easier. The shared story created a bond between them. He could still be bloody annoying, but knowing what he'd been through made it easier for Adrian. Whenever Billy could see Adrian getting fed up with him, he would remind him of the 'gun story' and grin from ear to ear.

Billy did not naturally take to art and would shy away from anything that was in the slightest bit demanding. He was much happier if Adrian did the work for him. Adrian went along with the 'watching is learning' bit, until he realised that it was probably as far as it was ever going to go. Billy had a nice folder full of Adrian's work signed by himself. Therefore, Adrian tried to think up projects that might engage him more in the lesson. He came up with tattoo designing, macho art stuff, and got some basic design sheets for him to look at, hoping they would inspire him. It worked.

Billy began his tattooing project by copying a traditional anchor design which turned out reasonably well. In fact, it was so reasonable that Jabba wanted it on his forearm. Billy began to redraw the anchor in biro, on Jabba. However, he soon discovered that drawing it again, exactly the same, was more difficult than he initially thought, the second one was proving hard. Jabba, whose brain was directly connected to his mouth and never stopped talking, was piling on the pressure. There was no humour in his voice.

'You better not fuck this up. Biro's a bitch to get off.'

You'd think he'd have picked his words a little more carefully under the circumstances. The whole class came over to watch. Billy now found himself struggling under the spotlight and wasn't happy. He needed a way out without losing face. So, having got thus far, he stopped, and announced:

'I need to personalise this a bit, so it fits your character, like.' He then drew a large W in front of the design and walked away, grinning.

Nobody got it, at first, a large W followed by an anchor. Suddenly, the first penny dropped and Robbie exploded with laughter, and everyone else rapidly followed suit, whether they understood it or not. Not surprisingly, Jabba was the last to get it.

'What? What's so funny? What?'

Billy had temporarily found his niche as master tattoo artist, and the next lesson began designing a wonderful piece of body art that was to stretch right across his back from shoulder to shoulder. The main part of the design comprised the words 'THUG LIFE', drawn in graffiti style - another kosher project - surrounded by scrolls, skulls and a car. The centrepiece, however, consisted of two crossed guns. Having had the graffiti designed for him, ninety-nine percent of the car drawn for him and so on, the next obstacle presented itself.

'I'm having problems with the guns, boss.'

'You haven't started yet; I'll help you when there's something that needs helping along. Give us a shout when you've done something.' Adrian freely would give any amount of instruction, encouragement or help, but he did insist, this time, that Billy put in some effort too. He wasn't there to just draw things for people. One line later: 'I need some help, this isn't working out. You'll have to do it.'

Reluctantly Adrian started to draw a gun. He thought it was turning out well and looking good, until Billy said: 'What's that supposed to be?' He was looking on in amused disbelief. 'Ha ha ha! Is that supposed to be a gun?' Billy would have been very indignant if Adrian had laughed at his work as he was now doing at Adrian's. 'It looks like a toy cowboy pistol. You've been watching too much *Toy Story*.'

He then began showing everyone in the room the stupid gun Ade had drawn. Adrian was surprised at how pissed off he was feeling. He tried to explain himself and save face.

'How should I know what a gun looks like? I've never actually seen a real hand gun, except on telly, that is.' Adrian snatched the paper out of Billy's hand. 'This is mine,' he said. Unfortunately it ripped in half. 'Fuck!'

A general, incredulous look descended on all faces around the room, except Adrian's which was smiling insipidly.

'Really? You've never seen a gun? You really have led a sheltered life, haven't you.' And then some reverse psychology kicked in and Billy began to instruct Adrian in the art of 'still life with guns'. 'They don't have handles like that. Here - let me show you.' He had found the confidence to show the idiot teacher something real. He drew a sketchy picture, telling Adrian the names of each component, and then said: 'Now can you do it properly?' Adrian could hear his own voice coming out of Billy's mouth. He had transformed into the teacher.

Billy having made the effort to draw something, Adrian then honoured his side of the bargain and began to complete the Luger, or whatever it was, as part of the tattoo design. Billy was delighted with the results of his teaching skills.

'You've learnt well,' he said, looking at Adrian.

Between them, they completed the extremely in-your-face piece of art. Billy told all and sundry he was going to have this put on his back as soon as he next got out. Having drawn about one percent of the design himself was enough for it to become his own work. He was elated by his own sense of accomplishment.

Billy left the classroom on a wave of congratulations. Adrian, on the other hand, was left in a sea of paint pots, which he had to clear away. He packed away his art things and gave the room a general tidy. When he went over to his chair, he found a bar of chocolate on it with a note. It read: 'Thanks.'

Adrian felt something move inside him, his heart, it felt like melting chocolate, he was truly touched.

The next week Adrian came into work, he discovered another, less pleasant, note with his name on it. It was a security note in his pigeonhole. He was to report to Security. Totally baffled, he went to the office where a rather severe officer took delight in being able to exercise his duty so unreservedly.

'I've asked you here to inform you that it is against the rules to make replica firearms with the prisoners.'

Adrian was dumbfounded.

'I'm not aware that I have.'

'You do work on D wing. You do teach Billy Bates?

'Yes, but...' The officer pulled out a cardboard cut-out of a gun that looked vaguely familiar.

'Oh, that.'

Billy had somehow or other managed to enlarge Adrian's tiny drawing, stick it on cardboard and cut around it. Pretty amazing in a place where there was neither glue nor scissors.

'Bates came out of his cell brandishing this imitation firearm,' continued the security man. 'The officers on duty, seeing it, raised the alarm and the prisoner was overpowered and the weapon was removed. He said the art teacher had shown him how to make it.'

Adrian explained it was for a tattoo design, but this only made it sound worse, as tattooing was strictly banned too.

Anyway, late, belittled and angry, Adrian made his way to the wing, where Billy came running over to him as soon as he entered.

'Look out! You're in trouble. I've stitched you up.'

Another officer beckoned Adrian to the wing office, where he was taken through an almost identical briefing. He tried hard not to take personally the officer's enthusiasm in exercising his duty.

Eventually, when everything had died down, Billy told Adrian what had happened. It was interesting to hear the other side of the story. He had decided it would be cool to enlarge the crossed gun design, cut it out and hang it on his cell wall. A kind of trophy above the mantelpiece. He had spent all evening making it, and was just taking the first one over to Mikey's cell, as he was doing A-level art, to get him to help colour it in, when....

'These fucking idiot officers jumped me and bent me up. I tried to tell them I was just doing art, but they didn't hear me as one had his fist in my mouth.'

Billy eventually did do his time (not for the first time) and was released. He walked out carrying a see-through plastic bag containing all his worldly goods, a head full of good intentions and his bus fare to the station. As fate would have it, he was delayed by a 'friend' who was waiting for him with a celebratory wrap of skag. He was back in three months. He had missed the boat to Fiji.

# 10 VISITS

*Before western missionaries came to Fiji, marriage, as such, didn't exist on the island. Women slept with whoever they wanted and lived together communally. Children were universally loved by all men, as each was, possibly, the father. Both sexes were regarded as equal in power because whereas men had magic in their thoughts and limbs and could catch wild goats; women, on the other hand, had strong magic in their stomachs, from which they grew babies. This was all about to change with the arrival of 'civilization'.*

Mikey, the lifer, once told Adrian while he queued at the hot water sink to fill his flask, that he never had any visits. When asked why, he said it was because he didn't want any. Adrian thought this strange and asked why again.

'They remind me of all the stuff I'm missing. The last one upset me for ages. It took me weeks to get over it, so I'm not going there again. I think it's best to forget all those people while I'm in here and anyway, I don't think it did them much good seeing me either.' He shuffled off across the wing back to his lonely cell to loose himself in a cup of regulation tea.

This opinion wasn't shared by everyone, however. Jabba, for instance, couldn't wait for his next visit. As the days rolled by, and the visit got closer, he worked himself almost up into a frenzy.

'*Yes*! My missus is coming on Friday and she's bringing my kid to see me.'

'Really! That's nice. How long since you last saw her?' Adrian said glibly. It was the third time he'd heard it that morning.

'Well, the last time I saw Jen was about a month ago, but I haven't seen my kid since I came inside, it's nearly a year now. Jen don't like bringing her to prison. It's not really a place for a child, is it? Here, I've got a photo of them.'

From his pocket he pulled a dog-eared photo, staring out of which was a bubbly, bleached blonde babe from Barry with plucked eyebrows, nose stud, big earrings and a newborn baby. Adrian said they looked nice. He really was feeling glib. Jabba continued.

'She's a doll. Just looking at her photo turns me on.'

Suddenly everyone was listening.

'Can I have a look?' said the ever-optimistic Frosty.

Frosty was Jabba's mate and yet at the same time he was the one who argued with him endlessly. It was a kind of love-hate relationship. He also had a visit on Friday. Frosty stretched out to take the photo.

'Fuck off, my kid's on here as well. Get your own picture, pervert!'

Then turning back to Adrian,

'I can't wait till I'm out of here. First thing I'm going to do is shag her, then I'm going to shag her again.' For some reason, Jabba thought this was hilarious and starting laughing furiously. Adrian just sat there looking at him, waiting for him to finish.

He hated it when someone thought something that funny when he didn't get it. Frosty came to the rescue and brought all the hilarity to an abrupt end by delivering a sobering comment somewhere below the belt.

'Dream on! She probably will be living with someone else by the time you get out, if she isn't already.' Judging by the reaction from Jabba, this must have been quite close to the truth, for it evoked a considerable outburst. Frosty always managed to say things that led to this kind of fall-out.

'What the fuck you think you're saying? Get lost! She's not like that. She loves me! And she's got my kid. She'll be waiting. She's not like those slags you hang around with. Which one of your strung-out friends is coming to visit this time? Moron!' Then turning to Adrian he continued: 'You knows, I can puts my hands around her waist like this. She's so small.'

Adrian turned his attention to Frosty, while Jabba started one of his laughing fits again. Frosty was a strange man who, like so many others in here, had spent the best part of his adult life locked up. Being free meant trying to survive in a hostile environment. There was always some relief in being hauled back again. Today, Jabba's enthusiasm was really annoying Frosty. He also thought Jabba's response to him was undeserved. He wasn't going to let that go so easily.

'My mum's coming, actually.'

This really surprisingly bugged Jabba further. Maybe it was because his own mother walked out on him.

'God! Don't! I don't want to even imagine that someone actually gave birth to you.' Jabba was directing his smile at Adrian, but pointing at Frosty.

'Have you got anything to give her? You should give her something, you know,' said Adrian, trying to put the conversation back on line - and also get him involved in some work.

'I dunno. I'm too excited to do anything today. Can you helps me make a card, guv, and gets me an envelope?'

'I'll help you if you make a start, but if you can't do one yourself, then why don't you ask Steve and Mark?'

His face dropped, and Adrian remembered that Jabba had once had a card of Steve's. It was at a time when Cardiff (the Bluebirds) were up against Liverpool. Jabba wanted a card to share his support with his brother, who was a great Cardiff fan. He went to see Steve, who asked him to think of something to write on the card. After hours of thought and consideration, he came up with the staggeringly original *'Come on the Bluebirds!'* Steve didn't like doing this, it grated in his throat. Normally, he didn't have a problem with doing any football insignia, but this time, they were up against his team and he lived and breathed Liverpool. With every word he felt a betrayal most heinous surge through his entire being. He couldn't refuse to make the card, for then his 'safe' position would be questioned. He was subordinate to Jabba, who was higher up the pecking order. He resolved it, quite brilliantly, by writing *Cum on the Bluebirds*, which the none-too-literate Jabba didn't notice and happily posted the card. Steve played it cool and no one knew for sure, whether it was a genuine mistake or not.

'Yeah, I don't want one with their football crap on it. They can't even spell,' said Jabba, suddenly reliving the moment when it was pointed out by his brother.

'I want something like roses in a heart.'

Ready everybody? *'Aaaaah!'*

Frosty got up.

'Scuse me. I'm just going for a vomit...' sticking his fingers down his throat. As he waddled off to the toilet he turned and called over his shoulder, '...and a shit.'

As Friday approached Jabba got his hair cut, washed his best shirt, spent three hours ironing it over and over again and covered himself in half a bottle of Lynx.

'You scrub up well,' (should have used 'Bang Up For Men' for that unforgettable pheromone phenomenon) Adrian said encouragingly. 'She won't be able to resist you.' Jabba grinned, glowing with pride.

'Visits!' shouted an officer, and Jabba plus the more-sober-than-usual Frosty were escorted to the Visits Hall.

'Good luck!' someone called.

An hour and a half later, they both returned. Jabba didn't look like a person who had had a happy meeting. He was crest-fallen and wasn't talking to anyone. He went straight to his cell and would only come out when he was ready, which happened to be tea break. Adrian had to wait to hear what had happened. When he did emerge from his cell, he was dressed in his usual clothes again but he was definitely not his usual self. Frosty also came to sit at the table and, sensing a golden opportunity to avenge himself, chose this moment to continue the earlier banter and gain the upper hand. He said very loudly, so all could hear: 'God! Your missus was well out of order. I wouldn't let my wife nag me like that, in front of everyone. All that crap about the house and her selling your car. Why you let her talk to you like that? Jeez!'

Jabba began to redden with rage, but without the fire. 'Shut up, Frosty! Anyway, you shouldn't be eaves-dropping on other people's private conversations. Which part of "private" don't you understand?' Jabba was instinctively retaliating but had lost his fighting spirit; his repartee had also lost its venom. He was weighed down by 'issues'. Frosty, having his own need to prove himself, hammered on regardless, and wouldn't let the point drop.

'Private? That's a joke, the whole hall could hear her. There was nothing private about it. And that kid of yours didn't like you much, did she? She screamed every time you tried to go near her, like you were some sort of beast.'

'*Fuck off!* She wasn't scared of me, she was having a bad day. Seen too much TV last night, and she was frightened of prison.'

Adrian was making noises like, 'Calm down, boys,' and, 'Let's take it easy.' But no one seemed to be taking much notice.

'Frightened of you, more like,' said Frosty with a smirk on his face.'

Jabba dug his fingernails into the plastic seat.

'*Piss off!* You know nothing about anything. I'm her dad.'

'Who was that other bloke then, outside? She seemed to be OK with him.'

Adrian got up.

'OK, Frosty. Off you go! Go and sit somewhere else!' But something got twisted, because Jabba got up instead and made to go to his cell. It was all too much for him. As he left he said almost absently:

'Fuck knows who he was...'

All the time he'd been arguing, he had been wringing his hands. In the ash-tray on the table he left a ripped up photo. It was the one of the bleached blonde babe and the baby. Adrian was angry with Frosty.

'That was a really bastard thing to do,' said Adrian. 'I thought you were supposed to be his friend.'

'I am. He's probably my best mate. I was only telling him the truth. Better than sitting here being all sugary sweet. He knows what I mean. If I didn't tell him, who would?'

'Yeah! Well even so, you could have been a little more understanding.'

'That's how he understands. He knows what I'm saying.'

Adrian never completely comprehended the complicated relationship between these two men. They showed their affection for each other by swearing and arguing constantly. On the other hand, they were not that dissimilar to certain married couples that Adrian knew.

Seeing the space created on the table, Mikey, the lifer, shuffled over and sat down with his horribly stained tea cup.

'What did I tell you. No good, visits, no good at all!'

They sat and finished their tea in silence, and for the first time Adrian felt sorry for Jabba.

# 11 GLOBAL CONNECTIONS

*'Do not try to find literal explanations for why natural disasters happen. Some are caused by quite minor things, far away. For instance, when a butterfly flaps its wings on some tropical island, mountains fall elsewhere. Everything has its effect, we just don't always see it.'* World Ecology – A Spiritual Investigation

Adrian had always been of the opinion that if you wanted to succeed well at something, you first had to understand the rules. Ignorance of any system greatly increased the possibility of failure. Structures needed to be securely in place for initiative to flourish, because like new shoots they needed support to grow up against. All this seemed like common sense, but when it came to Feldon Park, Adrian scratched his head. Just when he thought he had understood something about the prison system, the rules would suddenly change. Nearly every colleague that Adrian met seemed to have their own personal version of them that always boiled down to... 'Well that's what I was told.' Also,

Adrian working part-time didn't help, he got the distinct feeling that it was used as an excuse for keeping him uninformed. One day he could be teaching here, another there. One day he could have equipment, another not. One day he had six students, the next, fifteen. One day the men could go to the library during lessons, then not. There was no logic and no explanations. The only consistency was that if you didn't know about it, it was your fault. Adrian assumed that the prison had adopted the same approach to life that he had, 'Live in the moment,' though he somehow doubted it.

Dealing with inconsistencies on a daily basis was one thing, but what worried Adrian equally, was what the long-term effects of all this 'not knowing the rules' would be. What consequences would eventually manifest? There would definitely be consequences, he thoroughly believed that. Every deed has an eventual outcome, all that goes out, comes back, in one form or another. It was a kind of divine justice, a kind of karma. Where was all this dis-information, and all its resulting frustration and anger, going? He was mulling over such things as he drove home.

Most of his friends pitied Adrian his long drive back and forth to work, but he valued it because it allowed him time to either plan or reflect about the day. Today, his reflecting had reached a dead end, so he switched on the radio and heard an interview with Richard Jenkins. This young man from Brecon had been brutally attacked, for no apparent reason, whilst on a gap year in Fiji. 'Maybe,' thought Adrian, 'this was the outcome of all that bad feeling that seemingly went nowhere in Feldon Park?' The radio spoke...

'Richard Jenkins arrived back to his parents home in Brecon last week, after having endured what looks like a ritualistic attack by the tribes people of Fiji. He was set upon by several painted warriors in what police are saying appears increasingly like an attempted form of pagan sacrifice. Richard was fortunately physically unharmed. A statement from the British Embassy in Fiji said that the lack of rain on the island this year had possibly motivated such desperate means. With me in the studio now is Richard Jenkins and Professor Don Hope of the Anthropological Institute of Polynesian Studies...'

Adrian listened. It was as if the radio was answering his question. Perhaps this really was where all the overspill from Feldon Park was going. It was hitting other people far away elsewhere, in the world. Adrian listened more attentively. Apparently, the people of Kaduva, a small island lying in the south of Fiji, had been waiting all year for the arrival of the rains.

'...every June the clouds usually blow in across the turquoise ocean, quite ferociously, but this year, for the first time ever, they failed to appear on Kaduva, whereas everywhere else was getting a soaking.'

Then the actual interview began, 'Richard, you're lucky to be alive. Do you think that your being attacked was in any way associated with the lack of rains?' The interviewer pressed on: 'Were you aware that this sort of thing was a possibility?'

'No. not at all. In fact I was getting on very well with the local people. Why only two days earlier, I had been playing "Dragon Slayer" with the men of the village.'

'These were the same men who attacked you?'

'Yes.'

'What's "Dragon Slayer"?'

'It's a game on my console, you know, my Game Boy®. It was a great ice breaker, it got everybody laughing.'

'You don't think that the game might have had something to do with the attack?

'I don't think so, they loved it. We all had so much fun.'

'Professor, What do you make of this? Judging from the way these warriors were dressed, it seems this was some sort of ritual. Is human sacrifice common in the South Pacific?'

'No, not nowadays. In the past many people believed that bad weather was how the Gods expressed their displeasure, should they have been insulted or the like. But those days are long passed. Then it was believed that to change the weather, one had to appease the Gods, one had to make a sacrifice. I can't understand, if it was a ritual why they went for an outsider, a stranger.'

'Richard, you don't think you offended the Gods in any way, do you?'

'No! Like I say, me and the locals were getting on fine.'

'How did you first meet the tribesmen?'

'Well, as I said, when I arrived, I went to the nearest bar, and started playing my computer game. All the local boys were amazed and wanted to see it. They acted like they'd never seen one before.'

'When you say boys do you mean children were trying to play?'

'No! You know, men! The first match I had was with an old guy. It was so funny. This bloke didn't have a clue what to do. He was useless. He just kept pressing the buttons. He got so frightened when the sound effects kicked in. He threw the console across the mat and cursed the warriors dancing on the screen. Fortunately, he didn't break it, but the knock must have hit the right button, since he did manage to score two points in the first round. Unfortunately, he also lost all his lives.'

'Did you try and explain the rules, afterwards?'

'Yes! I told him it was all over and he had no lives left. I don't think he got it though. He just kept shaking it. It was well funny. '

'Did the old man have a ring of sharks teeth around his neck?' asked the professor.

'Yes he did. I tried to swap my magna-light torch for them. They were so cool,' answered Richard jokingly.

'That was the tribal chief you were playing with. He is a direct descendent of the Sun-God, who is regarded as invincible. For him to lose in battle is serious. He would have lost his soul. I think we know now you were attacked.'

'You were lucky you were not more hurt. They could have seriously damaged you or worse.'

'Yeah I know! But they still didn't have to throw my Game Boy in the sea.'

'So, Professor, you don't think it had anything to do with the lack of rains then?'

'The Fijians believe that the weather is directly associated with human thought. Bad weather from afar is a manifestation of bad thinking. Interestingly, it was because of all the bad storms they experienced each year, that the Fijians knew that other civilizations existed. The weather didn't match their own peaceful way of thinking. Thus it was no surprise to them when they were so-called *discovered.'*

Adrian froze. 'Exactly!' he said to himself. 'This is the big picture! This is global! All things have consequences! This lack of rain in Kaduva was probably caused by Feldon Park. We are making the crops in Fiji die. Let alone all the world's starvation, the disappearing rain forest and global warming. It's all the prison's fault, they cause everything bad in the world.' Adrian suddenly realised that he was acting like a man under stress.

He was feeling increasingly sleepy. He always found that he was able to engage in a completely different way of thinking in this state. It totally immersed him, and his vision, along with his understanding, seemed to extend globally. Not only had he realised where all the unanswered questions went, but he also realised how easy it could be to do the wrong thing and upset a 'god'. Although he had now been working in prison for three months, he still, every day, felt himself walking through the 'unknown'. There seemed to be no permanent rules, there were no warning signs, no training. He felt he was being set up to do a 'Richard Jenkins'. It could be so easy to get the wrong man to do the wrong thing at the wrong time. He turned off the radio and continued his drive in silence.

* * *

The next day at Feldon Park it suddenly stopped raining. It had been raining forever, a weird sort of rain that covered all the cars in a thin film of brown, sandy dirt.

'It's not our normal rain,' said the Officer on gate duty that morning. 'They say it comes from the Sahara or somewhere, that's what all that crud is. Sand!'

'Really?' said his bored companion. 'It's a bloody pain wherever it fucking comes from. I've had to wash my car three times this week already. Oh, come on, 11 o'clock, I can't wait for second breakfast.' He rubbed his copious, billowing stomach. And as he did so, he stared out into the car-park. Something had caught his eye, something that was shining between the cars.

'What's that there? Look - over there. There's something shining by that Volkswagen.'

He walked over to it cautiously, remembering his post-9/11 Prevention and Awareness training, and kicked it with the side of his foot.

'Bloody Hell! It's a Game Boy. Someone must have dropped it going on a visit.'

'Really! But you can't take them in. They're illegal. You can't take Game Boys in even if you're on a visit.'

'Better keep it here then. It'll be safe here. Hey! We're in luck - it's got Dragon Slayer on it. And it must be the new version - look! There's a new character, some weird voodoo warrior.'

'Great! Set it up. Prepare to have your arse thrashed.'

The soul of the old chief stared out of the screen at the grey concrete world of Feldon Park. Never had he seen such a place before. He wondered if this was 'the Hell' that the missionaries had talked about when he was a child and wished he'd lived a better life.

# 12 BIRDMAN

*The islanders on Fiji were generally of a happy disposition. Their beaming smiles were natural and genuinely reflected the outlook of their souls. To be sad was thought of as unnatural and was associated with pain and suffering. It was something to be endured, which would eventually resolve itself. To be unhappy unnecessarily was considered an affliction that needed curing quickly as it could turn to illness or even lead to death.*

When most men joined Adrian's class for the first time, they found it rather intimidating. Walking into an established group wasn't easy, and neither was doing a subject that possibly one hadn't ever attempted before. Adrian witnessed many different strategies used by different men to cope with this potentially embarrassing situation. New pupils seemed to join his group on a weekly basis, whilst others disappeared, and a few 'chosen' ones, (though never chosen by Adrian), seemed to remain for ever. The idea of anyone ever achieving a degree in art seemed ever more impossible, unless they could do it in about six weeks maximum, that is!

To make it as easy as possible for new students to join the group, Adrian always would make sure he talked to them individually, first, to avoid spot-lighting.

'Have you ever done art before?' he would ask.

' I'm crap, guv. I've not drawn anything since I was a kid,' they nearly always whispered through the corners of their mouths. Nobody wants to appear a fool in front of so many people, so, to make it easier, Adrian set up master classes where he would spoon-feed newcomers through the first few weeks until they felt comfortable enough to work on their own. He would lead them line by line, stroke by stroke until, by the end of the lesson, they all had an accomplished, finished piece of work in front of them. Most men were amazed at what they could achieve. It was necessary for such guidance and instruction, otherwise, many vulnerable areas could be exposed in a very public place. These early days were delicate for new students and the last thing Adrian wanted to do was to scare anybody off.

The beauty of art over more scientifically-based subjects is that there is always room to find something positive to say, no matter what is laid before you. It's always possible to be objective. But when Steve arrived, for the first time ever Adrian found himself lost for words.

Several men had joined the class at approximately the same time. None of them had done any art before and all needed the 'introductory treatment'. All except Steve that is. Steve was in his sixties, he wore black horn-rimmed glasses and had a shock of white hair. A bit like an older David Hockney, but unfortunately this was as close as the similarities got. Cleanliness was not one of his strongest points. He used lashings of 'Bang Up For Men', and this definitely contributed to his being a loner. The other men in the group all seemed to dislike him as soon as he walked in. The seats next to him were always the last to be taken, and no one went out of their way to welcome him. His voice was harsh, loud and rough. It had the quality of a lung full of clinkers. He was unkindly known as Trolly.

Adrian led the newcomers through several sessions, showing them how to use watercolours, how to use shading, taught them basic colour theory, and how to build up a finished piece, until eventually they felt more or less at home in the group.

Steve always followed everything that Adrian said and did, but something wasn't working quite right. He always managed to end up with something that looked completely different. His pictures never even vaguely resembled anyone else's. It defied logic. Adrian felt a little sorry for him, as he never asked for help and said little. Adrian thought he was enduring the lessons, going through the motions but not really enjoying it much. One day, holding up what was supposed to be a church nestled among green rolling hills, Steve, who never passed any kind of judgement, announced for everyone to hear:

'You know, if you had told me I could have done this a few weeks ago I wouldn't have believed you. I think I'm ready to start working on my own.'

'Shut up!' shouted Billy, then added under his breath, but not so quiet that you couldn't hear it: 'You *should* work on your own, though...'

'Enough, Billy,' said Adrian, making a mental note to have a talk with him later. Of the whole class, Billy in particular seemed to dislike Steve. Steve didn't take any notice anyway, and Adrian thought Billy was probably equally as vulnerable, if not more so, in a different kind of way.

Adrian was really taken aback by Steve's confidence and, not wishing to discourage him, agreed he should have a go. He asked:

'Is there anything in particular you think you would like to try? Anything you're interested in?'

'Yes,' he replied, 'there is.'

From that moment the revised version of the *Observer's Book of Birds* came into being. Steve began copying every single page of the original volume with a scary, obsessive determination.

The first painting corresponded with the first page of the book. It was a magpie. Adrian guessed as much by the colours. However, nothing else was recognisable. It was either a magpie or a king penguin. Its huge black bill was half open as if it was trying to say something. Probably, 'I *am* a magpie, honest.'

Towards the end of the session, Adrian came over to give him some help, thinking, 'Poor sod, it's not easy painting birds, especially when the artist you're copying is Archibald Thorburn.'

Suddenly Steve stood back and sighed. 'Well, what do you think?'

'It's fucking crap,' said Billy from the periphery.

'Enough, Billy.'

Adrian stared at the magpie's vaguely recognisable face and wondered how he could take this forward. He was about to suggest that maybe Steve should try something a little less ambitious - after all it was his first attempt - when Steve fortunately got there first.

'You know, I think it's actually better than the original. Somehow I think mine is clearer. It's easier to see what it is.'

Adrian was speechless. Surely Steve was taking the piss. But he continued:

'Mind you, they're nasty birds, magpies. They kill lambs, you know.'

'Nonsense,' Adrian retorted, glad not to have to comment on which was the better painting, Steve's or the original. However, now he was dealing with an ornithological expert instead.

'They do, they peck out their eyes, I've seen them. You have to shoot them or they'll have your lambs.' Not wishing to go into this too deeply Adrian backed down.

'Really?' he replied.

'He's a total dickhead. You don't have to be nice to him,' said Billy, very loudly this time, for all to hear. 'You are allowed to say the truth, you know. What's crap is crap.'

When all the other students had gone back, Adrian took Billy to one side.

'Can I have a word?'

'Which one do you want?

'Look, I'm being serious! I want you to quit giving Steve a hard time like this. I want you to stop it from now on. OK?'

'Why? I hates him.'

'This is not how to deal with it. Anyway, what's he done to upset you so much? Has something happened?'

'No. I just hates him.'

'Well, that's no reason, it's got to stop. If it happens again I'll be forced to make a choice as to who's staying in the class and it won't be you. One of the conditions of the classroom is respect for the other students as well as for the teacher. You know that?'

'Yeah, but I'll just hates him quietly then. I can't pretend to like someone when I don't, I can't be two-faced, like you.'

Adrian must have looked hurt. Billy smiled.

'Sorry! Only joking. I didn't mean that.'

'I've a lot of respect for you actually, Billy, but this bothers me. You're bigger than this. I want you to apologise to Steve.'

'You're joking! No way!'

'No! I mean it. You can do it.'

'I knows I can, but I'm not going to.'

'Please. I'm asking you.'

Adrian and Billy were standing face to face, eye to eye. They were both completely in the moment. A lot of stuff was silently exchanged in a few seconds. Adrian was suddenly acutely aware of all the issues that lived inside Billy. Billy had let down his barriers. It all happened so suddenly, so much in such a little time. Like transferring a load of computer files. Adrian just stared at him and realised that this was as close as two people could possibly get, short of having sex. There followed a few moments of silence.

'OK! I'll do it. But only cos you asked me. I still think he's a twat.'

'I knew you could. Thanks!'

Billy and Adrian shook hands. It was sealed. Adrian felt a huge change had come about between him and Billy. He now knew what it meant to be 'safe'. Adrian and Billy went to the wing where the men were sitting around having tea. Adrian watched from the periphery as Billy went over to Steve and said something to him.

Adrian turned to leave and caught Billy's eye from across the wing. Billy's look said it all. He gave Adrian the thumbs up.

* * *

The next lesson brought Adrian the delights of the jay. Steve worked on it all morning until it was finished. He presented it to Adrian for his approval.

'You probably won't believe this,' he said. Adrian still wasn't sure where Steve was coming from: either he was extremely clever or incredibly stupid. At this point in time Adrian didn't feel like taking any risks.

The jay is like a magpie: it's also in the crow family, but it's blue, russet, black and white. What Adrian hadn't realised was that they were both identical in shape, size and the way they sit in the same tree, in fact they were identical in every way, except in colour. Its massive bill was half open as if to say, 'I *am* a jay, really.' The background differed from Thorburn's in that there were several sheep in the field behind the bird, and the landscape fading away into the distance had been replaced by a very vertical, flat hedge.

'Did you trace this picture from the magpie?' Adrian casually asked, knowing full well that he had. Billy was about to say something, looked at Adrian, then looked away, shaking his head in disgust.

'Yes,' he answered, astonished. 'However did you tell?' Lowering his voice, he continued: I think that's how the originals were done, because if you look closely they're pretty much the same too. Most people wouldn't notice. You have to study it. I wouldn't be surprised if no one's ever seen that before.' Adrian was too flabbergasted to speak, but now knew that Steve wasn't taking the piss.

'Mind you, they're also nasty birds. You see that sheep there? Well, if you could see the other side of its face you would find that it only has one eye. Nasty birds, jays.'

* * *

Throughout the next whole term, many pages of different British Birds were painted. But there were far too many for Steve to do them all - even *his* sentence wasn't that long - so Adrian suggested that Steve narrow down his choice to doing only those he could see from his cell window. This would personalise the project and extend it to observation as well.

'I've started to feeds them, you know. We're not supposed to, but someone has to look after them. Sometimes in the morning they wakes me up for their breakfast.'

'Shame vultures don't come and eat you, you big twat,' said the up until now silent Mark. It seems that he was now carrying the talking stick for the group and would again have to be dealt with. Once someone was labelled punch bag, it seemed it was impossible to shake the role off.

The next few paintings he completed were of various finches, tits and robins. He was now putting several different birds on one page, connecting them together with a common background, usually fields, sheep, motorways and waterfalls, all miraculously interwoven, without a single trace of perspective anywhere. All the birds still looked like the magpie, but were either smaller or facing the other way, and unfortunately they all had developed a liking for killing lambs. Robins, though, only indirectly: apparently they steal the sheep's food in winter.

When he started painting guillemots and puffins, golden eagles and snowy owls, Adrian started to question how often these birds regularly visited the prison yard. He would imagine, whilst driving home, extraordinary gothic pictures of Steve throwing out his meagre crumbs to passing flocks of snowy owls, as they landed on the windowsill in the dead of night while everyone else slept.

One day Steve had a brain wave. He was going to stick all his paintings together and construct a wall chart, thus making easier quick identification out of the window. However, there was also a darker side to his reasoning. He whispered to Adrian in his lowered, grating voice: 'In about ten years hence there won't be any of these birds left, you know, and they will use this chart to find out what they looked like.' Probably they would have been culled because of their regular attacks on sheep...

One day, as he walked down the wing, Adrian caught a glimpse of Steve through the half open door of his cell. He was sitting on his bed, totally immersed in his *Observer's Book of Birds*. All around him, pasted on the walls of his cell, was the endangered species chart. Adrian called to him and Steve beck-oned him in. He was studying a picture of a collared dove. He had to hold it about three inches from his nose, just to read it. He was not looking happy, and when he spoke Adrian noticed a quiver in his voice.

'God, their lives are so simple. They fly where they please, have no responsibilities. No police, no juries, no fucking judges and definitely no prisons.'

'Oh, I don't think life is as easy for them as all that,' Adrian said. 'Some of them are kept in tiny cages all their lives, lots are shot at and many are hunted. In some cases it's not that dissimilar.'

'Yeah, but that's only because man is interfering, getting in the way again. Left on their own they can do whatever they want. Arctic terns fly all the way from Pole to Pole, every year. Think of that.'

'You sound like you understand birds, Steve. Maybe something of the arctic tern lives in you.'

'Yeah, right! The only bird that lives in me is the jailbird. This is my fucking cage.'

'Hang on in there, Steve, you'll fly again one day.'

Steve looked at Adrian with more watery eyes than usual and croaked: 'Yeah, but my wings are all broken and clipped, I won't ever fly again.'

Adrian took his leave. It was a sad, crumpled moment. Steve had the weight of the world on his shoulders. Adrian brought it to the attention of the officers that Steve, the birdman of Feldon Park, was on a downer.

# 13 ANT'S RANT

*The native people of Fiji made a huge distinction between intelligence and wisdom. Wisdom was greatly revered and respected, whereas intelligence was seen as deceptive and dangerous.*

Anton was an angry young man who one day appeared in Adrian's classroom after some dispute or other on the wing. He was looking for sanctuary. These things do happen, and sometimes a little distance between people helps. Billy Bates liked him and also put pressure on Adrian to let him join. Having another younger man in the group could make it easier for Billy, so Adrian agreed he could stay for the day. However, Anton soon became a semi-permanent feature. He was from Romania and had only been in Britain for a short time when he was arrested and sentenced for armed robbery. When he came to prison, he hardly spoke any English, having hung out with fellow Romanians since his arrival. While in Feldon Park, awaiting his court appearance, it was realised that he was an illegal immigrant.

Anton quickly picked up English from the other men. It was a weird dialect of prison-speak and Romanian that Billy christened *'romaniac'*. The first word he learnt was 'fucking', which he must have thought was a compulsory adjective and adverb in English.

One day he was particularly agitated and he gave a lecture. It was the first time anyone had heard him string so many words together at one time. Adrian called it 'Ant's Rant'. It summed up a lot about prisoner psychology, politics and social studies better than many learned books on the subject. It began with a question to Adrian.

'Does you think I'm a bad person?'

'How should I know. I only met you recently.'

'So you thinking I mights be, is that what you're saying?'

'What I'm saying is I don't know. Just like you don't know if I'm a bad person.'

'That judge said I was a bad person. He said I was a menace to society. He told me the world woulds be a better place without me roaming the streets. How could he say that when he didn't even fuckings know me? What sort of fuckings logic is that?'

Adrian was just about to say something about maybe it had something to do with what he had done, but Ant continued.

'You says you don't know if I'm a bad person and you's known me longer than he has, so how could he says that, when I'd only been there in dat court place a couple of hours? He coulds be a bad person but I don't go round slagging him off.'

'Well, he is a judge. I suppose that's his job.'

'In Romania we calls that kinda person a *sadista* that goes around telling others you're a bad person when you're down. I bet he wouldn't say it to my face on the street, like.'

Adrian thought he'd better try to contribute something constructive to this one-sided conversation so he asked what had he done to end up in court.

'I robbed a post office. It was in Gloucester City...' He noticed Adrian staring at him. 'Why are you looking at me like that? I knows I broke the law but that doesn't mean I'm a bad person.'

'I'm not looking at you any way. I'm not a judge. I'm a teacher.'

Adrian didn't know what this last thing had to do with anything; it just seemed good to answer something to this string of questions. Obviously Anton's character had been slurred and this was not to be taken lightly. It outweighed everything else; he had been insulted. It must be a Romanian thing.

'I didn't hurts anyone if that's what you're thinking. If I had wanted to, I'd have used a real gun. It was only a toy. You know, an imitation. I didn't hurt anyone. I just told that granny to lay on the floor, that's all. It was a fake. I didn't hurt anyone.'

'Oh! But how did she know that? You could have given her a heart attack. Frights can be really serious, especially to older people.'

'Yeah, but I didn't give her a heart attack. If I had that would be wrong, but I didn't.'

Adrian fumbled for words, but Ant continued: 'All Post Offices are insured anyway, so she'll have got the money back. It wasn't as if I'd taken the money directly from her, was it? In fact, if it wasn't for people like me who robs, there'd be no insurance companies and all those people who works there would loses their jobs.'

Jabba couldn't bear being left out, and decided to chip in:

'That's the same with prison officers. If it wasn't for us they probably wouldn't have work. They'd all be on the dole. The Government should pay us money. We're a kind of job creation scheme, we keep these boys off the streets. They couldn't get any jobs anywhere else, they'd end up doing crime, like us.'

'Yeah, they should shows us more respect and be more grateful. Anyway, most of the big business people are on the fucking fiddle all the time. It's not just in Romania, you know. They're always connings people out of their money. Like all those pension scams lately. You know all those poor old peoples now with no pensions. That's far worser than anything I've done. A lot more grannies are suffering because of that. But I'm the one doing this bird thing, while those company people are out there driving big cars with big houses, and people probably say 'good morning, sir' and all that crap. That judge is probably like that. I bet he's committed loads of bad things but I don't go judgings him, like, do I?'

A space was left for Adrian to speak.

'But, like you said earlier, you broke the law.'

'Have you never brokens the law? Of course you have. You just haven't got caught, that's all. Everyone has broken the law at least once. Even Mother Fucking Teresa's broken the law at some time. Have you ever broken the speed limit?'

'No, I always try and keep to the limit.'

'Yeah, right. So you've never gone over it, not even once?'

'Well...yes.'

'"Well...yes" - exactly. You might have hit a granny trying to cross the road because you were goings too fast. You wouldn't have been ables to stop. You could have killed her.'

'Yeah, but I didn't - that's hypothetical'.

'Yeah. Exactly, that's it, it's hypothetical. I didn't hurt the old lady in the Post Office neither. I might have given her a heart attack but I didn't. It's the same.'

'You should be a lawyer.' Adrian said, amazed at the mental gymnastics, before he realised he had probably just insulted him.

'No, you're fucking joking, aren't you. I'm not good enough for that, guv.'

'But what *do* you think about yourself? Do you think you're a good person?' Adrian asked, completing the circle.

'No, I'm not a good person,' he replied, 'but I'm no worse than anybody else.'

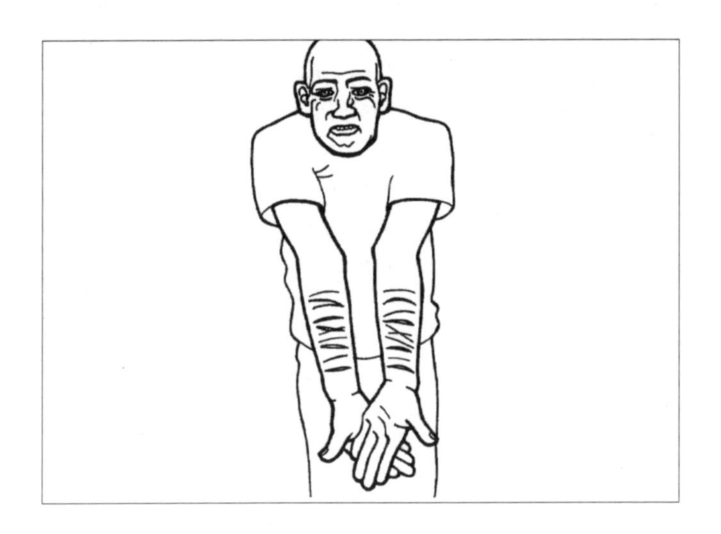

# 14 UNANSWERED CUTS

*The indigenous peoples of Fiji believed illness to be a kind of possession, that resulted from floating spirits becoming trapped within the human body. Unable to escape, they became increasingly embedded in the flesh. The prescribed remedy was to cut the forearm and bleed. This would create an exit. And bring immediate relief.*

Adrian had never been able to understand why some people deliberately hurt themselves. He had seen plenty who did and he'd heard all the text book reasons why it happened, but he still didn't really understand it. He supposed that was because he had never found himself in that same dark recess and couldn't find the same motivation to do it. It required a desperate condition, one so numbing that the only thing left that connected you with the world was to cause yourself pain. It seemed so extreme that it almost had a religious quality to it, reminiscent of medieval flagellants.

The last few times Adrian had been come onto A wing, the topic of conversation in the officers' room had always been the same: a new inmate who, in their opinion, shouldn't be there. His presence was causing them alarm.

'They've moved that Dunaway over here. What the fuck are they playing at? He's a liability. He should be in seg.'

Adrian was intrigued. Who was this terrible man? Nobody ever spoke to Adrian directly and therefore he assumed it was none of his business. Another characteristic of Feldon Park was that you were supposed to know everything without anybody telling you anything. An advanced state of clairvoyance was a job prerequisite. Hence he was surprised when he arrived one morning and was given his register - which again sometimes happened and sometimes didn't - to find, halfway down the page, the name Dunaway. Adrian definitely hadn't overheard that. He went to his classroom expecting to meet a missing Kray brother. He couldn't have been more wrong. What arrived was a tall man in his thirties with a high shaven head who looked very down and nervous. Adrian's self-generated image of the hard man didn't fit him very comfortably. He wore it like an ill-fitting suit. A soft man trapped in a thug's body.

Dunaway was the last one to arrive that morning and the only chair remaining was right at the front. Adrian introduced himself and shook the hardly-proffered hand. There was no eye contact and Dunaway's handshake was incredibly limp.

When all the other men were working, Adrian went over and spoke to him. Dunaway was very unhappy and hardly ever lifted his chin off his chest. Adrian asked him if he was alright, to which he replied.

'I can't do this, I'm really crap, and the drugs I'm on are doing my head in. I can't think. Sorry!'

'Don't worry about it, what drugs have they given you?'

'I don't know. They did tell me but it didn't mean anything and I've forgotten, but they make me really sleepy.'

'Crikey! You just do as much as you can, and when you've done enough, stop. I certainly won't push you. This is for you to enjoy, not to make anything worse.'

Dunaway entered what can only be described as an almost trance-like condition in which he seemed to focus on a point of nothingness about three feet in front of his face. His expression was painful. He suddenly looked up and saw Adrian watching him. He beckoned him over.

'Sorry, guv. I can't do any more.'

It was then that Adrian noticed the insides of his arms. They were covered in a mesh of white scars that disappeared up under his sleeves. Each one representing a pit of despair. He saw Adrian looking at them.

'I'm a self-harmer. I hurt myself.' He said, quite nonchalantly, in answer to Adrian's unspoken question. 'These ones are all old ones. The most recent ones are up here.' And with that, he raised his sleeves. There was a huge chunk missing from his elbow, as if a shark had bitten it off. Adrian gasped. For the first time Dunaway laughed. Adrian's face must have said it all.

'I didn't do that. That happened when I came off my motorbike. These here are the most recent.'

He pointed to some thick, ruby red lines that looked like they were in the final stage of healing.

'Bloody Hell, when did you do this?'

'I can't remember when, but I did it with a biro.'

Adrian became very aware that already this morning he'd given him a paintbrush with metal on it and a 3H pencil, and had lent him a pencil sharpener. Adrian was both amazed and pissed off that he had been put in a room, for six hours, without any information or advice, with a man who was so evidently capable of hurting himself. If Feldon Park showed Adrian so little professional support what could this guy expect? Adrian felt very sorry for him. They immediately became friends.

One strange quality of Dunaway's vulnerability was that he had no self-respect, and seemingly did not care what others did to him. As a result, he was defiant in the face of authority and would answer back all officers, even when harder men would back down. His biggest enemy was himself. Everyone else paled next to him.

Unfortunately, Dunaway was not very good at art, but he did try, and even though he kept putting himself down and ridiculing his own work, he was at least laughing a lot more than before and was generally happy.

'Hey, Adrian! Bet you haven't seen one this bad before. Be honest now. No bullshit! You better get over here before it gets any worse.'

When Adrian was helping him with his work, Dunaway always began to talk - about his family, his kids, his addiction, everything. Adrian found there was something about sitting next to someone, not opposite them, that encouraged talking. It was less confrontational. Also, because they were working on a shared piece of artwork, it was less of an 'interview' situation. The point of attention was indirect. Adrian called it sideways conversation.

One day Adrian was faced by a security problem. The class had been painting all morning and Dunaway, in particular, was in high spirits. It had been what Adrian considered a good morning and when it was over, the men began to clear away. As Adrian put everything in his bag he became aware that certain art things were missing. Some things he didn't mind being taken. However, anything that could be dangerous, like pencil sharpeners and putty rubbers, were always meticulously accounted for and on this particular day there were several paintbrushes missing, with their metal ends attached, and this could not be ignored.

'There are several paintbrushes missing. Does anyone know where they've gone?'

'Accusing us of theft now, are you?' Billy jumped up at the first opportunity for confrontation.

'No! I didn't say that.'

'Come on then, search me. I dare you!' He pranced around in front of Adrian with his arms akimbo. 'Come on!'

'What are you going to do?' said Derek.

'I don't know,' Adrian honestly replied. 'Just sit here and wait, I suppose, until they turn up. Can we all check our folders again to make sure we haven't picked them up by mistake?'

Billy was now verging on the hysterical. He was bent over double with his butt facing Adrian.

'Come on, search me, search me, if you think I'm the thief.'

'Go away! We'll just have to sit here until the officers come over. I can't let you go until they turn up. Not only will you get in trouble, but so will I if they don't reappear soon. There'll be a lock-down.' Until the missing brushes were found all doors would be locked and movements suspended while everyone was searched.

A silence descended on all those present. Suddenly Dunaway spoke as if enchanted.

'I know where they are,' he said with that faraway look again. 'They're in my cell.'

'How on earth did they get in there?'

'I took them at tea break.' As if in a trance, he got up and went and fetched them. Adrian counted them and they were all there. He let everyone go. They left grumbling. Dunaway, however, stayed behind while Adrian finished clearing away. He was subdued.

'Are you pissed off with me?' he said eventually .

Adrian realised he had probably been frowning the whole while. He smiled.

'Not at all! I'm fed up cos I'm late. I'm not angry with you, quite the opposite, actually.'

'Really? Why?' said an incredulous Dunaway.

'I'm really pleased that you could own up. It takes courage in this place.'

'I was just going to do some painting. I know I'm not very good but you know, when I paint, I actually forget that I'm in prison. It's the only time that I do.'

'I can well believe that, because I actually forget that I'm in here too when I'm teaching!'

This was very true. There had been several times when Adrian had totally forgotten where he was. In fact, the longer he worked in prison the more this seemed to be happening. It obviously had something to do with familiarity, but he also realised that this was another quality of art. It had the power to completely absorb you, to suck you in and make the surroundings temporarily disappear. This was what was made it good for somebody like Dunaway, who needed as much time out from his overwhelming 'issues' as possible. It gave him respite from his collective hurts.

'Are you going to tell the officers?' he asked. 'About the brushes?'

'Not necessary! You've given them back.'

'I just wanted to use them in my cell…' he saw Adrian's concerned stare '... for painting.'

'Well, next time just ask me. You don't have to steal anything. If I can give it you I will.'

'Can I have a paint brush then?'

'No. But you can have a pencil.'

Dunaway laughed.

'Yeah, a pencil.'

Dunaway didn't stay in Adrian's class long, which was a great shame. His education package included four days of other subjects which were more exam-oriented and put pressure on him, so he dropped out altogether. However, he would still come over and talk whenever he could. He trusted Adrian, and Adrian realised that he actually enjoyed talking to Dunaway, who seemed to be getting on and settling down well. Then one day, Adrian was held up and arrived on the wing later than usual. As he waited for the automatic door to open, he could see Dunaway prowling up and down the landing looking very disturbed. He hadn't gone to work. Something was wrong. When the doors eventually opened, Adrian walked in and went over to him.

'What's happening?'

'I'm in a bad way. I'm in a mess,' he hissed, as if he was out of breath.

Adrian noticed, for the first time, that Dunaway was wearing long sleeves. Poking out from under his cuffs were bandages.

'Have you hurt yourself?'

In reply, he just rolled up his sleeves. His arms were bandaged all the way up. He could hardly speak, he was so short breathed.

'I did it with a razor. Do you want to see? I can show you if you like, or maybe you'd find it too upsetting?'

Adrian felt this was an invitation and a challenge. This was a test of their friendship. Adrian had to give the right answer. Dunaway was staring him in the face.

'OK.'

Dunaway began to unravel himself and the first stitches came into view. The neat little lines ran up his arm. Adrian wondered how many times this poor skin had had to heal itself. He looked on. It was horrific.

'For God's sake, why do you do this?'

This was not the best thing to have said.

'Don't you start to lecture me too; I've had it up to here. They don't know what it's like, none of them.'

'I'm not lecturing you. I'm just really shocked and upset to see a really nice bloke like you hurt himself. It's difficult to see a mate in this state.'

Something very unexpected and extraordinary happened. Dunaway started to cry.

'That's the first time anybody has said anything nice to me the whole time I've been in here.' His breathing became shallow again.

'Do you want to sit and talk a bit?' Adrian said. 'I'll get you a tissue.'

'No, I'm going to my cell. I don't want anyone to see me like this.'

He went behind his door. Adrian went to the officers' office. They were complaining about how selfish Dunaway had been, causing them all this unnecessary headache. 'We told them he shouldn't be on this wing,' was the gist of it.

When Adrian eventually got his class out, Tony, Dunaway's cellmate and friend, told Adrian how he had found him. Apparently, Dunaway had been up all night, unable to sleep, pacing the cell. When Tony awoke in the morning, Dunaway was laying on the toilet floor covered in blood. Tony had rung the alarm.

Adrian did not see Dunaway again that day, and the next time he came, he was gone. Dunaway had been taken to Healthcare, the medical wing, for high-risk inmates, where there was increased surveillance. Adrian asked if he could go and visit him and was told that it wouldn't serve any purpose, so no. 'What do you want to do that for?' they'd said.

On leaving Alpha wing at lunchtime, Adrian found himself walking past the Healthcare exercise yard, and lo and behold, there was Dunaway, sitting on a bench on his own in the pale sun. He seemed to be meditating. Then, all of a sudden, he smiled, got up and came over to the fence. There were two officers walking just behind Adrian, so he turned around and asked: 'Can I go and talk to him?'

'I suppose so. But don't put your fingers through or he'll bite them off.'

Adrian didn't laugh and went over to Dunaway.

'How's it going, butt?'

'Alright. I feel a bit stupid now.'

'Well, don't let it bother you. I always knew you were a dickhead.'

They both laughed loudly.

'Seriously though, you could have killed yourself, you know. You're lucky you're still alive, the number of times you've done this.'

Dunaway smiled.

'Don't worry. If you want to kill yourself, you do the cuts up the arm, not across it.'

Adrian was shocked and his mouth fell open. Dunaway was so matter-of-fact and took no account of the risk of septicaemia. Adrian was about to point this out, but something else flashed through his head, and came out of his mouth as: 'Can I ask you something, as we're mates, like. I've done a lot of thinking, and I think I know why you did this. You don't want to go out, do you? And you're up for release soon...'

Dunaway smiled again, and leaned over. He put his head close to the wire and almost whispered.

'You really have got me sussed. I've got a lot of enemies out there, you know. I grassed on a lot of people and they know I'm coming out. They're going to be waiting. I want to stay here. I don't want to go back to Gloucester.'

'God! That's awful. Can't you go somewhere else instead? Get Probation to relocate you to somewhere where no-one knows you?'

'I can't. My family is there. And, anyway, I couldn't cope with a whole new move like that either. But don't worry, I'll be back. I'm not staying away for long. I'll nick a car or something.'

'You take care of yourself. I mean that! Are you sure you don't want me to have a word?'

'No, don't bother, it's sorted. I appreciate all what you've done for me, though.'

'But I haven't done anything.'

'You have, you've been my mate, I really appreciate it.'

They touched fists through the wire fence and Adrian went to lunch with a great sadness upon him. Over lunch he told Mr Nash, his head of Department, what had happened, and how depressing he thought it all was.

'Oh yeah, many long-term inmates are completely institutionalised. They've been in so long they can't function outside prison. They need the structure and the routine, otherwise life spirals downwards.'

The conversation didn't help. It only made Adrian realise that the art classes on the wing were as good as it got for Dunaway. The whole day became even sadder.

Dunaway, true to his word, was back in just over two months. He had stolen a car and then turned himself in. He was strung out on heroin. It was his twelfth time inside. He was unable to cope with the long, rough journey to Fiji. He paddled his leaky, broken craft out to sea, but once Feldon Park began to disappear, he panicked, turned around and swam back to its familiar shores. The gaping gates and Bang Up for Men waited to gobble him up once more.

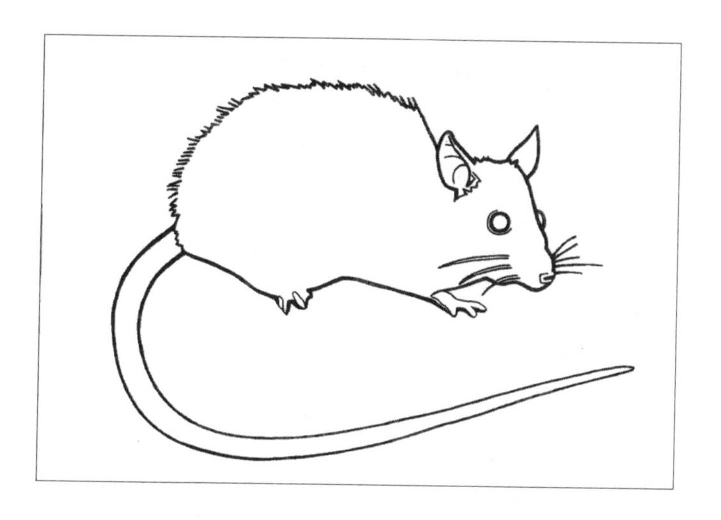

# 15 MEET THE INVISIBLE MAN

*'An unanswered question resembles an unanswered "hello". It leaves one feeling ignored and hurt. Such a denial of existence usually leads to a breakdown in friendship.'* From the maxims of Chief Hanu-dova of Kaduva, 1893

Adrian had been working at Feldon Park for four months and although his perception of how the prison was run was never really clarified, his relationship with the prisoners was definitely improving. Generally he was feeling more confident around them, though he had been warned not to mistake confidence for complacency. The apparent ease that had developed with some prisoners, was perceived by a few staff members as a kind of betrayal. There was this great divide: us and them. It arose from the siege-like mentality that permeated the entire gaol, on both sides of the bars. It necessitated taking sides and being permanently vigilant. There were many unclaimed mistakes floating around looking for possible unsuspecting 'owners' to attach themselves to. There were always several hovering above

Adrian, it seemed. One thing was always certain though, it was always somebody else's fault. The inmates blamed the screws, the screws blamed the management, the management blamed the education department, the teachers blamed the prison allocations unit, who in turn blamed over-crowding and so and so on. The buck never stopped moving and everyone seemed Teflon®-coated. Adrian found himself adopting the same non-stick attitude. He was in as much danger of being compromised by the staff as by the inmates. The realisation left him feeling very alone and very vulnerable.

When he first began working in the gaol, he had excused the apparent mistakes or contradictions, thinking they were part of some huge master plan, the Big Picture. Now he was beginning to think that maybe, there just wasn't any plan at all, or if there was one, maybe security management thought Adrian wasn't ready to be given the rules yet. Maybe they still didn't trust him. However, it seemed that these rules were so secret that nobody knew them. As a result, Adrian decided he needed to start making up his own, and like everybody else, rule number one was 'watch your back'.

As he checked behind him, the class began arriving, He could hear them coming and knew straight away that something was wrong. His newly discovered, self-defence, force-field clicked on. He could sense potential danger. Jabba's voice stood out above the rest.

'I fucking hates him, the filthy twat. I tells you there's going to be trouble.' As they arrived in the classroom Adrian greeted them but they were so agitated that they hardly noticed him. Jabba momentarily looked at Adrian and carried on.

'Hi. Why did they put him with me? What was wrong with Billy?'

Adrian guessed that Jabba had been allocated a new cell mate and he obviously wasn't pleased.

'I don't want him in with me. He isn't clean and he snores. He kept me awake all night. I had to shake him three different times.'

'You shouldn't do that,' said Adrian, who, being a snorer himself, knew the agonies of being woken up by an irate partner in the night. 'You should always gently turn a snorer on their side.'

'Like fuck! The last time I just shouted, 'Shut the fuck up' as I shook him. That stopped it. He was too frightened to go to sleep again, the bastard! The trouble was, I had gotten so worked up myself, I found it impossible to sleep after that. We spent all night just listening to each other. Fuck it! I want my own cell!'

'You'll be lucky in this place,' said Frosty. 'You have to be a screw-boy or a psycho to get one on your own.'

Adrian pondered the word screw-boy, it was a title of absolute contempt within the gaol. It was someone who sucked up to the officers, a grass, someone who broke rank. It also had a horrible sexual overtone that made Adrian's buttocks flinch.

'Yeah! These cells are not big enough for two people.'

The truth was, though, that space in Feldon Park's commodious design did meet all European Union requirements. The problem was they were designed for one man per cell. The days when that had been the case were short-lived and were now part of ancient history. An adult male prisoner supposedly needed at least four metres by six to maintain a healthy mind, body and soul. Adrian ashamedly, recalled how he and his wife had discussed, only the previous evening, how their three bed-roomed, large gardened house was too small for them nowadays. He was convinced he would go mad if he had to spend any time in one of Feldon Park's spartan cells. He had only been in one twice, and the over-riding memory was the heat. It was so hot in there. The cell windows only opened wide enough to chuck your rubbish out, they let in very little air. Here Adrian became immersed in the full complement of 'Bang-Up'. The effect made him gag.

'Who decided he should be two-ed up with me? Asked Jabba. 'They knows I'm a light sleeper.'

Adrian didn't have the heart to tell him that probably no-one gave it any thought at all, because nobody cared.

Adrian wondered though, who actually did decide on whether it was ok to put two men in a one man cell. On what grounds did they make that decision? He recalled an experiment he'd read about years ago at school. It was about the effects of over-crowding and how one needed a certain amount of space to remain healthy. The tests were done on rats. The rats were continually deprived of space until they became pressurised. After being squashed into ever smaller boxes, the rats' peaceful co-existence soon began to break down. They started to attack each other. Unfortunately - for the rats - the boffins had been in their formaldehyde world too long and repeated the experiment thousands of times. Adrian remembered his father commenting at the time: 'If they want to study over-crowding they should come over here, for a bit, to where we live. They don't need to waste their time on stupid experiments. They could experience everything first-hand. Far more relevant.'

Also, there was one slight thing they overlooked that annoyed Adrian intensely, and that was being compared to a rat. They always assumed that rats and people were the same...

'Hoy! Adrian! Wake up!' said a voice next to him. 'What are you on?' Jabba was staring at him as he reminisced.

'Can you do me a favour and put in a word for me. Can you ask the screws if I can have my own cell?, I'm so stressed out it's making me ill. I've got a rotten headache coming on.'

Adrian's heart sank and he doubted that asking would do any good.

'It would be better if you put in an application first. Tell them about how it's making you unwell.'

'I have, but they haven't done anything. Please! They'll listen to you.'

The men seemed to think that Adrian could do anything. He hated being the go-between, crossing the great divide. It rarely bore results and often only lead to both sides becoming increasingly irritated with him. For Adrian, it was a no win situation. Before he could answer, the shopping list began.

'Could you ask them for a paracetamol as well. Jesus, Ade I've got such a headache.'

Adrian knew what it felt like to have a headache in Feldon Park. A headache in the land where there is no access to pain-killers. It had happened to him once, and he only had to wait till lunch-time to get relief but that was bad enough. Adrian knew how migraine and tooth-aches, or any illness for that matter, took on monumental proportions in here. And then to be locked in with someone you didn't like... You weren't even allowed the dignity of suffering in privacy.

Adrian's newly enhanced sense of self-preservation told him he should be saying 'no', but he found himself answering automatically instead. He questioned the wisdom of the words falling from his mouth: 'OK! I'll do my best.'

He knew to refuse was tantamount to taking sides and he wanted to be above all that. He didn't want to be a screw-boy. He gave himself another squirt of non-stick spray and stood up and surveyed the office. He wasn't hopeful. The officers were shouting at each other within their glass box. Adrian thought he could see a floating problem being tossed around. Adrian left his students who were all still in full blame mode. Problems were being resolved, people were being accused and heads should be rolling.

Huddled together, in their measured requirements, sat six officers. They stopped arguing as Adrian approached the door. They eyed each other in silence under the scrutiny of their leader, the dominant male. No one spoke. Adrian wondered whether it would be less painful to just commit suicide on the doorstep instead of going through with this. There didn't seem to be much charity in the air. They had obviously spent the morning letting off steam, trying to deflect a cock-up somewhere else, but the free falling 'problem' began to settle, deeper and deeper in their court. It was now way past the blaming someone else stage, the glue had begun to stick. Once realised, it was only a few seconds before they had started on each other. This was almost a daily ritual. If you want to stay clean then you need to put your muck elsewhere. (Survival rule number two.)

Adrian approached their door and opened it. He knew they had all seen him coming, but they preferred to pretend not to. Adrian could have cut the air with a knife, if one were allowed one in prison, that is. He waited for someone to acknowledge him but nobody did. They all were suddenly totally engrossed in silent, intense work. Adrian felt that he wasn't welcome. He thought, 'If it's like this for me, then how must it be for the inmates?'

He didn't have time to find an answer, because mayhem broke out all around him.

'You fucking dickhead. What you want to do that for?'

At first Adrian thought he was being addressed. The adrenalin began pumping. However, whatever gave him the idea that they should want to talk to him? It was actually aimed at Mr Ruddock, an officer who must have broken rank.

'Yeah, dickhead!' mumbled the others. The group found comfort in the shadow of the dominant male.

The outburst exploded all around Adrian. The shouts weren't loud but managed to carry maximum aggression. Adrian couldn't help feeling shaken, but his new Teflon® suit offered a surprisingly high degree of protection, so he decided to bite the bullet and ask.

'I hate to interrupt but Jabba needs a paracetamol he's got a splitting migraine. He can't work...'

Nobody even acknowledged Adrian. Did somebody speak? Two of them stood up and said to the chief, over Adrian's head, 'We're off to visits now, shall I pick up the post while I'm over there?'

Another officer answered the phone. Another looked at a clip board. They all walked passed him. He had become one of the invisible.

Adrian felt personally insulted. He turned and walked out.

'Fuck you,' he thought, as he closed the door behind him. He rejoined his expectant class who again all wanted to ask him what had happened.

'I tried,' Adrian said at last to Jabba. 'But you know what it's like.'

Adrian recognised he was increasingly talking like one of the prisoners. He was sounding more con-like as he sympathised, as he began to blame. Together, he and the men worked through the rest of the morning angry and fed up.

Adrian returned a changed man after lunch. Over the rubbery chips, he felt he had gone through a barrier. No longer would he just stand and accept all the prison's crap. The word 'screw-boy' niggled his consciousness. The officer's behaviour was just too awful for words. Over lunch, he even contemplated just bringing in a couple of pain-killers for Jabba. Be defiant, just go over their heads, but then the thought of being caught and labelled a drug-smuggler. Adrian was dreading having to be with an in-pain Jabba all afternoon. Although he felt sorry for him, he also knew he wouldn't suffer in silence, but to his surprise, when Jabba arrived he was in fine form..

'How's the head?' Adrian asked. 'You looked terrible this morning.'

'Yep it was awful, but it's nearly gone now,' he replied. 'Mr Ruddock brought me a couple of paracetamol at lunchtime. They worked a trick. Thanks for asking for me.'

Adrian was in shock. They had heard him after all. He now understood what it felt like to be gob-smacked. Mr Ruddock was now probably known to the other officers as a 'con-boy'.

Jabba continued, 'They'll probably give me my own cell too, now that you've asked.' Adrian shuffled nervously. He had forgotten to ask about that bit.

# 16 AN ASIAN RAP

*'The people of Fiji were unanimous in their acceptance of each other as equals, as they were all children of the Great God. Problems began when different Gods appeared.*

The most talkative man Adrian ever met in his class was Khalim Kazim. He could talk himself through anything. Khalim was Muslim. He had a broad cockney accent, though he told Adrian he originated from Pakistan. There were two threads of thought that ran continuously through whatever he was talking about. Sex and Islam. An unlikely combination, one would have thought, but it seems Khalim was an expert in both and could use either as a weapon if necessary. He could turn everything and anything any way he chose. As is so often the case, his listening skills were, unfortunately, minimal next to his enormous speaking capacity.

The first day he arrived, he spent the whole morning arguing that it should be prison policy to allow prostitutes in jail. The other men thought this a wonderful idea. He argued that this would greatly reduce much of the pent-up anger that many of the inmates felt, which subsequently led to problems for the authorities. It would thus reduce the necessity for added security and would ultimately be cost-effective. Also, it would give unemployed women the opportunity to earn extra cash. As a greater incentive, he generously put it forward that officers and staff could also use the facilities, should they be allowed. It could be paid for by the inmates themselves from their wages. The conversation went all around the houses and threw up many other questions en route, none of which Khalim expected Adrian to answer.

Once this subject had been exhausted, he moved to the next related topic. 'Life Drawing', and in particular, its vital role as an artistic discipline and the need for it to be included as a subject within the prison curriculum. And consequently, the necessity to bring in nude models. He pointed out that female models, because they were more curvaceous, were logically more artistic in form and were therefore preferable. Should this not be possible, however, a male model would be adequate - people aren't fussy when pushed. To back up his argument further, he also surmised that had life drawing been withheld from many famous artists they would have remained in obscurity. As he realised this was going nowhere, he compromised and suggested that Adrian could, at least, bring in some pictures of nude paintings for them to copy.

'Yeah, bring in some porn,' growled Alan.

Having established that this was not going to happen either, Khalim asked if the class could do an architectural painting that showed perspective. An excellent idea, Adrian agreed, but his enthusiasm was short-lived, as Khalim wanted to paint the Twin Towers in New York under attack. He didn't think this was inappropriate: as he pointed out, the class could learn several different techniques all at once - perspective, fire and smoke, atmosphere. Adrian said he thought this was insensitive and wouldn't allow it. Khalim argued that as artists we should be above politics and not be sentimental. He argued that historically many great and generally well-respected pieces of work were of battle scenes. Didn't the British Government actually employ 'War Artists'? Therefore he couldn't see why Adrian should have any objections. When Adrian still refused, he said that the only possible reason left why Adrian was stopping this project must be because he was a racist. That was where Adrian put his foot down, and for at least fifteen minutes Khalim stopped talking. Briefly, the class were able to work in earnest - and in peace.

Racism was a hot potato in prison. Posters shouted at all who passed, on every landing, corridor and classroom to *report it if you see it*. Trouble was, with the exception of extreme cases, you rarely did see it. Because racism was usually invisible. It lived in people's heads and hearts and sometimes got so strong it erupted and produced the visible stuff. It lived in looks, in silent nods, in thoughts and body language. It came out in whispers, in attitudes, in the choice of where you sat, in multiple, multiple ways.

Adrian had often met racism in it's various guises. White against black, black against white, Welsh against English, everyone against Moslems.

Adrian asked himself why was there so much of it about. He had always thought of himself as international and multicultural, but he had a revelation that wasn't that pleasant. It resulted from that same *blame* culture he had now entered. Everyone blamed someone else. And the reason was because they all felt threatened, they felt scared. The Nazis were scared of the Jews, the whites were scared of the immigrants, the Welsh were scared of the English. Everyone was scared of the Moslems.

Adrian looked at Khalim who had just called him a racist. Was Khalim scared of him.? Did he feel threatened by Adrian?

Khalim looked away and started talking again. He wanted to know why Adrian was a vegetarian. Was he a Buddhist? He asked Adrian what he thought of the officers. It was endless, and getting boring. And then he said, 'What is the point of education in prison, anyway? What use is all this?' For the first time Adrian thought there was something here worth answering.

'There are many reasons why I think education should be taught in prison. It brings confidence, it can bring qualifications, it improves the mind and above all, it gives you opportunity.'

'To do what?'

'To take it as far as you like. You could end up with a degree, you know.'

'I wouldn't mind that actually. I would like to study.'

Adrian noticed that his usual ranting tone had taken on a more thoughtful, quieter quality. Could Khalim be his first potential degree student? To obtain such under these conditions seemed almost impossible. Khalim seemed to be thinking along the same lines.

He snapped back to his old self.

'Yeah! Well! I'd want to study Islam and there ain't anyone here to teach that and I'm only in for a few more months anyway.

Several of the other men were voicing their irritation, and started mumbling, they genuinely wanted to proceed with their work.

'Let's be quiet now, Khalim. Give your tongue a rest and let's get on.'

'One last question though! Can I go to the toilet?'

This was another of his exhausting habits. Khalim was always trying to find reasons to leave the classroom and go walkabout. If he wished to go to the toilet, he would go via everywhere and return via everywhere else. Unfortunately, due to a weak bladder condition, (yeah right!) he needed to go at least once every thirty minutes. The officers on duty were becoming really fed up with him casually strolling round the wing. They regularly exploded at him, with little effect, and told him he could only go to the loo at break times like everyone else, unless it was an emergency. They firmly informed Adrian not to let him leave the classroom. The onus was on the teacher.

After lunch, they resumed their lesson, but when Khalim came into the classroom he was fuming, he was really mad. Something had gone wrong since Adrian last saw him. He was back on the racism issue.

'Who's the racist officer in this prison?'

Alan burst out laughing.

'They all are, mate. Take your pick.'

'I want to speak to the officer who's responsible for complaints about racism. Where do I get an application form?' The question was directed at Adrian.

'They're on the wing. You can get one at tea break.'

'No, I need one now. I need to report a racist incident.'

In view of the fact that he would invariably go several other places too, and that Khalim cried wolf at least three times a day, Adrian thought it probably best to wait an hour.

'No, you can't leave the classroom now. Not until tea break.'

'Are you going to stand up for racism and block me making a report?'

'I'm not blocking you. You can do it in an hour's time. It makes no difference whether it's now or in an hour's time, does it?'

'You're supporting them and standing up for them. Now we know where we really stand.'

'No I'm not. Anyway, tell me what happened?'

'At lunchtime the screws spun my cell and they took away all my Islamic posters. It's a blatant racist attack. It's because I'm a Moslem. They can't do that, it's part of my culture.'

'I'm surprised they did such a thing. You can fill in a report at tea break.'

'No, it'll be too late. I've got to do it now.'

'NO.'

'I need to go to the toilet.'

'No, you don't. Just wait.'

Suddenly Alan, Khalim's friend, spoke up:

'Which ones did they take?'

'My favourites, the one with Osama Bin Laden and the Mujahadin, and the other one I like with the freedom fighters on it.'

'Oh no! Not the 'Kill the Infidels' one...'

Khalim took this as a cue and began giving a lecture on Pakistan and all its virtues. It would have been fine but, unfortunately, he had to compare every positive attribute of Pakistan with some negative one of Britain. The food, the weather, the women, the politics, the countryside. Some of the other men were becoming defensive. Adrian told Khalim to stop. His opinions were inverted racism.

'I'm not giving my opinions; I'm only stating what is fact.' It was all sounding horribly arrogant. 'You can't deny that one country might be better than another and pretend that they are all the same, just for the sake of being politically correct. All you people know about Pakistan, or any Moslem country for that matter, is what you read in your newspapers, and they're all biased.'

'Well, I'd rather live here than in your fucking desert,' erupted Andy, unable to contain himself anymore.

The situation needed defusing immediately. Adrian decided to turn it into a very boring geography lesson. Nothing like good old-fashioned teaching to put everyone to sleep.

'There are bound to be good and bad points about any country. For example, there is a fantastic desert in Pakistan, which stretches into both Iran and India, and which can be very beautiful, However, the north of the country is very mountainous and green - the Swat Valley is a bit like Snowdonia as I remember.' Many years ago, he had travelled overland to India and spent considerable time in Pakistan, Afghanistan and Iran.

'You ain't been there?' said an incredulous Khalim. Adrian nodded. 'You've actually been to Pakistan?'

'Yes, I've been twice, actually, but the second time I was only passing through and didn't stay long. Whereabouts are you from?'

'Well, I've never been there myself. I grew up in Enfield.'

There was an unexpected silence. (For two whole seconds.) Adrian was aware that it was silence and not just a pause for breath. He could hear the difference.

'Where did you go over there?'

'Lahore to start with, but mainly Peshawar.'

'Peshawar. Why? That's near the Afghan border. That's Taliban country. What were you doing up there?'

'I stayed there, having just come from Afghanistan. Over the Khyber Pass.' Adrian didn't tell him this was nearly thirty years ago.

'You were in Afghanistan?' He paused for thought, and then asked with all sincerity. 'Are you a Moslem?' Adrian answered No - in a way that could have said 'maybe'. Khalim looked at him through half-closed eyes and continued:

'Are you one of those white Islamic militants?'

The rest of the class were looking at Adrian with that same silence, that Adrian had been thinking about earlier. It made him feel physically cold.

Adrian didn't know how to answer so just raised his eyebrows heavenward and the subject was closed, at least temporarily.

By tea break the racism had retreated back beyond thoughts into attitude and remained unconscious. Khalim was up-beat and rapping to himself, loudly. Adrian couldn't catch the words because it was so fast - something about frustration, probation, illustration (rapping isn't Asian). It went on and on till eventually Adrian told him to stop, as he was getting on everyone's nerves, again.

'Wasamatter? Don't you like modern music, boss?' (Let's turn this into a weapon...) 'Who do you like then?' (...stab...) 'I bet you like that old guy in the rocking chair...' (...punch...) 'Yeah, I bet you like him, innit?' (...slap...) 'Come on, who's your favourite singer, boss? Val Doonican?'

Adrian stared at him and wondered whether Khalim was feeling threatened by him again, although this time it was ageism not racism. Adrian remembered that only the night before, he had been listening to Nusrat Fateh Ali Khan, the Qiwali singer. He wondered whether he should tell Khalim. He took him to one side.

'What! Amazing! You're one of us,' shouted Khalim. Adrian felt flattered, but realised how divided the world was for Khalim. The poor man must feel threatened by so much to be so defensive. Adrian couldn't think of an appropriate reply so gave himself up to the spirit of the moment, which he did under such circumstances and hoped for the right answer..

'Yes Khalim, I am and you're one of us too.'

The spirit never failed. Adrian was glad he had a clever angel.

# 17 A BABE CALLED LEE

*The most respected man in Fiji, other than the king, was the shaman. The shaman could see into the future. He did this when the spirits entered him. Being bisexual, he offered himself up to the supernatural. The spirits exchanged their insights into the future for carnal knowledge of the ladyboy, The shaman was both deified and feared.*

Lee and Dean joined Adrian's class at the same time. There seemed to be little rhyme or reason why people joined the class. They seemed to be of all ages and from all the various wings. Supposedly it was adults in the morning and Young Offenders in the afternoon, but there were so many exceptions that you'd never have guessed. All Adrian saw were people coming and going to and from his class. Almost every week, there was a change in the classroom constellation that had to be incorporated into the teaching. One consistency was that every other Young Offender was usually called either Lee or Dean (or Darren). Adrian, who had never been good at names, naturally muddled the new men up regularly, though he tried desperately not to. The new Lee didn't mind, but the new Dean did. Lee was 27 years old, friendly and chatty, and Dean was about the same age but quiet and reserved. Lee was the seemingly easy one. He had lank, rather greasy hair, was slightly overweight, had stuck-out, buck rabbit teeth and round, gold-rimmed glasses. As Adrian got to know him better, he realised that Lee suffered from rather violent mood swings. He was usually found extremely high or extremely low or extremely whatever, but never in the middle. Lee needed to find some equilibrium in his life. Any one of these extremes was difficult for anybody else to endure for more than a few minutes. He was either over-friendly or aggressively in-your-face. Nevertheless, whatever he was at any particular moment, there was one thing you could always rely on and that was a running commentary. He could always manage to talk and talk and talk. There were so many things going on in his head that there was never any space left over, unfortunately, for art.

The day Lee first arrived he was already in full swing. In the short walk from the cells to the class, he had managed to argue with everyone else in the group. The reason for this became obvious as time went by and was always the same. Lee wouldn't, or couldn't, let anything drop. If it had to be said then out it would come, regardless of whom he was talking to. This was not a good way to join an established class. A bad atmosphere already wafted around the men when they entered the room.

Today Adrian had planned to paint a mining village scene. It was a little ambitious and needed a fair amount of concentration, but the class had been making progress lately. However, there was obviously something else, more important, on Lee's mind as he dragged himself through the work, and it wasn't art. He copied all of Adrian's brush strokes, while at the same time managing to continue his argument with everyone else in the room. The end-result, needless to say, was not that brilliant. It was only what Adrian would call a token job, done with little enthusiasm in an environment that was hardly conducive to work. What Adrian had planned to do today - his *pièce de résistance*, if you like - was a lengthy instruction on how to paint the sky using many thin layers of cobalt blue applied on top of one another. Lee looked at Adrian as if he was listening, but then just slapped on the paint about three inches thick. Adrian looked on in disbelief.

'Lee,' Adrian called from across the room. 'Did you hear what I just said about the sky?'

'No, not really. What was it?'

Adrian realised that this was probably the first time Lee had actually 'seen' him that day.

'It's too late now, but please try and concentrate on what you're here to do. Painting, remember?.'

'I am trying.'

'You can certainly say that again, Lee.'

'Ade, I am really. And another thing - can you stop calling me Lee.'

A deathly silence fell on the group, as it does when something monumental is about to happen. Adrian thought maybe he'd muddled Dean and Lee again. He checked the register quickly.

'But you *are* Lee.'

'I know I am...sometimes. But I'd feel a lot more comfortable if, from now on, you would call me Angie.'

'Angie?'

Adrian looked around the table at the other inmates. They were all staring at him; some were nodding their heads knowingly.

'OK, if that's what you want, but why Angie?' Thus the key turned that unlocked the door to the world of a remarkable person.

Lee was gay, but to complicate matters he was also a transvestite. Being gay was almost accepted, but being a 'tranny' as well was pushing it a bit far in prisonland. Apparently he was quite convincing and had no problems passing himself off as a woman as this story illustrates. He had been arrested in Southend, in drag, and had been put into a women's holding cell for the night with several other real women. He never told Adrian why he'd been arrested in the first place, and Adrian thought it impolite to ask. It was only when he needed the toilet that the police realised their mistake and, according to Angie, he was then transferred to an all male cell with that particular evening's catch of blokes. Talk about throwing the lamb (maybe that's too innocent a word) into the lion's den. This story was listened to with relish and went down well with the class. Everyone was smiling. Adrian was obviously the only one in the room who hadn't heard it before. The story ended with: 'Southend is a shit hole, guv. Do you know it at all?'

Adrian replied that he did, and that he had actually grown up in Essex and had been there many times since. This was all that was required for their souls to be united for eternity.

'We're both Essex boys!' he exclaimed with glee. He lifted his sleeve to Adrian's ear.

'If you hold this shell-suit to your ear you can hear Dagenham High Street.' He grinned. 'We Essex boys have got to stick together. Ain't that right, Ade?'

Ade nodded. Strangely this camaraderie, was not just about coming from Essex, it was to do everything that Essex stood for; the council estates, the easy girls, the gold chains, the orange cars. It was all the stuff that Adrian hated. The stuff that had made him leave, no, run away from the bloody place as soon as he could. All that crap, that macho, loud, opinionated crap that represented so much pain in Adrian's life. That was what bound him and Angie together. They had a shared hurt. Adrian ran away to another part of the country, Angie ran into himself. For the first time ever, Adrian valued that ugly part of his life, for without it how could he understand anything. How could he understand Angie?

No more explanation was needed, Adrian now had a new soul brother (or sometimes sister).

Now that Angie's true persuasion was out of the bag, it was quite OK to talk about anything at all. When Lee took leave to go to the loo, Mike P., who had been sharing a cell with Angie, started telling the class of the huge amounts of make-up that he had managed to acquire, which beggars belief in an all male prison.

'He's got half of fucking Boots up there.'

When Lee returned, Andy, always ready for a wind-up, asked: 'Do you wear make-up, then? In your cell, like?'

Lee was completely un-phased, and replied amicably: 'Not all of it. I only totally frock up for special occasions. But I usually wear a little moisturiser every night, and again, I put a thin base of foundation on in the morning. I've got some on now, actually. It covers up the spots.' Then he added in a Mae West voice: 'I didn't realise you were interested, though. Why don't you come to my cell at lunchtime and I'll show you what I've got.'

Andy's gibe had totally backfired; Angie was definitely master of this situation. Others thought twice before going there. This was a perfect example of how things were when they were going well for Angie and he was on top - so to speak. He was clever enough to realise that the more open he was, the more a lot of the others were terrified of him. This led him to getting some respect as well as a lot of stick. Surprisingly, the most vitriolic slander came from those who were the least macho, and were probably the most gay. Adrian again realised the strongest prejudice came from those most threatened.

Prisoners are body-searched every time they enter or leave the wing. Angie's open pleasure in certain officers doing this was possibly how the make-up managed to get circulated. He would move around in the queue while waiting, in order to be frisked by particular hands, manoeuvring himself in place so that the chosen officer would get the pleasure. This usually resulted in a quick, token search.

Alan was the king of gossip. He had at least ten stories about everybody and at least three hundred concerning Angie. Alan worked in the laundry. His duties included once a week collecting everyone's dirties, left hanging in plastic bags on the cell door handles, washing them, and then returning them, if possible, to their rightful owners. He told stories which one hoped were embellished. He began one now…

'He hands out all these black frilly knickers for me to wash every week. Once I was in a terrible rush - everything was behind time. By mistake I got some of the washing muddled up (again) and a pair of Angie's frillies ended up with Sherwood's stuff...' (Sherwood was probably the person you would least like to play a practical joke on, especially if it in any way threatened his male pride) '...I expected Sherwood to go mad. However, he didn't say anything. He must have noticed them, but obviously he was keeping them for himself. Angie, on the other hand, had received Sherwood's Y-fronts in return and definitely didn't want them. He came to me as soon as he could, armed with Sherwood's pants, and very vocally demanded his frillies back. I told him they had probably gone to Sherwood by mistake, as I was doing their stuff at the same time...' (Stir it up, stir it up.)

Angie, finding the least appropriate time (the queue at lunchtime), had gone up to Sherwood and asked: 'Have you got my knicks?' The entire wing awaited his reply.

'You what?' Sherwood was not pleased to have all this attention from Angie in such a public place. But Angie, the master of linear thought, wasn't going to back off now.

'You've got my best undies, and I want them back.'

'Fuck off, faggot.' This was not the best thing to say to someone who is openly gay. It acted as a red rag to a bull. Angie was well out of the closet, and woe betide anyone who used that against him.

'I know you've got them. There's no need to deny it. And anyway, aren't these yours?' He held up the Y-fronts for all to see. 'If you want to borrow mine just ask, and I'll try and get you some of your own, but I want that particular pair back now as I've run out of cleans.'

'I don't have them. Why should I want your underwear? Pervert.'

'To wear, of course. As a result of this I'm not wearing any at all today - which I don't mind occasionally, but I don't want to do that too often, in case I lose my sensitivity.'

This conversation was very loud, against a deathly, expectant hush. Sherwood was shuffling around, turning a lovely shade of red. He was greatly relieved to get to the counter, grab his food, and make a hasty retreat.

As he left, Angie threw his Y-fronts at him. They landed on his shoulder.

'You forgot these,' he shouted. Sherwood almost broke into a run.

Later that day, according to Angie, who told Alan, the frillies were found stuffed under his cell door. No questions asked. But Angie, unable to keep anything so eventful quiet for long, informed everyone of their return. He also said that they had been worn. He could tell. He knew about such things. Not that he wished to put any names forward, like. But it began with an S.

* * *

All these stories Adrian took with a pinch of salt. However, one day, having taken his lunch, he returned to the wing to find the officers having an extended break. He sat at a nearby table and began to set things up. He overheard them laughing and joking about having just 'spun' Angie's cell and found, as well as make-up, all sorts of sex toys. Apparently, they were carefully modelled from bars of soap.

'It was probably Fairy,' they roared.

As every star that rises must set, so too did Angie wane , though it appeared more of a plummet. The time arrived when everything got too much for Angie and all felt his down side. The pain of too many insults stored up over the weeks, the cell searches, the isolation, combined with a cocktail of, or absence of, medication was pushing him close to the edge. Like Khalim, who played the racist card irresponsibly, so too did Angie play the sexual orientation card at times like these. Adrian was sure there was some truth in what he said, but it was all getting very muddled and Angie needed professional help. Such help was there, but it seemed to take forever to kick in. Angie was extremely needy *now,* and waiting patiently was not his strength He decided that the powers-that-be were all against him, which was possibly true. In an act fuelled by paranoia, he took the situation into his own hands. One morning he proudly told Adrian: 'I'm leaving soon. I've applied for a transfer to A Block.' A Block is the ordinary adult prisoner wing. Angie had been put on the 'protected wing' because it was thought it would be less of a problem for him there. A Block can be dangerous for someone so open-minded and open-mouthed. This was not sounding good.

'God, Angie, you'll have to be so careful. There's a lot of blokes there who won't accept you. They'll be openly hostile. Are you sure that's where you want to go?'

'Too late now, I'm already going. These bastards are so sexist.'

'I think they're more homophobic in your case.'

Angie grinned. 'I knew a homophobic bloke once. He never went out. He always stayed at home.' Angie still retained his wit, even under stress.

'Don't worry, I can be discreet when I want to be. I did it for years before I came out.'

This didn't ring very true. Adrian hadn't been aware of any discretion to date.

'You wouldn't believe what goes on, on this wing. I could tell you a thing or two. Who does what to whom. And I'm not just talking inmates you know. They make me sick. It can't be any worse over there than this shitty place.'

Adrian looked at the sweaty, twitchy face in front of him. Here was someone with so many problems. Rather than react to what he had just said, Adrian couldn't help thinking that this man must have been a kid at some time, and wondered what his parents had been like and how they treated him. He wondered whether he still had any contact with them.

That was the last time Adrian spoke to him. Angie moved to A Block and from there was subsequently moved to another prison where he would have to reinvent the wheel yet again. Adrian heard what happened to Angie on A block after he had been shipped out.

The story circulating around the prison was that when he arrived on Alpha he was told that he would be sharing a cell, and that prudence would be the best policy. He was told to keep his personal life to himself. Angie agreed and for the first fifteen minutes all went well, as he was feeling down and quiet anyway. Apparently his cellmate was expecting a little more conversation than this and began pressing him with questions about where he came from and so on, to which Angie replied in pure Angie style: 'I can't talk at the moment. I've got too many problems to deal with regarding my sexuality.'

The mythology surrounding him lived on.

# 18 FIGHTS

*Angry men make good warriors. So the people of Fiji treat their soldiers badly. They deprive them of all comfort and luxury and keep them locked in camps. When needed they are unleashed on the enemy.*

The boys had unexpectedly arrived early and were sitting around while Adrian was flitting about getting ready for class. As they waited, they chatted. The testosterone count in the atmosphere today was high. Whenever these levels of concentration were reached, the conversation invariably focussed on 'fights I have won', and the boys jostled for the most entertaining anecdote.

(When similar levels are reached in Fiji, the warriors of the Kaduva tribe act out a similar ritual. They compete by dancing ancient war dances in their regalia, each one being a little more ferocious than the last.)

The inmates were about to begin. Their voices and language, as was customary on such occasions, transformed them into some peculiar hybrid accent of black New York mixed with various colloquial English dialects, that became more and more pronounced as the conversation progressed. The most unbelievable one Adrian ever heard was NYC meets west country Somerset. It was a case of 'don't listen to him, listen to me - I'm further up the pecking order than you.' The first young offender (Y.O.) got the ball rolling. Being a 'muppet', he didn't last long.

'Der's nuttin better dan a good fight. You knows it don't matter dat you's hurt yourself, it just feels so good inside. Der was dis...'

'Yeah, yeah...' that's as much as he was getting '...I loves it too, but it's gotta be a real fight if yous wants to feels really fucking alive. Once I was in dis fucking club and dis bloke he's staring like. I goes over and I stands next to him and den I just fucking flicks my fist like dis and I hears dis fucking clicking sound in his nose.' There was laughter all round. 'He's dis big bloke and he cries out like a fucking baby. So I punches him again...' (Adrian was filling up the water jars and he needed one more yoghurt pot. It was incredible where they disappeared to.) The first Y.O. tried to get back into the picture: 'Well, I likes it best when you's really in der with da proper punching. It's like you sprung, mun. You's alive. Dere was dis...'

'Yeah! I's talking now...' another lad with more credentials again pushed him aside '...I once had this fight with dees tree blokes in Newport. God, dey's so fucking stoopid man. Dey says I've nicked der car and dey're going to rearrange my face like. But while he's talking all dis shit man I just fucking kicks him in de balls man. Rearrange my face, I'm going to fucking rearrange his testicles, da dickhead. I den punches dis udder guy in the fucking face and he fucking falls over dis concrete wall onto dis car and puts a fucking dent in it. And it's his own fucking car. He'd just parked it der and forgots where. He tinks I fucking nicked it. I beats de fucking shit out of dem and den I really does nick it and drives off in it....'

'But what yous wants that for, bruv? Ain't it got a dent in it?' The original Y.O. was questioning the story. WHOA! This was tantamount to rebellion. The comment was not acknowledged. But neither was it ignored. (Adrian was now sorting out twelve decent brushes; it was amazing how ruined they got if left in water.)

'Yeah, so when I'm nearly home I's torches it like. Teach dem stupid fucking fuckers not mess wiv me, cos I really don't take kindly to...' he was staring at the Y.O. that had interrupted him '...people interfering wid me.'

Suddenly the spotlight turned on Mark Jones. Everyone listened with more interest.

'If you's talking *real* fights, de best ones are at de stands, mun. Jeez! I've had some fucking good ones dere. Dey takes any weapons off us like when we goes in, but we takes newspapers and rolls dem up like dis - dey's really hard, feels it! - and we punches it just here, on de temple. There's nothing better to do on a Saturday afternoon dan get tanked up and have a fucking good fight...' (There was no lemon yellow watercolour left, so Adrian had to mix up some more. It was always the colour that ran out first.) The stories were coming thick and fast.

'Der's dis guy I knows and he's a dealer and has got a lotta money and he drives his car every week to get more smack. So I waits at the traffic lights and I has dis crow bar and I knows he's going to stop at the lights so I just jumps out and smashes his windscreen. He looks so fucking funny. He has bits of fucking windscreen all over him. He dunno what's hit him. He's like a shock monkey. I pulls at his bag but he won't release it so I hits his hand with the bar. His fingers all snap and he soon lets go. But in de back of de car ders dis big fucking bodyguard and he's lying on de back seat wid his bitch, mun. Any way he jumps up so fast he hits his head and gets out of de car still wid his dick sticking out. He's a fucking gorilla and grabs me and starts punching me. But he's all fat man. He's all jelly. I hits him and my fist disappears. I cracks him wid de bar, man. I splits his head open. His bitch is screaming, she's getting on my nerves so I tells her to shut de fuck up. And den...' (The paper wasn't as thick as the last batch. Adrian hoped it could take the water if he stretched it and fixed it with gumstrip.)

The conversation was cranking up a gear and the big boys were now coming in. But still the original Y.O., who didn't seem to understand the rules, kept interrupting. He was looking for an opportunity to try his story again, and once again to take the floor. Some people couldn't take hints. Was he stupid or did he want plastic surgery?'

'How comes you knew he was going to stop at the traffic lights? What if it had been green? Surely he'd have just driven on?'

There was a moment of incredulous silence.

'Yous calling me a liar or what?' The very logical question about the traffic lights was ignored. This was a question of protocol.

'Jeez! You've gotta fucking nerve.' However, a bigger man took over, taking advantage of the interruption to begin his story. This defused the situation, as everyone was obliged to listen and to put off any grievances till later. He began: 'I once went into dis shop, man, and I's going to robs it. But dis guy, who owns it, has tree brudders who are all visiting him like. So when I goes in dere, dey all comes out of de back and dey're big fuckers and dey all comes at me. So I pulls out dis big fucking gun, man, and I tells dem dat I kills dem if dey comes near man, but dis guy is so stoopid he just comes at me so I shoots him in da, leg man. You can hears da bone breaking inside, it sorta snappin sound, and den I...'

Another voice butted in - the stories were beginning to jump from one to the next with increasing speed.

'I had dis great big gun, man, it was an evil fucker, and I goes into dis chemist...it was dis great fucking ting, man, it was more like a rocket launcher...'

Adrian at last had everything arranged and was ready to begin. He looked around the room. The angels with dirty faces were reminiscing about times gone by, leaving their bodies below in the Art Room, eyes vacant and glazed. There was something quite *Jackanory*-like about the way they sat and listened. However, it was time to interrupt their conversation as the moment had come to commence the lesson. The world of art was to bring them crashing down to earth, leaving the angels, armed to the teeth, to sort it out among themselves.

'OK, boys! We need to get started. Can you look this way!' They stared at Adrian blankly as if he'd stepped off another planet and was speaking Martian. So to help them understand Adrian translated for them: 'Todays, bro, weez gonna paint de fuckin still life wid da bananaz an dat teapot shit, OK?...'

The men looked offended. Was he taking the piss?

Adrian looked at his class. He hadn't realised how sensitive they were. Sometimes the hardest nuts have the softest centres.

# 19 BALLET BOY

*The people of Fiji love to dance. It is as natural to them as talking. A man that didn't dance was considered impaired and was pitied.*

In the middle of the prison lies a little cultural oasis called the library, which is open to both staff and inmates alike. It is manned by dedicated staff, assisted by a group of prison orderlies, who together maintain the atmosphere of dignity and calm befitting such an establishment of learning. The room is found amidst the turquoise, soul-less corridors of the amenities building, offering hope and possibility to all those who find their way to its door. It is generally regarded as the most 'normal' place in the nick, and is often used as a place of sanctuary from the trials of prison routine. One day, sitting at a table with his head in a book, Adrian temporarily forgot where he was and thought he was outside. He was completely immersed in what he was reading. When he did come out of it and realised what had happened, it made him uneasy. Around him were hundreds of books, neatly stacked in long, catalogued lines. They extended around the walls, infusing the atmosphere with knowledge and learning. With such a wealth of information, surely there were enough resources, here in the prison library, for an inmate to get a degree. It wasn't lack of materials that prevented people trying. Here there was a brilliant asset. The verticality of the books mirrored the bars on the windows and to some extent helped camouflage them. This was another reason the place seemed somehow less 'prisony'. As Adrian pondered his lapse of consciousness, he became aware that each title offered the possibility of a temporary release, a quick escape - assuming one could read of course - and the library, like his art class, could be therapeutic.

Today, as his eyes ran along the shelves marked 'Art', they were momentarily distracted by a chart pinned to the wall. He strained to read it, but it all appeared as a blur since he had earlier put on his reading specs. Beholding his puzzled squint, one of the staff spoke.

'It's a list of the most popular books in the prison. A kind of literary top ten.'

Adrian moved to an optimum distance and scanned down the charts, and couldn't help noticing that all the titles were either about prison, or about famous prisoners. It seems that rather than use the library to escape for a few hours in fiction, the majority of readers preferred to use it to deepen and enhance their already malign situation. Adrian reflected on certain animals that have been brought up in captivity and then find, one day, that the cage door's been left open. Rather than go through it and escape, they stay in the cage, too frightened to leave. Who needs great fiction anyway when you've got Ronnie Biggs' life story... Adrian thought that if ever he was to write a book, it should be about prison, because that way he could guarantee certain sales.

Regularly, new consignments of books arrived at Feldon Park from the Central Library. Every week the crates of convicted literature, containing the next batch of sentenced volumes, came to do their time in Botany Bay. On this one occasion, however, there was a stowaway, lodged between Chopper and Ian Brady. It meekly sat there cowering next to these two heavyweights. It was a gentle, slim volume with elegant gold lettering on the cover, entitled *Teach Yourself Ballet.* It was a sophisticated, genteel kind of book and seemed out of place in such rough company as its neighbours. Maybe it was trying to escape the world. Or had it been forced to flee like a refugee? We shall never know.

'Why on earth have they sent us this? Is someone taking the piss?' (Or words to that effect; librarians, even in prison, never use such bad language.) 'I can't imagine anyone taking that out in here.'

After considerable debate, the collective librarians decided to keep it anyway. It was too much hassle to send it back. The book was given a home on the shelf labelled 'Keep Fit', where it was shoved, uncomfortably, between weights and circuit training. However, it didn't have to endure such rowdy companions for long, because by the end of the day someone had taken it out.

When I say 'taken it out' I don't mean gone to the counter, had it stamped and given the orderly the card. No, no, I mean it was taken out. Stolen.

'Well, at least I hope whoever took it enjoys it and doesn't vandalise it.' Kidnapping is one thing, but torture...?

This should have been the end of the story, and the little ballet book put on the missing person's list. However, several days later, one of the orderlies noticed something quite significant on the wing where he lived, which made him suspicious. There had been a change in the ambience.

If ever you have the pleasure of strolling in a leisurely fashion along the landings, on any of the wings, on a moonlit evening, you can't help noticing the gentle voices of countless cicadas chirruping behind all the cell doors, a hundred CD players jostling with each other to be heard. As controls are imperceptibly turned the collective volume creeps ever upwards. The noise level spirals higher and higher until the authorities bang their cans and all the cicadas scuttle back to their holes and hide. Silence reigns until the coast is once again clear, and they re-emerge to start the chorus over again. This happens every night and is part of the evening routine.

What the orderly noticed on that particular night was that one of the cicadas was not quite right. It was singing a different tune to everyone else. Someone was not playing the game and was being different. Amidst the rapping, rock and reggae, the hip hop ranting and brutal guitars were heard delicate strings singing a lilting, ephemeral song. The orderly froze and listened. His trained ear could pick out every note. All else seemed to fade away as the sweet melody cut across the wing. He recognised the music immediately. It was Swan Lake.

Homing in on its source, and picking up a few other puzzled inmates on the way, he stood outside cell number 8 and cautiously lifted the flap. Inside stood a Welsh inmate known as Insect. He was balanced on one leg, holding onto the table, with his other leg sticking straight out behind him in a dying-swan position. The stowaway book sat on the table in front of him, open at the appropriate page, egging him on.

A collective gasp came from the audience. Not only because of the wonderful grace of the dying swan, or its fantastic fluttering hand movements, but mainly because Insect had been wheelchair-bound for eight years and was now standing up.

At the sound of their amazement, Insect leapt with incredible agility across the cell and with one pirouette hopped back into his chair. He called across the orchestra pit to his now clapping fans.

'Fuck off, you bastards! Is there no privacy left in here?'

'Bravo, encore, bravo!'

The seeds had been sown for a life of torment. From that day on, Insect was titled and known forever more as 'Insect, the Swan(sea) Prince'.

# 20 BRING ON THE CATWALK

*Beauty is an indefinable phenomena that bears no reality in the physical realm because it lives only in the eye of the beholder. The world is therefore full of beauty, as long as there are people around to look at it.*

Daytime TV was something that Adrian knew nothing about as he was always at work. Even on the rare occasions he was at home during the week there were always so many other things to do, that the television was never switched on. It really was designed for those with masses of time on their hands and no gainful employment. Adrian wondered if the TV planners realised how many regular viewers they get in prison. Television was also a common reason for disputes. Adrian recalled incidents in his own home that were all about the bloody remote control.

Imagine replacing your family with a complete stranger and restricting yourself to a small room that you can't leave. Finally, put that stranger on edge, give him a short fuse, and a criminal record, and you can judge how explosive the situation might become. It's surprising there aren't daily riots. It's true that television is the opium of the masses, but recall how, once hooked and then deprived, the addict often turns nasty.

However, there are certain programmes that are universally appreciated inside. Well, almost. There'll always be exceptions. One of these that occurs annually, and is totally politically incorrect, is 'Miss World'. Adrian's attention was drawn to it when asked by Alan Driver if he would like to place a bet. He agreed, though at the time he didn't know what he was betting on. He felt, however, that being asked was a further sign of acceptance and therefore would never have turned it down. In the days running up to the show, bets were taken, syndicates set up and huge quantities of Mars Bars (MB, prisonland currency) were exchanging hands as a result. 1 MB was about 40p at time of press. 'Miss World' night was the one night you could guarantee there wouldn't be a breakout. (So if you were planning one it's probably the best time to try.) The show was avidly watched, every year, as the girls strutted their stuff and answered the highly predictable questions: 'How would you help the world if chosen to be Miss World?' In prisonland many more precise and explicit questions were being asked and thoroughly discussed behind locked doors on the block. The answers could only be imagined, and are - most vividly so I've been told. Adrian didn't win anything. Miss Fiji was knocked out in the first round.

In the aftermath of the current show Alan Driver came up with a brilliant scam. He was going to become the Robert Morley of his own extravaganza. The first ever Miss Feldon Park, as voted for by the men of D Block. The only difference between this and the real McCoy was that the candidates for the title didn't know they were in it - and therefore wouldn't get any prizes either.

A planning meeting was set up at association time and the candidates were officially nominated and seconded. You might think there would be a shortage of entrants, but since Feldon Park was an 'equal opportunity employer' and 'an investor in people', there was a huge pool of potential. The short list included: Sam the social worker, Nurse Phillips, Miss Reid in the library, Apeface, Claudia the English teacher, the 'lesbian woman in the gym', the 'lesbian woman who works in Healthcare', the 'lesbian woman who works in administration'. (The last three were all nominated by Ricky Evans, who had a certain obsession and a vivid imagination.) Sixteen stone Sian, Psycho Sue in Maths, Miss Rutter the Nutter, Big Mamma, Foxy Bev, Jan the Mouth. The list went on and on. An assortment of teachers, female officers, nurses, social workers, librarians and several others. The most unlikely entrant was Sister Veronica, the 108-year-old Roman Catholic nun.

When asked to place a second bet a week later, Adrian realised he was in on some sort of scam. His suspicions led him to finding out more than he wanted to, but crossing the threshold of inclusion, was more valuable to him than any embarrassment and sense of betrayal.

'Put a Mars Bar on for me then. Whichever you think best.'

Alan Driver, having listed the candidates, now set up his syndicate and the bets were placed. The first part of the competition was to be based on appearance, and marks were given out of ten for hair, face, breasts, arse, legs. The second part was based on hypothesis, each prisoner being asked to 'use his imagination' and then come back with marks out of ten.

Adrian pointed out that this alone was not enough and could so easily be rigged. Incredible, the importance of laws in a prison. They needed further tests that were unpredictable. They would have to ask questions and the answers evaluated.

The problem here was that the candidates didn't know they were taking part, and were not to find out either. The questions, after lots of consideration, were agreed upon, and were remarkably similar to those in the original competition. Most of the popular alternatives were far too explicit to be asked unnoticed.

The first question was: 'What changes would you make if you were put in charge of the prison?' This was equivalent to the usual: 'What would you do to improve the world?'

The second was not really a question but more a reaction test. 'How would you behave if a prisoner had left something in his cell and then asked if you could let him go and fetch it?' This would enable the panel to evaluate the candidate's level of compassion and co-operation.

The answers were to be evaluated by three different individuals: Alan Driver (who had an executive position), Khalim (probably to make the panel multicultural) and the third one, because he had a calculator, was Adrian.

'No, no, no!' was his reply on being first asked, but his protestations were futile as he had already been agreed upon.

'I can't do this. They're my colleagues. I work with them you know.'

'O come on! They won't even know. All you got to do is add up the votes.'

Adrian reluctantly agreed, though he felt an enormous weight of guilt descend on him.

'After all, Ade, it's only a bit of harmless fun,' said Alan as he walked away, mission accomplished.

That night forms were distributed, and then collected after breakfast the following morning. Once they had been handed in, Adrian had the honour of adding up the scores. He sat at his table and pretended to be marking papers. He was shaking, because he was in full view of the officer's window. His fingers flew over the calculator keys. He handed the results to Alan and left as soon as he could.

The final results were quite surprising. Firstly, for 'hair', the winner was Bev, a respectable 42 points above any rival. For 'face', again the winner was Bev, but this time by a slim margin of 2 points ahead of Claudia. When it came to 'bosoms' there were two favourites: Big Mamma and 16-stone Sian. They both had 26 points - they were abreast (Ricky Evans's joke, of course). Big girls were this year's preference. The same applied to 'arse', where yet again Big Mama and Sian were cheek by cheek. (Sorry!) The 'leg' count was the most varied and there was no obvious winner. It seemed that people's choices differed in this category or they just didn't care.

So when it came to results Bev was in the lead, followed by 16-stone Sian, followed by Big Mamma. The perfect woman, as voted by the men of Feldon Park, would have straight, shoulder-length auburn hair, a cute oval face with a little turned-up nose, DD cup breasts and a large bottom. This woman would float above the ground like a hovercraft, as legs were obviously not that important.

Once the results had been read out they were returned to Adrian for safe keeping.

'I don't want them! I've done my bit,' said Adrian trying to shove them back.

'You have to look after them, I don't trust anybody else, you have to keep the figures and add them all up at the end.'

Adrian, discretely put them in his bag, and dreaded somebody, official, finding them. What would they think, a list of staff members with numbers next to them.

The next part of the competition was the hypothetical bit. It was to do with something known on the wing as 'shagability'. Again, marks were given out of ten, and again the winners were the same as above, though this time Big Mamma was in the lead. Later analysis put this down to her having been seen only in uniform, which gave her the edge. The scores of all the candidates were extremely high: most were in the 8-to-10 range. There was one spoilt ballot. That was the one where Sister Veronica got all the votes and spurted ahead. (God, the jokes were getting worse!)

Having now established the results of the second round, Alan, as executive member, had to ask the three leading candidates individually: 'What changes would you make if you were put in charge of the prison?' It was brilliantly timed as all three women were in on this particular day. Unfortunately. Adrian was also there. He wished he wasn't. Bev was teaching Maths in the morning, 16-stone Sian was in before lunch to collect a medical report and Big Mamma was on an all-day shift. She was one of the female officers.

The first to be examined was Bev, the maths teacher. She arrived after Adrian, and came and sat right next to him. Knowing what was coming Adrian had to think fast and move faster, without seeming rude, but he wasn't quick enough.

'Hi Ade!' she said 'You with this bunch of miscreants today?

Adrian nodded nervously. She had brought with her a flask of tea and began pouring.

'I need a cuppa first! Want one?'

Adrian declined and wishing he could move, he began to fidget.

'I hope they're going to be co-operative today, and take an interest, ask a few questions.'

Bev was used to getting a lot of attention at work but she was equally adept at getting rid of it as well. She had developed the technique of 'deliberately not encouraging anyone' to the limit by making herself extremely unpopular. She came across as being unapproachable, thus deflecting any advance. Adrian got up but before he could move, she turned and asked, 'I was wondering whether you would look at a drawing my son did, tell me what you think. Won't take a mo'.'

Adrian sat down again just as Alan took his opportunity. Bev saw him approaching in her peripheral vision, and was annoyed.

'Look out! Here comes trouble,' she said to Ade. 'God, can't I have five minutes' peace to drink my tea?'

'Excuse me, Miss. Can I ask you something?'

'What?' she snapped back. 'It better be important.'

'Well, it's like this. What changes would you make if you suddenly were put in charge of the prison?' Bev needed no time to think, she already had the answer dripping from her lips.

'I would pass a law that forbade you asking me stupid questions.'

This wasn't the kind of reply Alan had expected. He thought he'd better give her another Chris Tarrant chance.

'Final answer? Sure?'

'Fuck off, Driver, I'm trying to drink my tea.'

Bev scored nil points.

'God! He's so weird, that one. He gives me the creeps.'

Adrian shuffled uncomfortably,. He felt so guilty He was 'carrying' information.

Having ballsed that one up, Alan decided that when 16-stone Sian arrived, he would take his time and build up to the question with small talk, and thus slip it in less obviously. He would be more subtle.

'Try not to ask them when I'm there,' pleaded Adrian when he was alone with Alan. 'Don't do it when they first arrive, wait till I'm sitting right over in the corner so I don't have to be involved.'

But when she did arrive, Sian too, seeing Adrian sitting way over there, made her way to him. She obviously thought this was the new 'staff' table. She plonked down next to Adrian and began sorting out her paperwork. Alan, ignoring Adrian's subtle hand gestures, began to saunter up to her. He had lots of silent encouragement from the others. Sian knew he was coming but didn't look up.

'God! Wait for it, here comes the dickhead.' she muttered to Adrian out of the side of her mouth.

'Yes? What do you want?' she asked in a thoroughly bored voice.

'I was just wondering how you were today?'

'Fine, What's it got to do with you?'

'Oh, just wondering. It's a nice day today, don't you think?'

'It's actually pissing down. Have you looked outside your window at all?'

'Really? Do you have a lot of work over here today?' Sian was now looking at him suspiciously. Alan continued: 'Can I get you a cup of tea?'

'What are you up to? What do you want?'

'Nothing, nothing at all.'

'Then go and worry someone else.'

'OK. There is just one thing though, Miss: what changes would you make if you were put in charge of this prison?'

'Is this a rhetorical question or what?'

'No, seriously.'

She turned to Adrian. 'Has he asked you this one too?

'Definitely not! I'm not...interesting enough,' he blurted

Sian returned her glare to Alan.

'Well, let me see, the first thing I'd do is build my own luxury office, with a big locked door so I could get some peace.' Sian had also won the golden zero. Again Adrian didn't need his calculator.

The last person left to ask now was Big Mamma. Adrian was in no danger of her sitting down next to him, as she hadn't once, ever acknowledged him. Adrian had stopped saying good morning to her ages ago. He told Alan to make sure that all questioning with Big Mamma was to be done far away from him. The best thing would be to dismiss Alan from the class, so he could pursue Big Mamma elsewhere.

Big Mamma was a big officer with big everything, including a big temper. She was very scary. Wrap this all up in a uniform and you get the picture. If she were to win, what would that say about Feldon Park's choice? Today she was particularly evil and was exercising her authority in a way similar to enemy officers in certain bad 1950s war films. Alan had to pick his time carefully. From the safety of his table Adrian watched her walk along the landing, Alan trotting after her. She hadn't gone far when she stopped to shout at Kenny, who was using the phone outside of association time (Imagine what that must have sounded like to whoever it was on the other end.) Alan stood back and tried to look busy. Suddenly, she took off again, with Alan once more in hot pursuit. She was looking to punish any who dared offend. Again she stopped, this time to shout at Ian, the cleaner, to get on with his work. Alan quickly turned his back to her as she turned around, and hovered in the wings, hopefully unnoticed. Big Mamma ignored him; she seemed to have her mind on other things, and was homing in on cell number 23, on the twos - the second landing - where someone had his stereo on far too loud. She threw the door open and screamed at him to turn it down, scaring the terrified inmate inside half to death. When she re-emerged she found herself face to face with Alan.

'What the hell do you want? You've been stalking me for ages? What is it?'

Adrian looked up, he could clearly hear all from where he was sitting. Alan must have felt really stupid trailing in the wake of this ferocious Amazon and probably wished he could disappear.

'Oh, nothing, Miss - but...' Alan took courage and blurted it out: 'Well, this may sound a little strange... However, what changes would you make if you were put in charge of the prison?' She looked at him with increasing suspicion.

'You *what?* Why do you want to know? What are you up to you?

'Nothing miss, I just wondered. Just curious like.'

'No, you ain't. You're up to something. Why are you asking me this?'

'No, it was just a passing thought...'

'...that made you follow me all the way up here, is it?' She stared at him with the eye of a cat about to kill a mouse. He became increasingly nervous, going bright red and shaking under such close scrutiny.

'It's nothing...' he said, and walked away as casually as he could, trying not to break out into a run, down the stairs, across the landing and into his cell, all under the piercing stare of the Big Mamma. Again, nil points.

Having thus failed miserably, to the amusement of the others, Alan handed the baton over to Khalim, the marathon talker. Khalim now had the task of pretending that he had left something in his cell and he needed to get it. Would the help be forthcoming and friendly or not? He first targeted Bev the Maths. She had been helping some of the students, but realising that a question of utmost import was about to be asked they all ceased clamouring for her assistance.

'Please, Miss, can you help me...?'

'Yes. What is it?'

'I seem to have left my maths book in my cell. Can I go and get it?'

'How come you're asking me now? We started thirty minutes ago. What have you been doing up until now?

'I was sharing with Alan, but it's too difficult, I needs my own. He won't let me share anymore.'

'Why not?'

'It is probably because I'm a Moslem, Miss. He's a bit of a racist when you get to know him.'

'No I'm not,' shouted out Alan, who had been listening to every word.

'You are, you xenophobic dickhead.' He gave Alan a sly wink.

Bev called over one of the officers to let Khalim into his cell. It was Big Mamma. This was an unforeseen complication. Bev scored two points, but these were contested since she also filled in a security information form about possible racist issues on the wing. Big Mamma was not a happy bunny either.

'Is there something going on? She asked Sian, who was sitting next to Adrian, 'they're all acting like they have some weird secret.'

Adrian laughed nervously. He got up and went over to Alan.

'This has got to stop. They've noticed something's amiss.'

'A miss world, that's what. Relax! Nothing will happen.'

Adrian felt the longer he was privy to all this, the deeper he sank.

The next person to be quizzed was 16-stone Sian. There was a chance, spontaneous opportunity as she unexpectedly came back onto the wing to collect something she had forgotten.

'Miss, Miss...'

She stopped and turned to face him.

'Miss, I need my fleece from out my cell. I'm freezing. Could you get one of the officers to open up for me, please.'

'But it's boiling in here. Are you sick or something?'

'I could be, I do feel shivery.' Realising this was something that would not be ignored by a health worker Khalim thought that he was on to a winner. He had several Mars Bars on Sian.

'You don't look ill.' But not wishing to take any chances, she added reluctantly, 'I'll see what I can do.'

On any normal day, there are at least four officers on duty on the wing at any set time, and more often that not there are more. Today there were six. So, by the law of averages there was only a 16 and a half per cent chance of getting Big Mamma again. It was Khalim's unlucky day.

'What the hell are you playing at, Khalim? Why didn't you get it earlier? You've already been back once.'

Avoiding the question, he replied.

'I think I'm coming down with something, Miss.'

'If you've got a chill then the best thing you can do is go to bed. You're excused from class for the rest of the day. Go to your cell and go to bed.'

This wasn't going to plan either. Khalim was banged up for the rest of the afternoon. He didn't come out again until suppertime. Sian did well on the scoreboard, gaining two valuable points, though there was some contesting whether Khalim had been completely fair by playing the sickness card.

The way the events of the day had unfurled made approaching the final contestant, Big Mamma, difficult.

Khalim was for abandoning it altogether, but others, who had bets on Big Mamma, insisted that it went ahead regardless of Khalim's complaints and protestations. The opposition's decision was set in concrete. Khalim would have to go and ask.

Big Mamma, on the other hand, had had a long day. Her shift had been seven hours and to top it all Khalim was now acting oddly. He kept looking at her. It was making her edgy. Khalim chose his moment.

'Please, Miss...'

'No, you can't. Don't even ask. Just turn around and go back to your table - and *don't,* OK?'

'But Miss...'

'*Go now!*' she bellowed so all could hear. Khalim, realising he was licked, turned and walked away. Under his breath, he muttered: 'Racist!'

Big Mamma turned and walked towards Adrian. For the first time she was going to speak to him. Adrian thought he had been rumbled and prepared to die. She walked over staring at him the whole time. A million excuses raced through his head, none of which would stick. She opened her mouth to scream at him, but it was just a gentle scolding.

'Try not to let them walk all over the wing during lesson time. This a prison you know.'

Adrian burst into a smile and almost fainted with relief. *So....*

*In third position - Big Mamma.*

*In second place - 16-stone Sian.*

*But this year, for the first time ever - MISS FELDON PARK 2004: Bev the Maths Teacher.*

Numerous Mars Bars changed hands, but Alan only ended up with an extra two when all was said and done, and furthermore he was being investigated for racist behaviour. Bev was now awarded the title 'Foxy Miss Feldon Park'.

'Fuck Miss Feldon Park,' mumbled Ricky Evans, having lost his entire sweet allowance for the next two weeks. His sentiments were generally shared by all the inmates on the wing.

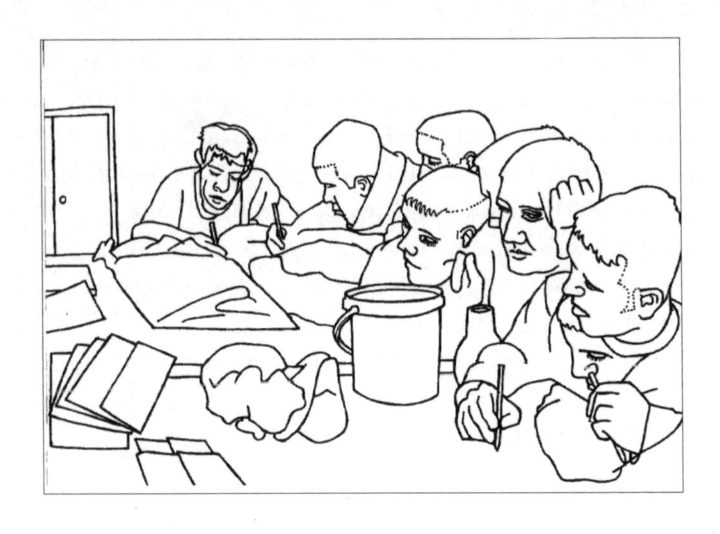

# 21 ADRIAN PREPARES TO GIVE A TALK

*Everybody in Fiji believed that the purpose of life was pleasure. To not pursue pleasure was considered wrong. Life was to enjoy, after all they were living in Paradise. It was considered a sin to work unnecessarily, so, as a result, they never ever prepared anything in advance.*

When Adrian first began teaching at the prison, he idealised the effect that art would have on his students and imagined them metamorphosing into academics overnight. Just show them a few rudimentary tips and off they'd go to uni. The reality was very different, it had little to do with whether they were intelligent enough, that was never in doubt, but they were hindered by all the other problems that got in the way and took priority. It all boiled down to whether anyone was focussed enough to do it. He soon realised that if he could get even one student to break the cycle of prison-release-prison-release, he would feel he had accomplished something. He also began to re-evaluate what the role of education actually was in prison and whether many less tangible attributes were being overlooked because there was no obvious way of measuring them. The rise in confidence, the relaxation, the channelling of energy, the improved communication. If education was just about obtaining qualifications, then it was failing miserably. Adrian knew there was so much more to it than this and consoled himself by thinking, 'Of course it's not about qualifications alone. After all, I don't have a degree and I'm alright.'

One day, whilst contemplating such educational complexities, Adrian was asked whether he would like to give a lecture on 'The Role of Art in a Custodial Sentence Plan' at the local college. He literally jumped, not because it was particularly frightening to teach at college, but because he was beginning to question the conjuring power of his own brain. This sort of thing had been happening a lot lately. He would just imagine something for a few seconds and then, Bob's your Uncle, it would happen. The lecture was part of a module on comparative teaching techniques. He accepted. After all, he had conjured it up, and it was an opportunity to take what he was doing out into the so-called real world and to teach so-called real students. The session was to be for two and a half hours. To Adrian's surprise it was part of a degree course.

Adrian began planning that evening. He took a pad and pencil and decided to make notes of things as they came into his head. The first thing he needed to clarify was what it exactly was that he and the education were trying to achieve. This was a very good focussing exercise and raised many questions that led him all round the houses, only to keep returning to those seven bloody points. Unless you could overcome drug abuse, friends who were criminals, years of being made feel inadequate and so forth, there didn't seem much point in education at all. You might just as well give up. When everything else had failed, he was expected to be able to educate. He looked down at his note pad and wrote in big letters:

*'Introduce the seven points.'*

The lecture could use these as a springboard to a myriad of possibilities. The problem was to pick one, stick with it and follow it through. He pictured each of his prison students in turn, sitting in front of him, and a warm smile crossed his face: he would introduce his mates.

*'What?* Did I just say *'mates'!?'* Adrian almost felt guilty. He frowned. 'I wouldn't use that word at work,' a little voice inside his head whispered, 'they're *in*mates, not mates.' Then why did he like them so much? Which way round was it? Did he like them because they were talented, or were they good at painting because he liked them? Hm! This was becoming interesting. He thought for a second longer and wrote down: *Getting on with the inmates.*

A lot of people had problems with such things, but for Adrian it was almost the opposite; if anything it was keeping some sort of healthy distance that was his difficulty. It was in his nature to get involved, especially where the underdog was concerned. He realised just how close he had become to some of the men when two inmates, on different occasions, and in all seriousness, asked if they could move in with him when they were released. He wrote another prompt on his pad: *Tell anecdote about moving in.*

On reflection, however, he changed his mind and rubbed it out. It sounded too egotistic, and he also felt somewhat disloyal. The first rule of the wing was you never grass on your mates. (There was that four-letter word again!) Having spent enough time on the opening part of the talk, Adrian moved on to consider what exactly education could achieve.

Words like confidence, expression and contact began to whizz around his head, but what he wrote down was: *Talk about exams.*

Adrian, for the second time that day, began to worry about his brain and the way it seemed to separate itself from the rest of him. His notes were almost writing themselves independently. A bit like automatic writing. He decided to give in to the spirit and go with the flow. So exams it was, and the floodgates opened wide.

Obtaining GCSEs, even if one agreed with them, was not going to happen for most of the inmates, as they were either not in long enough or their sentence dates didn't tie in with the academic year. Unfortunately, academic term dates were set in concrete even thicker than the foundations of the perimeter fence. (So if you want to maximise your educational opportunities in prison, you have to make sure you get sentenced in August or September and for at least a year.)

Exam results were for many people, unfortunately, the measuring stick for how well a department was performing. 'We want to see results!' To sidestep the problem, the Open College Network (OCN) was introduced, which devised short, project-based courses that resulted in copious certificates and that could be taken up at any time. So everyone should be happy. The good thing about them was it was great to give out the certificates. They were important to the men, if not of much value in the outside world, and Adrian always made an occasion of it, a little ceremony. Often they were the first certificates they had ever been awarded and it did brilliant things for their confidence. Because they were achievable, you could take as long as you liked to do them, and they were pretty hard to fail. This was a good thing, as there was far too much failure in these men's lives already. Even as criminals they had failed, as their presence in prison proved. The down side of these certificates was they were often given too freely, which undid some of their initial value. Adrian occasionally saw men carrying folders bulging with them, which always reminded him of pictures of people with wheelbarrows full of inflated, almost worthless money, during the Depression.

Adrian looked at his automatic hand. It had written EXAMS next to a strange little doodle of a brimming wheel-barrow-cornucopia. Within seconds the brain was off again. This time it went visual and recalled a conversation he'd had with the head of Art at the college several weeks earlier. All Adrian could see was a large, talking mouth. When the vision was over, he looked at his notepad and the whole conversation had been written out like a play.

*ADRIAN:* If you put these men in for external exams, it could prove really difficult for them to complete the work in the same manner as students can on the out. There should be some kind of allowance.

*HEAD OF ART (with irritation):* It's really important to remember that the men in prison should be treated exactly the same as other candidates. They need to regard themselves as students, not inmates, and be included in the broader college fraternity.

*ADRIAN (in an agitated manner):* All very well, but they cannot be put on the same footing when everything else around them is different. They do not have internet access. They do not have free access to the library. They cannot buy supplies easily. They don't even have a table in their cells to work on. You can hardly describe it as a normal student environment.

*HEAD OF ART (smugly):* But you forget many of the 'normal' students have to overcome enormous problems to get their work done too.'

*ADRIAN (going for the testicles):* Not quite the same, and to start with I don't think I've ever seen, in all my time at Feldon Park, a course actually start on time *(oooh!)* so the students are disadvantaged before they even start *(MIAOW!)*...

*HEAD OF ART (fading into the distance as he exits left):* It's important that you remember that the students in prison need to get to feel what a real examination is like, so that when they come out they are prepared.

*ADRIAN (shouting):* *If* they come out!! Consider SEN status!' *(aside)* Dickhead...

- Curtain -

Adrian snapped back to his study and tried to move on to part three of his talk. But the debate continued to oscillate in his head between the theoretical and the practical. Adrian wished the College would come and see his class in action and meet those so-called normal students, and actually witness the more subtle aspects of his classroom, which could not be measured quantatively.

His hand began to write again.

*'Time out.'*

Ah yes! Time out. This was an example of how therapeutic art could be in prison. Many men would spend hours engrossed in drawing while banged up. They could lose themselves in detail. Didn't Jonesy say, 'It's the only time I forget I'm in prison?'

The hand was taking control. (Speak to the hand: the face isn't listening.)

Adrian thought about all those detailed drawings eagerly thrust towards him every morning on his arrival. Each piece represented time out, time away from the pressure, away from the guilt, the anger, whatever. It was a means to cope with 'bang up', and far more constructive than going brain-dead in front of the telly, or mindlessly sticking match sticks together.

In contrast to the drawings done in lesson time, those done in the cells were invariably more detailed, as if they had been stretched out to fill the night. During class it was important that there was communication as well as instruction and demonstration. In fact, wasn't that what art was - 'communication'? Write it down, Ade, write it down.

It had taken a while for Adrian to realise just how important to the inmates these hours of contact with someone from off the wing were. One morning, he was in the middle of delivering a fascinating insight into Cubism when Frosty, one of his long term students, joined in:

'You've got new shoes!'

Adrian became very self-conscious. He now knew that he hadn't just been feeling paranoid every time he entered the wing. He had a distinct feeling of being peripherally studied whenever he arrived. Everyone would stare at him. He was the only unpredictable thing that ever came in. He was the one who changed, who was not part of the furniture.

'Yes, they are new, although they're almost identical to my last ones.'

As a result, he had changed the direction of his lesson and talked about the importance of observation in sketching.

Adrian was snapped out of his reminiscing by the sound of fingers drumming impatiently. The hand was becoming impatient and had written *Expression* on the notepad.

Adrian thought about the difficulty many men had expressing themselves. Bad education, misuse of alcohol and drugs, lack of real conversation, reduced dialogue to predictable clichés. 'Wicked', 'cool', 'sound', 'shit'... Often the most beautiful, sensitive artwork came from the most monosyllabic men. Some paintings spoke volumes more than any mouth could.

And finally (scribble, scribble) art, unlike maths or science, was never right or wrong. One could have opinions about art, but not pass sentence. There was far too much judgment in most of these men's lives. One could say, 'In my opinion that's shit,' but not just 'That's shit' full stop. This personalised approach was taken up and almost became a wing cliché in its own right. Whenever a comment was passed it would always be prefixed with, 'In my opinion...' 'In my opinion, you're an absolute arsehole,' for example.

*'Don't just focus on the negative all the time. Look for what's good.'*

Adrian recalled how he would always hang all the finished paintings on the wall to enable the men to appreciate them objectively. It was very rare that someone would refuse, even though it was by no means compulsory. What ensued was some brilliant criticism where the merits and failings of each work were discussed. Everyone had done the same painting, followed the same instructions and used the same paints, yet each painting was entirely different. Every individual spirit shone through.

Adrian's brain had begun to ramble. He found it hard not to go tangential. What he was thinking about is written below. If you don't want to read it you can skip it.

(This way of looking at things could never be applied to a piece of Maths or Science which is either right or wrong. Unfortunately, so much emphasis is put on this mathematical way of thinking. The prominence of sciences in education, the overuse of computers, with their binary, yes/no way of calculating, somehow was subliminally affecting us all. It resulted in things being labelled either right or wrong, black or white, good or bad, criminal or not - permanent labels, that don't come off very easily. You're this, you're that, and he's definitely that, and that's it. Labelled.

The main perpetrators of labelling culture were to be found in the media world, where tabloid headings reduce people to one or two words. 'Evil Monster' and 'Beast From Hell', and you don't need to read the rest. These were just two examples that sprung to mind that Adrian had seen recently in prison, where most of the men collect newspaper clippings of themselves. Adrian realised how unhelpful these were to the inmate, focussing, as they did, on everything negative and hindering the prisoner from change. Try convincing yourself you're an angel when you've got 'devil' tattooed across your forehead. There was something so fundamentally obvious, so sickeningly obvious about prison. Why, once inside, is the focus fixed solely on the negative? Everyone is a mixture, even the 'Beast from Hell'. Everyone is a potential criminal and a potential saint. What determines which has lots to do with upbringing, opportunity, environment, and those seven points. There but for the grace of God go I... (and you... and you as well.) What alarmed Adrian was that so many people working in prison couldn't or wouldn't acknowledge this basic premise and drew big white lines between themselves and the inmates, and saw their role as a cocktail of judge and policeman, rather than custodian or carer.)

Adrian was going to write some more when he realised that his right hand was turning the handle on the door. It was time to go. However, what he recognised was that there was a lot more potential with what he was doing than at first met the eye, and he wished that some of it could be supported and incorporated by others. Frequently, the probation department would comment that Adrian knew far more about the inmates than they did, because he was seen as non-confrontational. The next question surely was, 'Well, yes - why don't we work together then? And why do I feel so unsupported?' Adrian thought it had something to do with his having crossed that big white line mentioned earlier.

Feeling satisfied that he had covered enough ground to give a good lecture, Adrian looked down and saw that he had written half a page of one-line memory sound-bites. As he read through them he didn't exactly feel confident.

# 22 REAL COLLEGE, REAL STUDENTS, REAL DICKHEADS

*All the best teachers are also like students, forever learning. All the worst students think they know it all already. The Teacher's Handbook, University of the South Pacific.*

Arriving at the college on the day of the lecture was surprisingly intimidating. Adrian wished there had been a cattle grid and a big wall. The buildings were arranged in a kind of circle with a car park in the middle. This gave a weird prominence to the cars rather than the college itself. It was obviously built at a time when it was assumed the college population that could afford to run a vehicle was about six and every one else walked or came on the legendary 'public transport'. Trying to park his car was incredibly difficult and made Adrian's arrival stressful. It looked like the extra time he'd given himself to settle in was being eaten up by mindlessly driving around in circles. Eventually he found a parking place, but it was so far away from where he wanted to go that he felt he needed to take a bus to get there.

The classroom was white and strip-lit. It reminded Adrian of the prison but without the Bang Up - instead it had a sweeter, more feminine smell. This blend contained cleaning fluid too, but definitely no nicotine. It was not the smell of fallen angels but it did have a purgatorial quality, which was more difficult to define. To make the room feel less alien, Adrian began to customise it while he waited. He had brought with him thirty or so portraits he'd drawn of the inmates, which he Blu-tacked to the wall behind his desk. Their quirky, hard expressions were reassuring, and made him feel he had some support behind him. He found himself waiting to begin, and as he did so a sense of *déjà vu* descended.

When the students eventually arrived the similarity to that first lecture in prison was surprising. They blanked him completely as they entered the room. They weren't allowed to do this! Adrian felt increasingly pissed off as row upon row of students walked in and ignored him. He became aware of a sinking feeling in his stomach.

'Are we all here?' said a shaky, tinny voice that Adrian eventually recognised as his own. He felt himself breaking up again. All his various parts were deserting him like rats leaving a sinking ship. He consulted, for a final time, his half page of notes, while his stomach plunged into his boots and his lungs decided to shut down. 'Pull yourself together,' took on a completely new meaning. It was now or never. He introduced himself, and before lurching into the seven points, he asked:

'To start the session, I'd like to ask you this: what sort of person do you think ends up in prison?'

The students stared at him blankly. What are you asking us for? We don't do questions. There was a silence, until eventually one cocky, I'll-take-you-on student replied:

'Anybody and everybody. You get a cross-range of society.'

This was not the answer Adrian was fishing for. Shit! Now what?

'Well, you do actually find there are certain characteristics that are predominant. Some of which could apply to anyone at all, as you say, but others that are connected to poverty.' Adrian presented the seven points. All could apply to anybody from any background with the exception of poverty itself, but the thing was, they usually didn't. If they did they were the exception. Most people in prison come from council estates or whatever they're called nowadays and are from the unemployed class.

Adrian turned his back on the students and found himself under the gaze of his (in-)mates. They all seemed to be smirking, and looked like they were just about to do something 'unhelpful'. Adrian felt reassured. He turned, and returned to his talk. As each of the seven points were discussed, he could feel his confidence - and those missing parts - returning.

Adrian presented part two of the lecture: *exams, and the difficulties faced by the inmates as they tried to cope with them.* Instead, however, of drawing forth sympathy he heard the usual old grouse: 'I think they're lucky to have education at all. We have to pay for our courses.' The cocky student was passing sentence. Several other heads nodded in agreement. Adrian retaliated with:

'But it actually costs society far more if you do nothing and don't try to change these people. Firstly, they commit the same crimes again. The re-offending rate for Young Offenders is 72%, and they usually come out worse, more alienated, more disaffected than ever. And secondly, it costs society something like £92,000 a year each just to keep them banged up.'

Lots of heads were nodding disapprovingly. Nothing to get people moaning like money. Adrian fanned the flames.

'If we were to offer the men in prison half that amount each year and said, "we'll give you this if you put an end to your criminal activity," most of them would instantly become law-abiding citizens. What do you think?'

Adrian forgot that students don't do questions. Adrian felt a collective guffaw from the pictures behind him and psychically heard Billy's voice, in his head, say, 'Do you want me to deck him, Ade?'

When Adrian got to part three of his talk and brought up the subject of how therapeutic Art could be, and how it could be 'time out', one of the women, a bit of a tart with dyed hair and all dolled up, stopped pruning her nails for two seconds and said: 'I don't see why they should have time out anyway. I think they should be conscious of prison all the time. After all, isn't that what they're there for?'

Adrian felt himself glaring at her, and then felt ashamed for reacting. Instead, he smiled. 'I don't do questions,' he thought and ignored her.

When he came to the binary bit about the brain, he felt he had had it. This wasn't going as planned, so what the hell. The students seemed to have decided they didn't want to hear this stuff and a group of them started chatting amongst themselves while Adrian was still talking. Adrian stopped and just stared in disbelief. The students, suddenly realising it had all gone quiet, turned and looked at Adrian. They smirked.

'Sorry if you don't want to listen. But I'm going to deliver this talk, and if you really don't want to hear then I suggest you leave and talk elsewhere.' The students looked at him as if he was from Mars. The inmates were all shouting from the wall: *'Rumble rumble in the jungle, go it, Ade.'*

Finally, Adrian introduced the students to his portraits and explained how it felt to be drawn and what it was like to draw someone. He talked about walls coming down and bonds being made.

When Adrian picked up the pile of paper and began counting the pencils he noticed several students slipping out the door. He suppressed an impulse to shout 'cowards', and just thought good riddance instead. The tarty woman, being engrossed in her cuticle, missed her opportunity to escape and was given a piece of paper, much to her surprise. Adrian wanted them all to pair up and draw each other in turn, just to feel what it was like.

As there was an odd number, Adrian volunteered to draw Tarty.

'We don't do drawi—'

'Just shut it and sit.'

This was said in body language. Adrian started to draw - and what do you know, Tarty started talking.

'I don't agree with spending so much money on all this stuff you're talking about, but I can see it's something you can't ignore. So something's got to change.'

'Exactly,' said Adrian. 'Helping to bring that change about doesn't mean you're condoning what they've done. One has to step back, as it were.'

'I couldn't do that work. I'd feel so uncomfortable. I think that's what I'm trying to say.'

'Nobody's asking you to. You only do it if you want to.' Ade was feeling quite smug. The inmates on the wall were sticking their fingers down their throats.

Tarty, whose name was actually Megan, was staring Adrian in the face through lashings of mascara and shadow. It reminded him of the time he had drawn Angie-Lee. The two faces seemed to merge in Adrian's head and made him smile.

'Ah well, I'm glad we've had this chance to chat. Here, what do you think?' Adrian handed her the portrait. It was reasonable, thank God. Adrian thought he'd done her a favour.

She laughed: 'O my God, do you really think I look that bad?' and then added: 'Yeah, something has got to change. It's such a waste of money. I think they should bring back some sort of death penalty for some things - after all, that would cut down costs and act as a deterrent for lesser offences. Thanks for the drawing. Goodbye!' And she left.

Adrian was devastated. 'Bloody students! They can stick their degrees up their...' He was just about to turn round and give the pictures on the wall a piece of his mind too, when he noticed several of the students hanging round the door. They came over.

'We found that really interesting. It's such a big issue, and it doesn't seem to have any quick-fit answers,' said a young lady whom Adrian hadn't even noticed while he was talking.

'Yes,' said another. 'It seems to be a problem of society that's passed down to the individual.' Adrian wondered if these students had just wandered into the room from somewhere else, as he didn't seem to recognise anyone. 'And it's usually the ones who are least able to cope.'

They thanked him again and left, leaving Adrian perplexed.

On the way home, Adrian asked himself, once again, when he would ever learn. 'Don't just focus on the ones who are in your face all the time, look beyond them. There are others.' He was again reminded of his first time with the Y.O.s. He smiled.

# 23 A STAR IS BORN

*The shaman on Fiji was also the one you went to if you needed any sort of help or advice. He knew how to deal with things, because of all the people on the island he was the one who had suffered the most. He had been there and come back again. He was the one who'd had the most accidents, the most near-death diseases, the worst relationships, he'd been through it all and survived. Thus walks the shaman.*

The visit to the college left an aftertaste in Adrian's mouth that wasn't either good or bad, it was just there. It was an aftertaste that seemed to completely engulf him. When Adrian tried to work out what it actually was that was weighing so heavily upon him, he kept coming to the same conclusion; he was fallen in the great chasm, the divide, between the inside and the out. He was trapped in this huge expanse that separated polar opposites. The outcome of which was that he increasingly doubted his original notions of getting men through degrees, leave alone just like that! He began to question what this so-called education was all about. Was it not more like therapy than anything else?

Adrian arrived at work feeling quite despondent, and actually found himself thinking about what other work he could do, other jobs, when once again there was a divine intervention. It arrived in the form of a letter, inviting art departments to submit pieces of work for a forthcoming exhibition from men who resided in prisons. The name of the organisation behind this, was The Koestler Awards. The Koestler Awards were established at the request of Arthur Koestler who left a considerable legacy, on his demise, to promote art in prison. Adrian looked through the literature, there were hundreds of categories, each resulting not only in a certificate, but also in an exhibition. And best of all, Koestler had been in prison himself. He knew what it was like. He knew how it worked. He must have experienced the frustrations, the boredom, the pressure. He was *kosher*. This fact, and this alone, made Adrian sure that these awards were going to work. Adrian read a quote. 'If I hadn't been able to do art in prison, I think I would have gone mad. It kept me sane.' From now on, the Koestler awards became the main focus of all Adrian's endeavours.

'Star Pupil' was the nick-name that Adrian gave to Jimmy Star, who ended up shining in the art group for nearly two years. Everyone else just called him Star (or Ringo). It was an appropriate name because, with the help of the Koestlers, Jimmy lived up to it. Adrian wondered if another inmate, he had met earlier, called Matt Crook was also just the product of his surname. But Mr Star was a banged-up supernova hurtling towards the unknown. He was keen, and achieved much in the time he spent in education, especially in the realm of drawing. The title, by the way, was self-appointed, but seemed quite fitting considering the standards he reached. Having built up confidence, which wasn't always there, one of his favourite sayings, especially when other people were in earshot, was, 'It's a shame when the pupil's paintings are better than the teacher's,' followed by a wink and a cracked grin. 'You just can't get the staff these days.' All said in good humour. (If you ignore the time when the Board of Visitors was on the wing, that is.)

Star Pupil was another of the mass-produced tragedies of our present time. A question always hung around him like a sort of invisible force field. It seemed to permeate everyone that came near him, making them ask themselves, 'Why on earth does he have to be in here like this? Why him? He seems so *innocent...*'

When Star Pupil first arrived in Adrian's class, the star was dull. He was more like a black hole. He sat there unable to look at anything other than his shoes. Star had been in prison so many times that he had almost lost count, and the sad thing was that not only was he in the prison, but the prison was in him. He was a thirty-five-year-old professional inmate. His existence had been one long life sentence so far, peppered with short spells on the out, where he experienced anything but freedom. Included in his biography were all but one of the seven points. Drugs, a dysfunctional family, a failed adoption resulting in a childhood in care, low-level education, a history of crime, poverty and mental health problems. The only one he had seemed to escape was abuse. One break-time Adrian happened to mention to one of the officers on duty how sad Star Pupil was, and what a shame his life had been so ruined. To this he received the reply: 'I feel sorry for the girl he killed. He deserves everything that happens to him.' The officer left. Adrian was surprised to hear this and rather taken aback. Firstly, it was given to him as a tabloid headline, without any further explanation and secondly, he was angry with himself for maybe focussing too much on the good and not at all considering why Star was actually here. Why is it that criminals don't snugly fit the Vinnie Jones stereotype like they're supposed to?

When Adrian went back to his class he found himself wanting to talk to Star, but obviously couldn't. Star had never volunteered any information about why he was inside before, and Adrian didn't wish to pry. However, he got an indirect answer when he was talking to Billy about release dates and licenses and Star joined in with: 'I'm up for licence in three months. My Probation Officer thinks I stand a good chance.'

Adrian now knew that whatever had happened it wasn't, at least, first degree murder. Star was looking at his next taste of the 'out'.

As it happened, Star did tell Adrian eventually why he was doing time. It was not for killing anyone. That had been his previous conviction and he explained the tragic irony of it all.

'I saw it happening, but it was all like a film. I didn't think it was actually taking place, really.'

He had been a heroin addict, and on one occasion, having shot himself up, he prepared another syringe for his girlfriend. Unfortunately, it contained an air bubble and she died. In his words: 'It's so sad, she was the only person that ever cared for me, and I cared for her, and I killed her. What's wrong with me?'

The media had labelled Star 'The Smack Killer', (ignoring the fact that the girl he killed was also an addict who could have easily done the same thing to him).

Adrian wanted to stick another label on Star's forehead, something along the lines of 'The Prison Artist', as he was so good, though Star took some convincing to believe in himself. Adrian must have used the 'something positive to say' approach too many times with him, for one day he replied: 'You always say everything's brilliant. I could do any old crap and you'd say it was fantastic.'

Billy, to illustrate the point and be as provocative as possible, drew a scribble on a piece of scrap paper and went around imitating Adrian - 'Wow, fantastic, brilliant!' - much to the amusement of everyone else. Ignoring him, Adrian took the painting Star was working on and placed it in front of both of them. They began to discuss it together. As if on cue, one of the officers walked past and stopped to look too.

'That's really good, Ade. It must have taken you ages,' then turning to the class, 'You'll have trouble copying this one, boys.' He swaggered away on his rounds.

'See,' Adrian said. 'I don't think I need to say anything else.'

'You probably paid him to say that,' Star replied.

Adrian suggested to Star that this year he should possibly submit something to the Koestler awards. Star looked very nervous and then said he was not interested - that was until Adrian also mentioned that there was prize money and it was quite substantial by prison standards. He eventually decided to enter some calligraphy pieces, and much to Adrian's delight and Star's surprise he won two awards and a total sum of £45. The down payment on a one-way ticket to Fiji, possibly? (Incidentally, this was where the title Star Pupil took on extra kudos.) The effect of receiving a certificate from outside had such a positive effect on Star, that his whole presence seemed to rise up slightly. Later in the year, Adrian went to the exhibition of winning entries in London and took some photos of Star's pieces, nicely framed. Once these pictures were developed, Adrian gave one to Star that he'd mounted for him. Star told Adrian that he would send it to his mother. He had found enough confidence, in this restricted environment, to be proud of himself.

One day the flu bug struck and Adrian was sick, and couldn't teach his class. There was no other teacher free that day to cover for him, so the class was cancelled. When Adrian did next come in, Star looked very fed up and miserable and when questioned, told Adrian something that touched him very deeply. Adrian yet again was made aware of another aspect of his work:

'You know, I look forward to Thursdays all week. I was gutted when you didn't show up. My whole routine went out the window.'

Adrian felt another responsibility descend upon him, one that he accepted willingly, because after all this justified why he was there, though how anyone could measure it, God knew.

One of the by-products, for Star, of a life spent in prisonland, was that he had been on every course the prison had to offer trying to get himself in order. He had attended Anger Management, R and R, Offensive Behaviour, to name but a few, and he had spent countless hours with an army of probation officers, social workers, psychologists, criminologists, doctors. He'd done them all. Then one day he amazed Adrian and put it all to good use.

The previous weekend had been an all-time low for Adrian. He and his wife had had a particularly stormy time of it that had left both of them feeling extremely hurt and sad. That Sunday evening Adrian had to attend a study group, which under the circumstances he should have abandoned, but he was chairing it and had left it too late to cancel. It might be good to get away and do something else, anyway. The study was of a book by a well-known philosopher about heightened perception. Feeling like shit, Adrian managed the evening, hiding behind a thin mask of normality. An academic session ensued, with lashings of logic and cerebral activity. Everyone was so absorbed by the arguments that nobody noticed the emotional mess leading the discussion, being more preoccupied with the finer, theoretical subtleties of the human psyche.

The following morning Adrian was working in the prison. He went to the staff room where his colleagues were preparing themselves for the day. Pieces of paper were circulating the room. Adrian took up his register, went to his wing and began the lesson. All went well and he temporarily forgot the hurt he was carrying. At break time he went to get a cup of tea, and Star came with him. While Adrian was filling his cup, Star began to talk.

'What's up then?'

'Nothing. Why?'

'Don't lie to me! You're down, something's upsetting you. What is it?'

Adrian was amazed. He thought he was hiding his problems so well. Apparently not.

'How did you work that one out?' he asked incredulously.

'I can see it in your face, it's written all over you. You can't hide things in here. What is it?'

'It's personal, you know, domestic.'

'I knew it.' And then: 'I'm sorry to hear that. Do you want to talk about it?' Adrian smiled at Star, who had assumed a listening posture.

'I do know how to do it. I've had so much counselling in my life that I'm as good as qualified.' They went over to a table and sat down, but almost immediately Billy came over to join them.

'Fuck off Billy, I'm talking to Ade.' Without question, Billy about-turned and walked away. There was some unsaid message in Star's voice that said this was important. Adrian turned and faced him. He wanted to talk to him but knew this was not allowed.

'You know I can't talk to you about my private life. But you're right, I am down. I feel pretty cut up inside.'

'I knew it! Is there anything I can do to help, like? Do you want me to take someone out for you? You know - Deck 'em.' He grinned from ear to ear. 'No, really, what can I do?'

'Well, there is something. It helps just knowing there's someone around who understands and is looking out for me. Just be there! It gets difficult keeping it together sometimes with all these monkeys. I'd appreciate it.'

'Yeah, sure. I'm 'non-judgemental' and 'confidential' as well. It's safe with me.'

'Yeah, I don't doubt it.'

'Here, let me get you another tea.'

The rest of the day Adrian was looked after as never before. He didn't have to lift a finger, everything was done for him, he wasn't even allowed to sharpen a pencil. It made him think how extraordinarily kind and thoughtful, if given the opportunity to express it, many of these men were. At break time, Star gave Adrian a chocolate Wagon Wheel.

'I saved it from yesterday. I haven't opened it.' Star's voice suddenly picked up a beat, as he remembered something important.

'Oh! By the way, I could knock up a questionnaire for you, you know, help you with your relationship, only if you want it, like. You never know, it might be useful, though none of the ones I've ever filled in have been.'

# 24 PERSONAL HYGIENE FROM AN UNLIKELY QUARTER

*If you want to understand the holy man, pray with him. If you want to become the artist, paint with him, if you want to be the native, live with him.*

As Adrian was becoming increasingly aware of the gap that separated his two worlds, he was also conscious that prisonland had many peculiar properties that were different from the out. It felt, at times that it was almost enchanted. It was separated from the rest of the world in many ways other than just being physically cut off by a perimeter fence. Different laws operated in there, both human and natural, that caused things to behave differently from the outside world. Having over a thousand men concentrated together brought about distinct changes in the atmosphere (and the smell) that affected everything, including weather, time, values, gravity and, strangely, also conversation. The words were the same but their meanings were changed. They were imbued with a magical quality as they were spoken into the incarcerated ambience.

A conversation on male hygiene occurred one morning in June that was so ordinary yet so out of place that it took on this magical quality. Had it been in 'normal' circumstances, around a kitchen table for instance, it would have been dismissed as trivial, but here, on the wing of a high security jail, it took on a different quality. It was the best example Adrian could have given of how everyday things in life are distorted when people are banged up. Health and Safety signs should be attached to the main entrance: *Visitors be warned - you are entering a mystical land, where magical laws are in force once you pass this cattle grid.*

There were several inmates sitting around a table with Adrian, because for the first time, and again without any warning, they had been thrown out of their classroom by those running courses, and so found themselves, displaced, on the wing. This temporary solution, like so many of the others, soon became permanent. Adrian was beyond caring. There was no point in griping anymore, but he wasn't that fed up. He could honestly say he was happier to be sitting here on the wing than he had been earlier, sitting in the canteen with certain members of staff. Ever since the lecture in college, not to mention the meeting with Angie and the Koestler Awards, ( plus everything else,) he had felt a shifting in his outlook on prison. As he moved psychologically, so did he feel more comfortable with the men, and likewise they with him, generally. Today a kind of breakthrough in thinking, in consciousness, that Adrian hadn't thought possible before, happened. He was entering something greater, something more communal, which he later described as their collective group soul. It went beyond the individuals who were actually sitting next to him, but belonged more to the greater being of prisoners.

The students in the group, those who he shared this new experience with, included Rowlands, Driver, Star Pupil, Frosty and Billy. Today they were all working well, each one engrossed in what he was doing. It was an opportunity for Adrian to sit back and observe. He was sitting there together with five men with a collective 'bird' of fifty-two years behind them and forty-six before them. A shared total of ninety-eight years. Adrian noticed that at that particular moment they were entranced, as if sharing a moment of distant inwardness. They were wandering in their daydreams. Adrian believed that if he stared hard enough he would be able to see their thoughts flowing out of their heads. Above them, he visualised their angels, bald and tattooed, sitting in harmony amongst the clouds. They couldn't speak to each other directly, so they did so through their earthly mannequins. (Alright, Gabriel? Yeah! Fucking brilliant, mate.) The silent, preparatory meditation was reaching its conclusion when finally somebody spoke.

'I cut myself this morning shaving.' It was Billy. He was absently rubbing his cheek. 'It bloody hurt. It's these razors they give us here, they're crap. On the out, I use a Mach 3. Now they're fucking good.'

The enchanted talk was beginning. Let the flow commence. Eyes were glazing over. Harps were playing.

'They're a fucking rip-off. I went to buy some once and they cost about a tenner.' The angel that incarnated on earth as Mr Rowlands had just connected with his lower being, who was hard and one didn't argue. If he said something was good, it was good, OK? Cherubs don't argue with Archangels, right? He continued: 'There's nothing wrong with the ones they give you in here. You've just got to know how to use them properly.'

Being made of ectoplasm, angels find it hard to argue, let alone fight (or shave). Their only opportunity to partake in such things, is to do so through their earthly counterparts. They were now engaging.

'That's right. I always gets a nice smooth shave, but I have to start here first, otherwise it ends up rough.' Star Pupil pointed to a point just under his nose.

'Well, I start here,' answered Billy, pointing to his lower neck.

'That's why you don't get a good shave. The best place to start is here,' said Frosty, and moved his finger to his sideburn. 'Where do you start from, Ade?'

Adrian was overboard in a sea of inclusion.

'Here, the same place as you, but on the other side.'

'It's weird. We all start in different places. I wonder why?' asked a confounded Driver.

'I suppose I learnt it from watching my dad,' Adrian said. 'He used to have one of those shaving brushes and sticks of soap half-wrapped in silver paper. Do you remember?'

'No. We're young, Pops - hello-o?'

'Anyway,' says Star Pupil, 'I didn't have a dad.'

'Nor did I - well, not one worth talking about,' said Frosty.

'I did,' said Driver cheerfully, 'but then he had a beard. I always shave up good though, except I do have problems with the bit under my chin. It always remains rough...,' Then, giggling: 'My missus says it's like sandpaper. She says she likes it.'

'Oh! Here we go again. Let's pretend you're married. For God's sake. You ain't got a missus, you only think you have, she's in your head. Space cadet.'

Rowlands didn't like all these interruptions. *He* was talking now, and was going to finish his discourse on shaving undeterred.

'But anyway, the best way to get a smooth finish is to run a sink of really hot water, almost too hot, and then put your face in it for as long as you can possibly bear it. Then soap up and shave. It always gives you a good clean finish. It never fails, but you've got to know how.'

Rowlands had missed his vocation and was now making the most of a lost opportunity. He was on 'Blue Peter' and nobody was going to take his limelight.

Frosty also felt filled with inspiration and wanted to share in the glow of knowledge flowing from Rowlands. He decided to risk all and join in:

'I like that Gillette gel. It leaves you nice and fresh-feeling. You can get it in the canteen. There's the blue can and the green one. I like the green best.'

Mr Rowlands, however, wasn't in need of any side-kick muppet, and just wanted to get on with his presentation, and anyway, who said you could join in?

'No! *No! NO!* You don't want that crap, the best thing to use is pure natural soap. Simply Soap it's called, it does the job and you don't end up smelling like a ponce.'

'My missus likes Lynx Africa,' said Driver.

'For fuck's sake, Driver, stop trying to pretend that you've got a missus. We all know you haven't. You're probably some closet gay boy, anyway,' snapped Rowlands. But Driver wasn't going to step down - not because he was brave, he just didn't get it.

'I do have a missus. I'm no bum boy.'

'Why don't she come out and visit you ever, then?'

'She's too busy. Actually, she works.'

'What, collecting her benefits, you mean.'

'She's probably on the game,' said Frosty. 'Hey, I think I saw your Missus once on a Saturday night, down Portland Street. Big ugly slag, she was. But don't worry; she was still raking it in when the pubs turned out. Blokes were too pissed to care.'

'Shut up, Frosty,' said a half-hearted Driver. 'She ain't like that.'

'It's probably because she's so hideous she can only come out at night,' laughed Frosty. He wasn't going to waste this opportunity to regain some face with Rowlands.

'No excuse, she could always put a bag over her head,' said Rowlands, 'or come in one of those burhka sack things.'

The Fall was being re-enacted as Driver was thrown from grace into darkness. Black clouds of humiliation appeared behind his eyes where the fires of Hell had begun to burn.

'By the way, I've got a visit today. My missus (a real one) is coming this afternoon. I must get a haircut first. Are the hairdressers coming this morning?'

'Yeah, they're supposed to be. I don't want that bloke cutting my hair though, he's crap. The woman's alright. This time I want a number two all over with a little bit of a fringe to gel up.'

'I want mine shaved. It makes me look hard,' said Star Pupil. 'You could do with a trim, Ade. You're looking a bit woolly lately. Tidy Up!'

The mundane conversation had become surreal. Adrian found himself sitting with a rapist, two burglars, a drug dealer and an armed robber discussing, of all things, shaving technique. It was all so 'normal'. Again, things don't match the stereotype images. Adrian took Star's advice, and got his hair cut when the barbers arrived. He had the pleasure of experiencing, first hand, what it felt like not to look the part. He was mistaken for an inmate. When the barber (the 'shit one' - an inmate from another wing) finished shearing Adrian's 'wool', he asked Adrian what his cell number was. Obviously he didn't fit the teacher stereotype either. He no longer was separate, he was one of the mass. Adrian also now realised why officers wore uniforms.

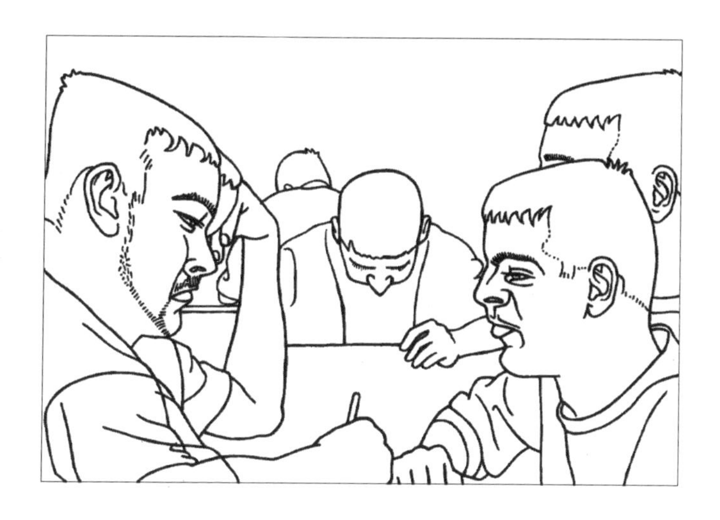

# 25 A FOLIO IS BINNED

*Mt Fiji is a dormant volcano. When last active it spewed lava all down its slopes, which over the years solidified into various types of rock. The lava nearest the summit cooled to form black, shiny obsidian, whereas, lower down it cooled to a black, less shiny rock, whilst that which reached the lower slopes turned brown. The black obsidian is greatly prized, and sought after but the sides of Mt Fiji are sheer and sharp. Many start the quest with great intention, but fail, and have to settle for second best; the dull black rock. Those poor souls who find the going really hard satisfy themselves with the brown rocks nearer the bottom. However, to the crippled man these are like jewels.*

'Staff Meeting, 1.00 pm Monday 2nd September, Room 6.' The piece of paper was pinned to the notice board in the staff room of the prison, where Adrian saw it at lunch-time. He wished he had gone straight out. Mr Nash was already in the chair, when Adrian arrived. This was just what one didn't need in one's lunch break. Adrian couldn't escape and felt his concentration going walkabout before he had even entered the room, let alone got to his seat. The faculty were assembled, those who were lucky enough to be in that day, that is. It didn't take long before the usual whingers began complaining. It was always the same and nothing ever got resolved. 'No one has it so bad as me...' was the general gist. 'When I asked the officer, he told me I had to have a blah blah, so I told him that the procedure for blah blah was so very blah blah...' Adrian had reached total shut-down. The last thing he remembered was 'I'll take it up with the blah blah and new forms blah blah.'

He was awakened from his semi-conscious ramblings first by a kick under the table and second by a horrible feeling that the present part of the conversation was aimed at him.

'The prison would like us to enrol as many students as possible this year for courses, especially art at GCSE and A-level. You have some men from D block who could benefit from such courses...' (And ones with long enough sentences to do them.)

Adrian smelt a rat and could almost see the certificates in the eyes of the management that were directed at him. Those heady days, when Adrian thought he could get them all through degrees. From this point of view an A-level seemed monumental. He pointed out that it would be quite a quantum leap for some of the men to take a formal exam course and that they would require time to build up confidence and good practice. This was acknowledged.

'Well, we've got a few more weeks before we start. The names should have been submitted a few weeks ago, so I will be needing them this week, but if you could start working in a way more GCSE oriented, then they should be alright.' Adrian was then told to keep an eye out for possible candidates.

'Also, if they do sign up for an exam then we will put a freeze on all transfers so that they won't be able to ship anyone out who's on a course.'

This was an added incentive that would definitely affect numbers should it leak out, which it inevitably would.

There was one man on the wing who had considerable skill, and he had been angling for some time to do A-level Art. (And - surprise, surprise - had been making a lot of noise about not wanting to be shipped out.) His name was Daniel Roydon. Adrian put his name forward. Jason was given the task of tutoring him, one morning a week. Unfortunately he was with Adrian the rest of the time. The problem with Daniel was that he didn't take to being a student very well. He didn't like anyone telling him how to do things, in fact he didn't like anyone telling him anything at all. One day he showed Adrian a drawing he'd done.

'You see this bit here, that's a bottle. And do you know what this is, here? Look closely. Can you see?'

'Is it a wine glass?' said Adrian hopefully.

'Exactly! This is a painting about alcoholism.'

'It has a bit of a cubist feel to it, around here. This bit.'

'What do you mean, cubist?'

'Cubism, it's an art movement that enabled the painter to unravel solid objects and make them flat. You can see them from all angles, if you like.'

'But you can't see behind this bottle. So it's not cubist.'

'True, I only said it reminded me of cubism. This bit.'

'But it's not.'

The next time Adrian met Daniel he had painted a cubist painting.

'I've decided to paint something cubist. What do you think?'

'It's very good...'

'Cubism sort of unravels solid objects and makes them flat.'

'Yes, I know,' said Adrian testily. 'I told you last week.'

'If you look carefully you can see this bottle from all sides. Because that's what cubist painters did,' replied Daniel, ignoring what Adrian had just said.

He waddled off to find someone else to show, leaving Adrian perplexed, wondering if this was some sort of weird joke.

But it wasn't. This was the only way to instruct Daniel. You had to give him the information in such a way that he thought he had discovered it all for himself and then let him lecture you. This was a very unsatisfactory teaching method, as it didn't give any teacher satisfaction, just lots of argument and criticism.

In addition, Daniel always wanted the materials that weren't available. He always wanted oil paints when there were acrylics. Acrylics when there was gouache. Gouache when there was watercolour. He always had to reluctantly make do and would then produce work with 'no help at all from anyone else'. He was doing this exam definitely on his own. One day Adrian thought he would get the upper hand. He took with him a complete set of acrylic paints. When he got there he said:

'Today I've brought over some lovely watercolours.' He knew Daniel would want something else, and true enough he did.

'Typical, just when I need acrylics. You can never get what you need in here. It's like they're setting you up to fail.'

'Oh, wait a minute! Yes - I do have some acrylics. Here, there are some at the bottom of my bag.'

'Good. You see, you don't prepare yourself properly for when you come in. You don't even know what's in your bag.'

Adrian had got Daniel to do what he wanted but he didn't feel any satisfaction in doing so.

Jason introduced the formal elements to him. He argued about all of them and then told Jason what the formal elements were. Daniel was left with a series of exercises to do by the following week, none of which he really understood because he had been so busy trying not to lose face by just listening. In the afternoon, he approached Adrian with a load of testing questions.

'Is pattern a formal element?'

'Yes it is, pattern is a formal element.'

'That's not what Jason said, he said pattern was *one* of the formal elements. You see, there are others as well. You didn't know that, did you, Ade?'

'Of course I did, I said it was a formal element.'

'Let me tell you what the others are. First there's line, then texture...'

Adrian was fed up with listening, and everything he said took so long. Nothing was quick. Adrian had loads to do this morning and felt his legs itching to go. He didn't want to play games.

'I gotta go, you need to get these exercises done.'

'Oh! Its different when you have to listen, isn't it? Don't like it when the shoe's on the other foot.'

Adrian left feeling pretty pissed off with Daniel. He was always so unappreciative. Adrian had gone out of his way to be helpful and bring him as much equipment and resource material as he could and yet all he ever heard were complaints.

'Sod him,' he thought as he drove home.

When the other prisoners had woken, the following morning, they found that Daniel had gone. He'd been ghosted away in the night. he was already on his way somewhere else. His cell door was standing open wide. All the signs were there of someone who had to leave in a hurry, Quick decisions about what to take resulted in a pile of discarded possessions strewn across the floor. Daniel was not given time or room to be sentimental.

'Jones! Clear out that cell,' called out one of the officers to the cleaning orderly. 'We've got someone coming in soon.'

Jones had never got on with Daniel, ever since he had tried to lecture him on keeping his cell clean, and so had set to the task with relish.

'What shall I do with all this stuff?'

'Bin it!' shouted back the officer without even looking at it. 'There's some bin-bags over there.'

'With pleasure,' answered the grin on Jones' face, 'with pleasure.' He picked up his folio and squashed it in the bin bag.

When Adrian, along with Jason, arrived the bin bags had gone. They desperately tried to find out where they had been taken too. The communications list, next to the phone, had column upon column of extension numbers, to every department you could think of but not one that was obvious. There was no 'Waste Disposal Office'. Adrian tried a few he knew to see if anyone could help him find the folio. But something in the tone of Adrian's voice set alarm bells ringing. After explaining the situation, the final response was always 'Oh! You shouldn't have lost that.'

Everyone began oiling their shoulders It was time to play the Blame game. Adrian kicked off.

'Why did you throw away his folio? You must have known he was doing A-level.'

'Why should we? You never told us.'

'But we told the wing managers. That's why Jason has been coming over here with me these last few months.'

'Yeah well! They never told me. I was only doing what Transfers told us.'

'But there's a freeze on transfers when men are doing exams.'

'You need to see them about it. Are you sure you told them.'

'I didn't personally, but education should have.'

'Anyway the bins should still be here, they don't get taken away till twelve. It was wrong them coming that early. If they'd been on time this would never have happened.'

Adrian decided to phone the Education Department. The voice on the other end, sensing someone's butt was about to be kicked went scampering off to cover their tracks.

'I'll check with Allocations. They should never have allowed this to happen. He's doing an A-level. He's supposed to stay until he's done his exam. I'll get back to you.'

Adrian looked at Jason in disbelief, well maybe not quite , they had both been there long enough to know it was all too very believable.

'All that work,' said Jason 'gone.'

They decided they needed to sit and think, before letting the class out. Was there anywhere they had overlooked? Whilst going through the facts again, in came Mr Nash. He was grinning as always.

'It's alright, it's alright. I've found him. He hasn't gone yet. They're bringing him back. He was over in a holding cell. He'll be here in a minute..'

It was true. Daniel was banged up in a holding cell, waiting to be shipped to Dartmoor. Weirdly, the delay was because there wasn't a vacancy at Dartmoor. They must have miscounted. Anyway, he was to come back. When he eventually arrived on the wing, later that day, he was confronted by his emptied cell and a very nervous Jones.

'Where's my folder?' he said coldly, though he probably guessed it had been thrown away.

Jones put in to be transferred to another jail that afternoon.

There was no way Daniel was ever going to catch up and do it all again. Not that he had any intention to do so. This was all conspiracy stuff. Adrian went to see Mr Nash to see if he could come up with the missing folder, but that was too much to ask for one day.

'No. I'm afraid that's gone. They don't leave rubbish standing around too long. It attracts rats. Anyway, in some ways it's a blessing. He never would have got that A-level anyway.' Adrian and Jason looked at each other in disbelief. Why were they teaching it in that case? They felt themselves becoming despondent as all feelings of self-worth left them.

The following day they set off, to teach the next module to the remaining two candidates with absolutely no enthusiasm at all. When they arrived, the first person they saw was Daniel. He was sitting on his own. He refused to look at them. Adrian felt really sorry for him and regretted feeling so pissed off with him earlier. They went and sat with him. It was impossible not to share everything he was feeling. All Adrian could say was:

'I'm really sorry!'

'They didn't want me to pass, you know! They were jealous. They couldn't bear the thought of me bettering myself. Sod them!'

'I'm really sorry!' said Adrian again.

'I really feel like kicking off. If one of them says anything, I'll deck him.'

'Don't do that. That's probably what they want. You'll be giving them *carte-blanche* to take you down even further. You'll be playing into their hands.'

'I know, I know. You can't win in this place.' He got up, went to his cell and banged himself up.

Adrian had the worst day ever. He couldn't work like this and vowed, that in future he would always try and remain focussed on the bigger picture, and not get drawn into petty things and miss the point. Stupid A levels! How could anyone seriously measure by the same yardstick, students in college and men locked up in prison. How many students had their work thrown out by the college? The obstacles that needed to be overcome! It seemed the longer the course the more likely it was to go wrong. With this in mind, Adrian tried to look forward to his next project, GCSEs, and wondered whether they would fare any better than A levels. It seemed that whenever prison and college collided there would be many casualties since both organisations refused to compromise. Something had changed inside Adrian, he realised, he had lost his sense of trust. He was not alone in this, the feeling was universally shared on the wing. Many men now started giving their work to Adrian to keep in his folder. He was being used as a safe deposit box and would be soon needing a pack-horse to accompany him to and from class.

# 26 THE WOMAN IN WHITE

*It is believed on Fiji, that when a man dies his soul, turns into a bird that flies away across the ocean. They roam forever on the wing, until once a year they return to lay their eggs. This is regarded as auspicious . The exception, however, to the rule are the souls of people who have been murdered. They turn into jellyfish and permanently float around the shallows trying to get revenge.*

It felt like it had been a long day even-though Adrian had finished everything he'd planned to do, a lot earlier than expected. There was still an hour left when Adrian began putting things away and contemplated leaving early. However, the men, anticipating early Bang-up. asked Adrian to stay on a while, so they could remain unlocked and associate. The day had been a lot quieter than usual, there had seemed to be less conversation even though the only person that had been missing was Insect who had reported sick that morning. It wasn't that he was actually ill, he explained to Adrian, it was because he hadn't slept.

'Been watching too much late night telly,' said Adrian.

'No, not this time I daren't sleep. '

He had been just about to explain why, when Daniel approached.

'I'll tell you later.' He had turned around and wheeled himself to his cell, Adrian pulled a quizzical face.

'He's been having nightmares about ghosts and ghouls. He's totally headshot, you know. Stupid little bugger!' explained Daniel. Adrian sort of nodded. Daniel was renowned for not suffering fools gladly so Insect had remained in his cell all day.

'Well, I will stay on for a bit. As long as you make us a cuppa,' said Adrian, thinking 'I may as well make the most of it.' Star pupil went off to make Ade a tea. Maybe having felt the change of atmosphere and increased 'chill factor', Insect now emerged from his cell, cup in hand, looking very pale. He looked to see if Adrian was on his own and made towards him. Daniel, seeing him from afar, called out 'WWWWOOOOO! Bring out your dead!' Insect, glared at him as he parked himself next to Adrian.

'God! Hello! You do seem really ill, ' said Adrian looking at the heavy blue bags under his eyes. and his dishevelled, almost matted, appearance.

'I'm not ill, I just can't sleep. I was up all night again. It's this place, its fucking *haunted,* and I think it's in my cell.'

'What is ? You're joking right?'

No I'm not,' said Insect emphatically. 'There is something in my cell. I don't ever joke about such things.'

'I hear you had a bad dream last night.'

Insect certainly wasn't making up his dreadful appearance.

'It wasn't a dream, it was her. It's that woman! The one that was murdered. You tell him Kim.'

Adrian turned round and saw a man he hadn't met before. His name, apparently, was Kim Dexter. He was tall and thin with hardly any hair. Everything about him was permeated with the smell of stale tobacco. Adrian also noticed that he clicked slightly when he talked. On top of all this, he had an I–told-you-so attitude that Adrian didn't much care for.'

'There is a ghost, actually. She's been seen quite a lot lately, round the prison. They won't be laughing now you know She always comes when the moon is waxing.'

'What? It's legs?' sniggered Billy.

'She is supposed to have lived on this very spot, in the eighteen hundreds, until she was murdered, that is, and she's been coming back ever since. You know, there used to be a nut-house on this site, before they pulled it down and built this prison. I've heard she used to scare the poor sods who lived there shitless. And now she's come again.'

'How do you know all this? asked Adrian sceptically.

'Cos my grandmother told me, she was a resident, here before. God bless her soul!'

'What!' threw in Billy. 'She was mad, Jesus! Didn't you ever think it might have been all in her fuckin' head.' He started to laugh, but was short lived because a very unexpected voice entered the debate...

'*It's not. It's all true*. Everything he says is true. I've seen her as well, with my own eyes.' All heads turned to Star Pupil who was staring wide-eyed.

'*What!* gasped Insect. 'You did? Tell us what she looks like.'

'I saw her last night., she was old and stooped with lots of dirty white petticoats. She's got grey scraggy hair and horrible arthritic hands that look more like claws than anything human. I definitely saw her and she is a ghost alright, one of the un-dead.'

Insect turned a paler shade of white than Adrian thought was possible.

'Well. That's proved it. Three of us have seen it. See I'm not making it up.'

Insect had been residing in cell 47 for nearly two years now. He was serving a six year sentence for theft with assault. The first time his biscuits went missing, he had been furious - they were his favourites, Jaffa Cakes. He accused his neighbour, Kim Dexter, of stealing them during association time. This lead to a long-term feud that had lasted several weeks. When it happened a second time, Insect was slower at accusing his neighbour, as he was in a state of shock.

Insect never slept well, he had far too many issues in his head, the biggest of which, recently, was his loss of biscuits. He always found it difficult to get a full night of solid sleep anyway, the best he could ever manage was a trance-like half-sleep that was more like a cat-nap than the real thing. He had also recently been put on a strong cocktail of medication for his various complaints (of which there were many). This left him in a very rarified condition a lot of the time. He often physically sat in the classroom, but he just wasn't present. Where he actually was, God knows, assuming he was anywhere at all. He was in one of these weird states of consciousness, vacant, when the moon had waxed to its set size, and The Lady In White had decided to visit.

At first, when Insect saw her walk through the wall, he thought he was just dreaming. He didn't react too much, as he had experienced similar sorts of things before. He knew if he just waited a bit, she'd disappear. But she didn't. Having now entered the cell, she paused at his bedside cabinet and began to cut an imaginary slice of bread. She had just been about to eat her basic meal, when she spied the Jaffa Cakes, lying next to the bread and began to eat them instead. At no time did she even look at Insect, whom she totally ignored. He remained seated on the edge of his cot with his back against the wall, petrified. Having polished off his Jaffa Cakes she had passed through the bricks only inches from where he sat. He felt the icy swish of her skirts as they brushed by him. The smell of decay then filled his nostrils. He retched.

Meanwhile, next door in cell 48, Kim Dexter had been fast asleep. He had been dreaming of his favourite subject: Kylie Minogue. She danced all around him, lifting what was left of her mini-skirt ever higher. Dexter liked this dream: it was one of his favourites. He always whittled on and on about it. It made most people feel ill, as Kim was about sixty something years old, going on eighty. The thought of him having such a lusty appetite seemed perverse. He would tell everyone how Kylie would eventually come over and slip into the sheets next to him, and unable to resist his alluring, male appeal a second longer, she would beg Dexter for satisfaction (as if). Unfortunately (for Dexter, not Kylie), this was always where the dream ended, and what happened next, he could never remember. However, last night things had been different. His wish had been granted and the dream didn't disappear, though later he wished it had. Unfortunately, what had started as the sweetest thing turned into a horrific nightmare. Kylie metamorphosed into a white, decaying hag. He spent hours screaming and trying to push her away, but she had wrapped her ice cold, corpse-like claws around his passionate body in a deadly, vice-like embrace and held him tight for what seemed like hours. He woke up, horrified, in a sweaty, soiled bed. There was the smell of death lingering in the room, tinted weirdly with the sweet scent of Jaffa Cakes. When Dexter had told everyone this dream over breakfast, Insect froze and went pale.

'*We have been visited by the woman in white! Shit!'* It really is true. She came to me too. I actually saw her.'

'What? Kylie Minogue?'

'No the hag-woman. I saw her too. She ate my Jaffa Cakes.'

'*Never!* shouted Dexter. 'Because I found this in my cell, this morning, under the bed. God knows how it got there cos I never eat them. I hates them.' He ran over to the bin and pulled out an empty packet for all to see. He handed it to Insect.

'*This is my packet.*' said Insect studying it. ' *I can tell.*'

The two men looked really scared. A few other prisoners sat around guffawing, but the majority were in an uncertain silence, unsure what to think.

'Well if three of us have seen her it must be true. I heard loads of creepy screams last night. That was her. Did anyone else hear it?'

A few nodded positively. No more proof was necessary .they needed none.

'What are we going to do about her?' asked Dexter.

'I wouldn't call it "her", I'd call it "it",' said Star

Billy laughed, 'It it.' He sniggered

Star was speaking in a spooky kind of voice, that somehow didn't ring true for Adrian. It was too theatrical. However, Adrian didn't feel confident enough to challenge him. But, it was obvious that, Dexter, like Insect had no doubts, whatsoever.

'I bet where your two cells are, is exactly the spot where she was brutally stabbed to death, otherwise she wouldn't hang about there. Ghosts do that. They always return to their final resting place. I bet if you were to dig, you'd find her remains.. I wouldn't try and escape by a tunnel. They don't take kindly to being disturbed.' Daniel couldn't help allowing a smile to crack his face as he spoke..

'I want to get a transfer. I'm not staying in this fucking haunted shit-hole. ' said Dexter.

'You can try, but even if you get it, it will take months.' replied Daniel.

'Well, I'm putting in for one, anyway. What about you Insect, you moving?'

'He's right! It's probably better to ask them to let us have other cells first and then try for transfer. But look, it's time for Meds now. We'll do it later.'

An officer appeared and began to shepherd the group of ailing men to Healthcare. Insect and Dexter both scuttled off together.

Adrian watched them go and finished his tea. The inmates, meanwhile, began to drift off to make phone-calls, play pool or go for a smoke in their cells. Star remained .

I'm gonna make another brew. Want one? Do you want a biscuit to go with it?'

Feeling peckish, Adrian agreed. In a short while Star returned with two steaming mugs and a packet of ...Jaffa Cakes.

Adrian made a puzzled look towards the biscuits and then at Star who, unable to keep a straight face, immediately burst out laughing..

'Don't look like that! I know what you're thinking?'

He sat down, opened the box and pulled out the last two remaining biscuits from the packet, laughing all the while.

Adrian was just about to ask whether they were legit or supernatural, when Star, with a mighty kick, sent the empty box scampering across the floor . It bounced into a cell, through an empty door and came to rest under a bed. The cell was Dexter's. Star roared so much that Adrian couldn't help himself laughing too,. It was so contagious .

'I hate that skinny, lanky git. This is so excellent,' he said through biscuit, tea and laughter.

Adrian paused long enough to ask...

'Really! He'll be so spooked when he finds another one there. Shame on you Star.' Adrian, nevertheless, couldn't help laughing.

'You ain't going to grass on me, are you?'

'Well, not just yet, as you've just shared your last biscuits with me.'

Star began laughing again even louder. Adrian asked what was so funny.

'They're not mine. I nicked them. They're his.'

He pointed to Insect's open cell, next door.

Later that evening, Dexter went to the office to ask for a different cell. He waited until Mr Griffiths, his personal officer, was on duty, before approaching and asking. He knew it would be a long shot as there were never any empty ones available. To confound it further, Dexter had a gammy leg, which kept him grounded. No flights of stairs for him.. The officer stared at him contemptuously.

'Why do you want to move? What's wrong with the one you got?

Dexter felt uncomfortable and decided to avoid too much detail.

'I just want to change. I need to. Please guv, I gotta move.'

The officer almost took pity on him, so rather than bawl him out, he decided to fob him off instead.

'Well, if one becomes free, we'll swap you. OK?'

Dexter wasn't expecting it to be that easy. The officer turned and walked back to his desk.

'God you'll never believe what he just asked' he said rejoining the other officers, 'He only wants another bleeding cell. Jeez! Not a chance.'

The nearest officer looked up, all bright-eyed.

'Well, we can actually. Let's do it. Insect also asked earlier on if he could move. There's a coincidence.' Don't ever let it be said we don't do our best. We'll swap them round tonight.'

# 27 JABBA FUCKS OFF (GOOD)

*When the people of Fiji realised they were not the only folk on the planet and that other places existed, some of them wished to leave. The king decreed that before they departed, they would have to stand trial enabling anyone who had outstanding business or grievance to settle to get what they considered their just desserts. Only when all debts had been paid, could they then leave.*

One morning Adrian arrived to find that during the night the Flu Angel had delivered its retribution on the staff of HMP Feldon Park and smitten them with a virus of biblical proportions. Take that! Many of the brethren felt the wrath of God, and those left un-smitten still suffered grievously by the hand of Man instead. Today there was an acute shortage of snot-filled teachers, especially in the art department, which meant Adrian had to cover another class besides his own, at least for half the day. Unfortunately for him, it was in the ceramics room. This was the one area of art where he didn't have a clue. Obviously, there were several projects going on involving clay, but Adrian thought he would just bluff his way through the morning and avoid getting involved. All went well until, after about fifteen seconds, one lad, Winston, asked: 'What glaze should I put on this, guv?'

To which Adrian replied, and thus sealed his fate: 'I've no idea! I don't know much about ceramics. You'll have to wait until George is back. Clay was never my subject. If I were you I would leave that and do something different today in case we mess it up.'

Immediately, the entire class, recognizing a chink in the armour, switched over to clay-based projects. Filling someone else's shoes is always difficult. It's like starting all over again: you have to build up trust and establish the rules.

The daily regime of the wing restricts social contact between prisoners to certain times, and always under the ever-watchful eyes of the officers, who supposedly see everything with their x-ray vision. If something needs to be said privately between prisoners, it's quite often done in passing, on the stairs, in the queue, through the keyhole, something like that. You need to be awake and take your opportunity when it presents itself. This gives little time for explanations and even less for comeback. But the boys, with lots of time on their own and little else to focus on, put a lot of hours dwelling on these fleeting social contacts. But beware! These tiny throwaway comments can get blown horribly out of proportion. An insult said by the wrong person on the wrong day to another wrong person can lead to getting a cup of boiling water thrown in your face, often long after the incident has taken place. The anger or humiliation has just sits there, festering, having been put on hold until the right opportunity should present itself. Then it's revenge time, the hour of reckoning - and all the while, Chinese whispers fan the flames of urgency.

If suddenly, in the middle of this complicated social string of events, someone's time is up and their release is imminent, you have to act fast. If you haven't got even yet, then all those stored up grievances and hurts need to be quickly avenged. You don't want to be the one left wearing the muppet hat, do you?

The other side of the coin is if it's you who's about to leave. It's advisable on the last day to keep your head down and avoid as much general association as possible. This is especially true if you are a mouthy little sod who has just about managed to insult everyone on the wing over the last few months. But Jabba seemed to have missed this point and, rather than keeping quiet, was *cavorting* all around the art room, right in everyone's collective face. Many of the prisoners present that day were just waiting for an opportunity to get even with him before he disappeared. In addition, here was Adrian, a stranger, in a classroom where he was out of his depth. It was going to be a rough three hours for him - and for Jabba. There was a lot of taunting right from the outset; stupid remarks for which Jabba, instead of ignoring, invariably had a comeback, which just aggravated the situation.

It was obvious that it would have been better to have kept Jabba out of the class today as apparently he was going to be released in the morning,. He was, naturally, as high as a kite. Adrian could never quite understand why someone so close to release, should have to attend classes at all. It was hardly as if they were going to start a new project or something, You would think there were other things that needed doing, but no! This was doubly confounded by the fact that his regular teacher wasn't in. Adrian was not surprised by anything anymore though. Number three rule: Make it up as you go along. Jabba was actually good at art and Adrian always wished he had been in his class. He would have got him through an A-level, he was easily capable of it. But as it was, he was leaving with the usual pile of OCN certificates. He could have done so much more, had his time been managed better and his sentence a little longer. Another missed opportunity and another missed A-level. The odds were definitely stacked against him. Short sentences and long course dates, with starting dates set in concrete, didn't match.

Also by allowing Jabba into the classroom hours before his release exposed him, (and Adrian) to another possible problem. Again no prior warning was given. If, by chance, an immanently to be released inmate manages to avoid most of the revenge attempts during the day, the un-avenged simply pool their differences and collectively give him a good pasting on his last night.

'You're going to get it tonight, Jabba, you twat.'

'I don't care, I'll be out of here tomorrow. Your wife's picking me up, by the way...'

The verbals would occasionally culminate in a nudge or a glare that only added to the price to be paid at the reckoning hour. Adrian decided to collect in all the tools. The tool cabinet, in moments like these, looked increasingly like an arms cupboard which has to be kept meticulously locked. Having just turned the key for the final time something splattered on the wall inches from his head, leaving a brown stain. It was a flicked clay pellet. Adrian spun round. Everyone was intently staring everywhere else but at him. Eye contact would have been an immediate giveaway.

'Whoever threw that pellet had better stop now and think again...' This was a ridiculous thing to say, and only acted like a red flag to a bull. They were completely unmoved by Adrian's threat, and whenever he turned his head for more than a few seconds, a pellet would be launched. It seemed that teacher target practice had momentarily replaced the revenge sessions as the sport of the day.

'If I catch anyone flicking or making a pellet, I'll give them a nicking.'

'No-one's flicking anything at you, boss. You're imagining it,' said Winston. 'You've probably taken too much LSD when you was younger. You're getting hallucinations.'

Adrian walked around the room, hoping to find the ammunition, but it was hopeless. Without the evidence, he couldn't really do much except maybe nick the entire class, but then Jabba's release would be postponed. Only later did he realise that once the pellets were made they were stuck under the table, unseen, ready for use. Eventually, by the use of his stealth or more likely because his threats sounded so hollow, Adrian came up behind a youngster with a pile of smooth round pellets, right in front of him.

'So, it was you. You're nicked.'

'Get lost! You can't nick me. This is art. This is my sculpture. I've been working on it all morning. Ask anyone.'

'It's not. That's a pile of pellets.'

'It's not. Do your homework before you come in here. I'm making a clay sculpture of a plate of food. These are the peas.'

The youngster then produced a clay pork chop and some clay chips.

Meanwhile, while Adrian's attention was thus engaged, someone had squirted a dollop of white oil paint on Jabba's chair, which he, not noticing, sat on. Jabba: nil, Avenging Angel:one. He was not pleased, he was wearing his best trousers, the ones he should have been wearing tomorrow. A few minutes later someone had furtively splattered oil paint down the back of Winston's jacket. There was a lot of tension in the air. Adrian locked as many things up as he possibly could and willed the clock to get a move on.

The clay pellets continued to fly about, several hitting Adrian on the back of his head. He consoled himself by thinking, 'Well, it's better they throw things at me than kill each other.' Or maybe not.

This cat and mouse behaviour seemed endless. Adrian's main concern was to get to the end of the lesson without serious incident, to keep all the tools under lock and key and to get the room cleaned up at the end of the day. The last objective was probably the hardest to achieve. No one would co-operate.

'I'm giving a nicking to the whole class if one more pellet is thrown. Now clean up this mess.'

'I ain't cleaning the fucking floor. I never threw nothing,' was everyone's response minus Jabba's.

'Me neither, I never chucked a thing. I'm not clearing up other people's rubbish,' he eventually added.

In the end, Adrian had to pick two 'volunteers'. This was his way of getting even with hyper Jabba and mouthy Winston. Adrian handed out the brooms and they began to sweep. But nothing was going to be that simple, and even this ended up in conflict. Winston was sweeping all his rubbish into Jabba's half, and Jabba then doing exactly the same back to him. This could go on forever. Adrian turned away for a split second - and knew straight away that something was going to happen. He just caught sight of Jabba wielding the broom at full throttle into Winston's face. There was a cracking sound as a tooth came out. They threw the brooms to one side and started punching hell out of each other.

'Break it up *now* - I said *NOW!*'

They ignored him and rolled around the floor, embraced in a tight clasp, banging into the tables. There was blood on them both. The other inmates retreated to the walls, as far away as possible. The fight continued.

Adrian acted on impulse and grabbed the nearest one and pulled him off. It was Jabba.

'Stop this now. How dare you fight in my class!'

Adrian had reverted to the old schoolteacher in him, he was back in primary school. They actually pulled apart from each other and Adrian went to the door.

'I'm getting an officer. Stay where you are,' he shouted. There was no officer to be seen. They were in their office.

'Can somebody get here, fast!' he shouted. It seemed to take forever for anyone to respond.

When an officer did eventually come, it seemed that the desire to get even before an inmate leaves also extended to the officers.

'Nick him, then we can give him an adjudication and extend his sentence for a week. I can't wait to see his face when he finds out he ain't going anywhere tomorrow.'

This led Adrian to make probably one of the biggest mistakes he'd ever made in prison, not because he thought he was doing the wrong thing but because he didn't follow the rules. (You know, the ones he was supposed to know.). He didn't nick either of them; he just gave them both a written warning. This did not please the officers and was noted by the rest of the inmates too. Adrian couldn't bring himself to prevent Jabba's imminent release. Adrian got it in the neck on several occasions from both sides as a result.

'Oh, and another thing: never ever get physically involved if prisoners kick off. You were lucky you didn't get hurt. Haven't you done a Restraint and Control course?'

The next day Jabba walked free.

'Send us a postcard,' said the officer on the gate.

'Yeah, right! I'm not going on a fucking holiday, you know.'

Jabba knew that Fiji was out of reach for him and he'd never make it. He would return to more familiar places, more familiar faces, more familiar habits. He had played safe and bought a return ticket.

# 28 AN ANGEL VISITS

*'Once the spirit has left the dead man, his house is filled with wood and straw and set ablaze. No trace of the deceased is left in this world. To leave personal possessions is thought to bring about great misfortune.* The Journal of Captain Cook, Fiji.

There was a particularly dark gloom hanging in the air the next time Adrian arrived to teach in the prison. It was not just the black, menacing clouds that heralded another wet February day, nor was it the general weariness he was feeling from a long week. It felt as if someone had replaced the normal strong light bulbs with 40-watt ones, both inside and out. However, the cause of the gloom was far more sinister. During the night, the Angel of Death had been summoned to Feldon Park. Unable to return empty-handed he had taken a soul back with him. He had hovered over the blocks all night, looking for someone to snatch away, but found that all were fast asleep. All but one, that is.

Steve, he of the magpie drawing, the bird wearing different plumage, had been up all night and had seen the black silhouette, soaring with the silent white snowy owls. Not recognising this giant raptor on his bird chart, he felt sorry for the migrating angel and threw him some crumbs. However, the big bird's appetite was huge and he wanted more than that. He wanted it all. Steve didn't struggle. Passively, he gave himself up to the clasping talons. Steve, the bird, couldn't endure himself any more, locked as he was in his cage, so he decided to release his spirit. He hung himself with his shoelaces.

News of this tragedy spread throughout prisonland on whispered breaths, from ear to ear, from cell to cell, along the heating pipes, through the grills and peep-holes. Steve, Troll man, Birdie - the names became meaningless now - had topped himself. No matter what anyone's relationship to Steve or to suicide was, they couldn't help feeling a dampening spirit descend. Adrian's initial thought, after it had sunk in, was ridiculous: Who was going to feed the birds now? 'Sorry, Steve, but then that's probably exactly what you would have said anyway.'

'I think people who do suicide are really selfish,' said one of the officers on duty that morning. Adrian couldn't get his head round that one at that particular moment, but even the officer had said it with only a fraction of the normal venom. Steve had finally got noticed, and now his gravelly spirit had expanded along the spotless, strip-lit corridors, under cell doors, filling every nook and cranny of the prison, while his soul joined all those others who had taken the same way out. Adrian stared through the window at the clouds just as a group of gulls were flying in from the coast. They were flying in formation in a giant V. They were delivering Steve's final message to Feldon Park: two fingers up to them all. Adrian smiled.

'Stupid bastard,' growled Billy that morning, making a pretence of not caring, but he was only talking automatically. It had shaken him to the core. Adrian watched him, he had sunk into himself in a way he hadn't seen before. He wondered, 'Who is going to be your punch bag now, Billy Boy?' Another door had been closed to him. The outlet for so much of his anger. He was his nemesis, and it was at this moment Adrian realised how much Billy needed him. Part of Billy had died too.

Suicide is an ever-present companion in prison. All those isolated hours, all those night vigils spent with the Grim Reaper as your only companion, waiting. All inmates have heard his persistent chatter. It's unsaid, common knowledge that each one carries close to his chest, and even if he thinks, 'I'd never do that,' it's there. When it happens and someone gives in and offers himself up, the entire prison shivers of one accord as if in sympathy. There wasn't one person that Adrian met who wasn't affected. Not that they necessarily talked about it, but it showed in the way they spoke, in the way they moved. It was as if, having kidded yourself, day after day, that everything's fine, I'm going to be the tough guy, you suddenly realise the truth. It really is that bad. In one fell swoop, all the masks come off. Adrian for the first time realised how thick his own mask had become.

The lesson that day, was very downcast. The men worked for long periods of the day in silence. Adrian noticed that although the same projects were being carried out as last time, a lot more black was used that day. Nobody sat in Steve's chair, it gaped empty. Until Billy decided to put his feet on it.

'Oi! Don't do that! That's Steve's chair. Get them off and show some respect! Insect glared at him. Billy, for once, did exactly as he was told and removed his feet. Though not without some protest, feeble as it was. 'It's only a chair.'

'It's Steve's chair. He could well be sitting there right now. After all this was the one only place, in this whole fucking nick that he liked to be. He liked his art, you know.'

The thought of Steve's presence still sitting there suddenly seemed quite plausible. Perhaps that was why nobody said much today.

At the end of the morning, Adrian went to his folder to put away the men's work. As he did so, he saw a scrunched up, scrawny picture of a bird, lying at the bottom. Totally out of proportion and beyond any recognition it was one of Steve's, so misunderstood. The crap picture now looked like a naïve masterpiece. Adrian carefully pulled it out and straightened it. He decided to take it home and mount it.

Later that afternoon, Adrian passed Steve's cell, and was surprised to find that already every physical trace of him had vanished, the wall charts, the stained plastic cup, everything. It was as if he had never existed. However, there would be no-one clamouring to get this cell in a hurry. It would probably stay empty for a while, well at least until tomorrow. Adrian paused and looked inside for a few minutes. He imagined the ghostly white Snowy Owls silently circling around the barred window as Steve threw them his crushed-up regulation biscuits. Under the watchful gaze of the moon, Steve's spirit had taken wing, had taken leave of his body. He had begun his migration to a place far away across the emerald ocean, to Fiji, without the burden of his clinkered body. Adrian felt himself almost in prayer.

He felt a hand on his shoulder, but he was so relaxed he didn't even flinch. It was Dunaway. He didn't say anything. He just stood there, turned, and then walked away.

# 29 LIFE WITH THE COMMON PEOPLE

*When travellers from the west first arrived in Fiji with a radio, the indigenous people were greatly puzzled. How could the white magicians keep the spirits locked in this little box. What sorcery was this? They filled their ears with wax so they couldn't hear the spirit's song. Those who did became possessed and began to jerkily move about.*

Adrian knew that if any of his teaching was to prove to be effective, he needed to connect and communicate, which meant he expected to be listened to. It was a peculiar prerequisite of his that he actually needed to be heard. In the early days he found himself in competition with a stream of endless drivel that spewed forth from the radio. There was one occasion, however, when the incredibly beat-up ghetto-blaster actually took on a positive role, and as if trying to make a point, showed what it was capable of, in spite of being tuned to the crappy local radio station… 'Get on down to Homebase today...' Yeah! All that sort of stuff. Well, today the radio found soul and spoke so profoundly that all who heard were transformed. Such are the powers of the airwaves.

It began as a usual sort of day with the radio murmuring quietly to itself in the corner at a predetermined, much debated level of volume. Paint slapped, pencils scratched and erasers erased, and the students moaned endlessly about proper prisons and fairness. Incredible, this need for fairness. Break everyone else's rules but don't touch mine... This particular morning saw a group of men sitting shoulder-to-shoulder around the table, all in their own little knotty worlds. Their barbed wire fences were beginning to rub together and snag. In a world where people are reduced to numbers and statistics, the need to impress one's identity into the world takes on a desperate urgency. *My* chair, *my* cup, *my* space, *my* thoughts, *my* ideas. Take them away at your own risk. But on this day all barbs melted away, all sense of isolation vanished as everyone in the room, for a whole five minutes and thirty three seconds, merged into a huge united mass of uplifted spirit. And the reason? One song. Pulp's *Common People*. It just started up unannounced...

*She came from Greece,*
*she had a thirst for knowledge,*
*She studied sculpture*
*at St Martins College,*
*that's where I caught her eye.*
*She told me that her dad was loaded;*
*in that case, I'll have a rum and coca cola.*
*She said, fine, and in*
*thirty seconds time she said,*

*'I want to live with common people,*
*I want to do whatever common people do,*

*I want to sleep with common people,*
*I want to sleep with common people like you.'*
*Well what else could I do,*
*I said I'll see what I can do...'*

It was that magical song. Everybody loves it. Adrian always knew it was special. This is our song. It summed it all up the estates, the comprehensives, the soaps, it's us, Essex boys of the world unite. The Common People.

All in the room were moved by the spirit. It was another Pentecost. Tony stood up and floated over to the dials and granted power to the message. It got fucking loud. Really loud. God was speaking in rolls of thunder and all raised their voices in praise. *YES!*

*...I took her to a supermarket,*
*I don't know but*
*I had to start somewhere,*
*so it started there.*
*I said, 'pretend you've got no money',*
*she just laughed and said,*
*'you're so funny', I said, 'yeah?*
*Well I can't see any one else*
*smiling in here...'*

Everyone in the class, including Adrian, started singing, hearts brimming to bursting, in a stadium-north-stand euphoria.

Billy, needless to say, was on the table again, whipping the crowd to a frenzy with his weird, jerky dance. This definitely wasn't chaos. This was shared religious experience. A vision of the virgin in sound, brought by that bloke with the glasses, but it could just as easily have been anyone in the room.

*But she didn't understand.*
*She just smiled and held my hand.*
*Rent a flat above a shop,*
*cut your hair and get a job.*
*Smoke some fags and play some pool,*
*pretend you never went to school.*
*But still you never get it right,*
*cos when you're laying in bed at night*
*watching roaches climb the wall*
*if you called your dad he could stop it all...*

If this were a film, this bit would be all in slow-mo and show lots of blurry smiles as the camera panned around the room. Oh, and there would be lots of meaningful looks as well. But back to the music...

*You'll never live like common people,*
*you'll never do what common people do,*
*You'll never fail like common people,*
*and you'll never watch your life*
*slip out of view.*
*and dance and drink and screw,*
*cos there's nothing left to do...*

Then, just as quickly as it had come, it was gone, leaving in its wake an afterglow that hung around in the hollow room for a few minutes. Tony turned the radio off as the door opened. It was an officer.

'You're in good spirits today, but keep the noise down, boys.'

We, the common people, who *knew*, just smiled as the tongues of fire descended (handy when you've forgotten your lighter) and we began speaking in tongues:

'That's so fucking wicked, so fucking cool. Innit?'

# 30 A DIFFERENT ANGEL COMES

*The Fijian whelk (phytostatus pacifium blanca) was close to extinction. The few remaining colonies clung on to life, and certain coral reefs, south of the Fijian mainland. These reefs, like many reefs elsewhere in the Pacific, were slowly dying. It was only a matter of time before the whelks had nothing to feed on and nowhere to live. Their days were numbered. Until one plucky little individual managed to attach itself onto a migrating turtle and stow itself away. It was carried across the ocean to Hawaii, where it then dropped off and found miles of fresh new corals. When the other Fijian whelks heard of this, they followed suit and began hitching rides too. Within a very short time they were off the danger list.*

The atmosphere which the Angel of Death hung over prisonland haunted Adrian, and many others, for a long time afterwards. He half expected to meet it every time he arrived, every morning. He would always prepare himself for the invisible tell tale signs, the shared gloom, the common isolation. However, what met him one particular morning was quite different though equally powerful. Another angel had visited the prison. The aftermath that this one left behind wasn't, fortunately, heavy and dark but was more exciting and buzzy. It produced a mixed bag of contrasting emotions, - joy, fun and hope, yet also anger and fear. The last two were coming from the authorities, the rest from the inmates. Adrian was greeted by a 'maximum security' regime when he stepped inside. Nothing like slamming the door when the horse has bolted. In case you haven't guessed, someone was missing.

When Adrian eventually arrived on the wing, after having been thoroughly searched (just in case he was trying to smuggle him back inside in his pocket) there was a whole welcoming committee waiting to tell him what had happened, as he was probably the last person on earth to remain unenlightened. It was all because of Anton, the Romanian. The 'I'm not a bad guy' guy had done the impossible and escaped. He had put into practice everyone's dreams. He had stuck his two fingers up at them all.

Apparently, he had seen an opportunity and taken it. A 'meat truck' (Reliance prisoner transportation lorry) had come into the campus with some new cons on board and, having been unloaded, was temporarily sitting idle. Some of Feldon Park's boys were going to be taken away as if in exchange. All eyes were on the door to see who was going to be swapped, including those of a group of inmates who were watching as they worked in a nearby workshop. The Angel of Fortune smiled down on the scene and created, for a split second only, a little window of opportunity .

'Here - take it, if you're awake enough,' said the Angel, 'and if you've got the balls.'

As the Feldon Park inmates who were to be ghosted away began to be mustered at the gate, Anton looked God in the eye, and knew that they were in agreement, that he had His blessing.

The angel, as God's messenger, was showing his approval and pointing to the van. Two seconds later, the lorry was reloaded and the transporter doors were locked. With two officers in the driver's cab, it manoeuvred its way to the main gates. Little did they know they were taking an extra passenger.

The angel had also provided Anton with some string from the workshop where he'd been working, which he gripped as he slid behind the tyres. He tied himself onto the under-chassis somehow and hung on.

The wagon was on its way to HMP Swansea, the most westerly prison in Britain, hurtling down the M4 at 70 miles an hour. How Anton maintained his grip was a miracle, but then angels are reputedly capable of producing them. Adrian tried to imagine what it was like to be tied by thin string between big fat wheels and not letting yourself get tired. Imagine letting your head go floppy, inching its way down to the scraping tarmac. It made him flinch. However, the gods were on Anton's side for once, and he stayed attached - and this in fact was the very difficulty that eventually faced him, and not at all what he expected. He couldn't get off. The only time the vehicle travelled slowly enough for him to take his leave was when, once off the motorway, it slowed almost to a standstill, on the roundabout directly outside the main gates of Swansea jail. Taking the opportunity, he loosened himself and dropped from underneath the lorry. This would have been perfect had not there been a bus stop immediately opposite, with three people waiting for the No. 49. They stared in disbelief as an inmate dropped from out of the bottom of the prison van. One of them had a mobile phone and called the police, but Anton didn't hang around to explain himself. He legged it and disappeared.

On the wing, Anton's escape had already reached legendary proportions. Television and tabloid frenzy had kicked in and cranked up. The most fantastic version Adrian heard on that first day was that Anton had managed to disappear by dropping down an open manhole as the lorry came to a halt. Indiana Jones eat your heart out. Adrian said there was no need to exaggerate or elaborate, what Anton had actually done was incredible enough. A large proportion of the joy among the inmates was that the Security officers in the prison were going to get their arses kicked for a change. The tabloids, with their usual ferocity towards the prison, put the paper boot in.

It appears that Anton, being an illegal immigrant, had nothing to lose. He had told several of the inmates that should he be sent back to Romania, he would be killed. A lot of people had it in for him back there, and had called his number. As this is what the Home Office intended to do, why shouldn't he throw his fate to the winds and escape? Having already negotiated many international borders, he was an old hand at hanging under lorries. Getting out of fortress Feldon Park was a piece of piss.

'You had better look under your car when you leave tonight. You might find me hanging on underneath,' said Insect.

'Hardly,' Adrian replied, looking at his expanded waistline. 'My car is very low off the ground. I don't think you'd fit.' Insect looked hurt, so to help him save face Adrian added: 'I think I also might notice your wheelchair trundling along behind me as I speed down the motorway.' Insect smiled.

As far as is known, Anton still is free and is probably bobbing around in the oceans around Fiji trying to land. Trying to sneak his way ashore underneath some bark canoe. Trying to find paradise.

# 31 BLACK ISN'T A COLOUR

*Until recently, all adult males in Fiji lacked one tiny part of a chromosome that caused them all to be colour blind. They could not tell the difference between red and green. They called both colours 'mui', meaning 'life'. However, all other colours were clearly perceived, in fact they had twenty-six words for blue. As Europeans settled and inter-married, their offspring began to see colours differently and the language changed accordingly. They now have twenty-two words for red and green apiece.*

When Adrian began to work on the GCSE course, it amazed him to find that the communion he experienced earlier, seemed to have evaporated overnight. It was as if it never had been. He hadn't wanted to teach these bloody courses. Not like this, something about the way they were structured, how they were set out seemed to separate and divide. They required some to succeed, some to succeed really well and some to definitely fail. This smelt like a set up. Adrian looked at his teaching notes. In most courses on art, the starting point is to study colour theory. *Yawn*! This is generally seen as a precursor to doing anything creative and is usually taught in a way more suited to the physics lab than the art class, and designed to put off anyone who is slightly non-academic or might have a more than vague interest in art. This year's GCSE course was no exception, and Module One demanded the usual collection of colour wheels and charts. The first part was to establish the concept of primary colours and then to pick one and paint a picture in its various shades. He stared into the group of blank faces around his table and knew this was going to be a lot more difficult than it sounded. They had that collective 'don't bother trying' look that sometimes showed itself as an omen of an imminent difficult day. Adrian was going to have to get them actively involved somehow. They seemed to be overfilled with regulation stodge breakfast. He was going to have to wake them up with a bit of audience participation. It was time for the class entertainer to step in. *Good Evening, ladies and gentlemen! Are we going to have a good time tonight? Oh yes, oh yes!*

This actually came out as:

'I want each of you to think of a colour.' Adrian waited a few seconds. 'OK, got one? Now ask yourself: Can I *make* this colour? Can I mix it?'

The 'don't bother trying' warning was confirmed. They were not playing. The 'difficult day' scenario kicked in. Adrian found his eyes locked on Insect, who was almost bursting to say something.

'What the fuck would I want do that for?' asked Insect.

'What's your colour?' Adrian continued, ignoring this red herring.

'Orange, that orange there, in that tube.'

'Well, how could you make it?'

'I don't know. What you getting at? I'm not going to make it. I'll just get it out of the tube.'

'But what if you didn't have the tube. Could you make that colour?'

'I wouldn't need to, I'd just have to go and buy another one.'

'But supposing you couldn't, supposing you were in prison, for instance, and didn't have it. How could you make it?'

'What? We *are* in prison. I don't understand what you're saying. Are you going to take it away or something? Cos I was going to use that.'

'No, I'm not going to take it away. However, you could, if you wanted to, take other colours and blend them together and make orange.'

'Really! What, any colours?'

'No, but there are two you could mix. What do you think those colours would be?'

'How the fuck should I know?'

'Well, let's try it. Here, mix some of this yellow with that red.'

Adrian squirted two healthy dollops of paint onto a palette and gave Insect a brush.

'Bloody Hell! Look at this. It's gone orange.'

*Thank you! Ladies and Gentlemen... (rapturous applause) ...and now for my next trick I will need a complete twat...*

Having established the fact that you can mix paints together to make new colours, they now had to tackle the point that certain colours cannot be made. Rather than ask further questions, Adrian thought it easier just to tell them:

'There are some colours you can't make. They are called Primary Colours because there is only one colour in them. Colours that are made up of two primary colours are called Secondary colours.'

'They're mixed race colours,' said Insect, 'like me.'

'Yeah, but we're not allowed to call them coloureds any more,' said Billy.

'Yeah, but we're talking about *colours*. They *are* coloured, they're not people...'

With this conversation, the men began painting their colour wheels and the concept of primary and secondary should have been established, at least Adrian thought so. They proceeded to the next step, which was to pick a primary colour and paint a picture in it, using different tones. There followed a huge debate about what colour really was. Adrian wasn't sure if the men were ready for this or not. He began to hate this riveting project.

'I think I'll do mine in orange,' said Insect nonchalantly. Adrian glared at him.

'No, orange is not a primary colour.'

'Who says? I think it is a primary colour, and anyway I like orange.'

'But don't you remember, we just made orange out of red and yellow, so it can't be a primary, it must be a secondary.'

'But I don't like any of the other colours.' Insect glowered back at Adrian. 'Well, if you won't let me do my favourite, I think I'll do black instead.'

Adrian was convinced that Insect knew more than he was letting on.

'No, I wouldn't do that. Black is not really considered a colour. It's actually a lack of colour or, more to the point, of light.'

'Of course black's a colour. There's a fucking tube of it over there.'

'I'm black,' said Mofty, 'but I ain't coloured, I'm black.'

'Look, if you want to get a good mark in your exam, then paint the picture in either red, yellow or blue. OK. If you want to fail, paint it in black.'

'Or orange.'

'Or orange.'

'What about white? White's a colour and it's a primary.'

'No, it's not.'

'Yes it is. You can't make white. Go on try it, make white. I bet you bloody can't. Or black for that matter.'

'White is the absence of colour.'

'You said that about black. Are you saying they're the same?'

'I'm black,' said Mofty again, 'I ain't white, for God's sake. Of course they aren't the same.'

Mikey, roused by the gripping conversation, woke up and said: 'I saw this programme on telly once that showed that if you put one of those triangle glass things in light you get all the colours. It's on that Pink Floyd album. It shows that white's got all colours in it, actually.'

'Yeah, that's right. But that's light, not pigment. That's Newton's theory.' Adrian replied already knowing he was setting himself up to be shot down in flames.

'What? If it's just a theory, why are we wasting time on it if it hasn't been proved yet, then?'

'Well, yes. There are several different colour theories. Goethe had another one for instance...'

'But it's still only a theory again. It's not a fact. It's not for real.'

'Well, yeah. I suppose so...'

'So in that case I'll have my own theory about it, and orange is a primary colour. Insect's theory of colour.'

Mr ('who put the lead in pencils?') Smith then presented his own theory about colour, one that involved alien intervention.

'I think colours only arrived on earth about 1940-ish. I think that before that there were no colours. If you look at all photographs, films or television programmes from before 1940 they were all black and white. What's that telling us? It's saying that maybe there were no colours before that date. So my question is where did they come from, and why? And that's why all these old people like Newton only had theories and not the real thing.' QED.

'Hang on! What about all those old paintings? The Moaning Lisa, for instance, they're all coloured in,' said Insect.

'They are now, but when they were originally painted they were done in black and white. They only became coloured in 1940.'

Fortunately, everyone else ignored Smith's tangential, extraterrestrial colour theory, though Adrian would have loved to have seen the examiners trying to mark it. The discussion continued.

'I don't think much of this GCSE. They want me to paint a picture all in one colour. Why? Life's all different colours. It's not just one, it's not how it is. What if I want to paint my jumper here, it's red. How can I paint it blue for instance when it's red?' Insect was not giving up orange that easily.

'Ah, but how do you know it's red?' Adrian was biting the bullet. 'If I was to put in different coloured light bulbs then it wouldn't look red any more. So what colour would it be then?'

'Ah, see! The colours are interchangeable. This only proves that they were once black and white,' said guess who, who by now was being cold-shouldered by everyone in the room.

'So what are you saying? Red doesn't exist? Jesus, are you trying to mess with my mind or what?' Insect was getting more animated than Adrian had seen for a while. Adrian decided they needed to stop talking.

'I think you just need to do it. This isn't going anywhere. Look, take one of these. Which do you prefer. How about red?'

'I hates red,' said Alan.

'Why's that? Why do you hate it?'

'I dunno. I just hates it.'

'It's because it's the colour of death,' said Insect. 'I hates it too.'

'Death? Why death? There must be a reason why you associate it with death. What is it? And if you hate it so much why do you always wear a red jumper?'

An alienated voice rang out from the corner of the room: 'It's because red is really black. That's why it's associated with death. All colours are either black or white...'

'It's the colour of blood. Spilt blood.'

'But not everyone dies splattered in blood. Some people just die in their sleep, peacefully,' Adrian reasoned.

'Yeah, but their eyes go red.'

'Do they? I think a lot of people have their eyes shut.'

'Yeah! But they're red underneath. If you look under the eyelids they're red.' (As one does.)

'And it's the colour of flames and burning alive.'

'Well, if you're frightened of death, then we'll try one of the others.'

'I ain't frightened of death. I ain't frightened of anything. I ain't frightened of death.'

'Me neither,' said Alan, 'I ain't frightened of dying. I'm frightened of living, I am. If I had a button that could end it all, I'd press it now. I ain't frightened of dying.'

'Look, it's almost tea break, let's leave it for now and try it again later. Jeez.'

Where had all the camaraderie gone from yesterday? Was it so cheap it could be thrown away that quickly. Adrian was unsure. He sighed and said to himself aloud, 'I didn't think teaching colours would be so difficult...'

'I heard that,' shouted Mofty. 'I always thought you were racist. You should be ashamed.'

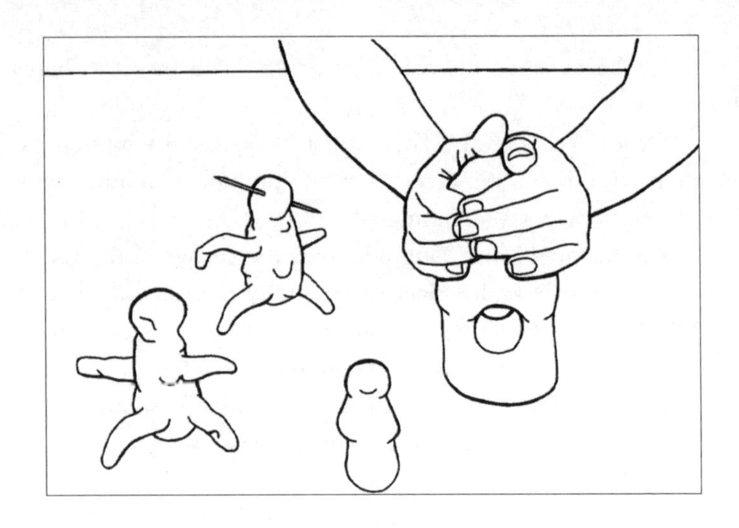

# 32 THERAPY

*When the first missionaries arrived in Fiji, they were pleasantly surprised by the numbers that attended their church without much coercion. There was an almost peculiar enthusiasm for it. Communion held a particular fascination, as did the crucifix that hung above the altar. There was much animated talk as they examined the hosts and the statue. The missionaries were delighted and thought they had discovered the Garden of Eden. The natives told the missionaries that there was very little difference between their existing religion and Christianity, and invited them to return a visit to their church. When the missionaries arrived, they were horrified. They were invited to a cannibalistic ritual, where little pieces of flesh were distributed among the congregation. On the walls of the temple images of their enemies were hung up with nails hammered into them, each pin brought sickness and disease upon them. The missionaries realised that conversion was going to be a lot harder than they initially thought.*

'It's not their fault, but they needs to sort it.' Frosty spoke. He was on one of his mental walkabouts. He was looking Adrian in the face but talking to someone else, someone who lived inside his head. Both Adrian and he were sitting in the Art room, though Frosty seemed to be somewhere else, probably Manchester.

'I tried to help them but it all went wrong. I didn't realise how desperate they were. It started all sweet, like. We spent all our time together. It was the best sex I've ever had. It went on for hours sometimes.'

Adrian was nodding and making affirmative grunts as one does, though he had no idea what Frosty was talking about. Frosty continued.

'Then the lies started, and those sneaky sidelong glances that go with them. I knew there was something wrong. They were always whispering together, which really pisses me off. Then that money went missing, it was the last straw. I certainly didn't know which one of them took it but it had definitely gone.'

Frosty was under stress and needed to go through his story once again. He was re-enacting how he ended up in prison. This story would never go away, and seemed determined to haunt him always. What had gone wrong? Whose fault was it really? Why was he the one in gaol? The questions jumped around in his brain as he tried to cut and smooth the corners off the more jagged memories. Could he make some sense of it all and still keep face? Every time he ran his review, it temporarily removed a little of his guilt and numbed away a little of his pain. And today we were getting the sound as well as the pictures. The mute button had been released and Adrian was hearing Frosty's random sound-bites.

Instinctively, Adrian picked up some newly worked clay and put it in front of him. It was grey and cold.

'We searched the entire house and still couldn't find it. Then when Sandy tried to blame it on my kid, I got really angry and kicked off. She was the one who had the habit, and she was acting so peculiar like. I tried to talk to her but she wouldn't listen and insisted she'd seen Liam with it, which I knew, wasn't true. He'd never stolen anything in his life. I wish I'd never taken them in.

Frosty picked up the clay and began pummelling it against the table. He didn't look at it. His head was engaged elsewhere. He continued talking the whole while, speaking his story into an empty space in front of his frozen eyes.

'I really disliked their new friends that were constantly coming round. It was far more likely that one of them had taken it. And I think I knew which one it was. His name was Will, a big bloke from Rochdale. I accused him when I saw him next and told him to hand it back. He went for me with a bottle. Bastard!'

The clay hit the table with a thump.

'The friends eventually moved out but the cash never turned up and shortly afterwards, she followed, but I did try, I really did.'

'I'm sure you did,' Adrian replied, not really knowing what it was he was condoning. How many times people in prison assume you already know everything, as if psychically, and get almost offended if you don't. Adrian acknowledged what Frosty was saying, while at the same time, he tried to redirect his energies into something more positive. As this jumbled story unravelled, Frosty was becoming increasingly keyed up. His face showed a mixture of both pain and anger as he squeezed and punched all his frustration, all his desperation into the lifeless clay that recorded each outburst with an imprint of his knuckles. The session was interrupted when one of the other students called for assistance.

'Ade, give us a hand, please.'

'I'll be back in a minute. See what you can do with the clay.' Adrian moved across the room but all the while he kept an eye on Frosty, who was muttering to himself as he fumbled with the grey mass. As soon as he could, Adrian returned to him.

'How you getting on with the sculpture?' he enquired. Frosty almost jumped out of his skin as Adrian redirected his attention back to the here and now.

'Oh, hi! It's going fairly well. I've nearly finished.'

Adrian looked down at a group of anthropomorphic shapes lying on the table and made a quizzical expression. Frosty began to explain. He pointed to the smallest one first.

'This one is Liam. He's all smooth and gentle. While this big ugly one is Will. Big, hard Will, at least he thinks he's hard, but see, there's a great big hole there where his heart should be. Big vacuous hole. And these two creatures represent Sandy and her friend. God, how they piss me off.'

He held up two extremely spiky, scrunched-up pieces of clay for Adrian to see. They looked vaguely human. Frosty punched the table in his rage.

'I'll enjoy putting these in the kiln.'

'You'll going to have to be careful that you don't damage these spikes. This one, for instance, looks extremely delicate. I think you may well have to reinforce some of this.'

Adrian passed Frosty some fresh clay which Frosty began adding to the two malformed women.

'She thinks she's so clever, but she isn't, that's why I've given her this tiny head. She thinks she's academic, but God, she's as thick as fucking shit. She can't even change a tyre.'

'Really! But if you hadn't told me that that lump was her head, I would never have known what it was. If you want people to understand what it is you're trying to say, it's got to be more obvious. They've got to be able to recognise it. Let's give it a neck and make it more human looking.'

Frosty automatically stepped back to allow Adrian to get involved.

'No, you have to do it, or else it's no longer your work.'

He began to squeeze around the model's neck with far too much force. The head nearly came off.

'Not like that. Be more careful. You can't get the effects we're after if you are so heavy-handed. Use the tips of fingers.'

He began to gently stroke around the neck and chin. The difference between his rampant emotion and his delicate manual work began to narrow. It became increasingly difficult for him to be angry and aggressive while doing such fine, concentrated finger work.

'That's much better. But if you are going to leave that huge hole in her chest, you need to make it smoother. Maybe also make the arms stronger so they can support the figure. Imagine she's lying down. You need to allow her to be more human.'

Frosty was now talking instead of ranting. His gentle, fine, hand movements were working the sculpture, caressing away the roughness of both the figure and the jagged surfaces inside his head.

'Try moving the piece around. What does it look like lying down?'

Once reclining, the sculpture looked far less threatening, and more vulnerable.

'Don't forget, a good sculpture looks good from whichever angle you view it. What does it look like from the back?'

'It looks like someone resting, like they might be reading a book while on the beach.'

'The small of the back doesn't look right though, does it? It looks more like a man from here.'

He carried on playing plastic surgeon.

Slowly the scrunched-up, spiky blob began to take on a new, more delicate form. Like a phoenix rising from the ashes, something not that dissimilar to a Henry Moore was emerging.

'Why don't we work on the other pieces in the same way. They need to be consistent.'

Frosty took hold of 'Will'.

'This bloke's so conceited. I'll start by making his head a lot bigger but I think I'll make a great hole in it, to show there's nothing inside.'

He began his alterations, and Will was restored to the world of human beings. The large hole in his chest was smoothed, the large hole in his head was smoothed, the large hole in his genitals was smoothed (with difficulty). Meanwhile the rest of the body became more Incredible-Hulk-like by the minute as Frosty gave extra substance to the body. 'Will' was growing in bulk, yet looking less threatening as he did so. Frosty was taking care; he was concentrating and had virtually stopped talking. He was giving his enemy loving attention, caressing him with the tips of his fingers - though Adrian, of course, knew better than to mention any of this. Frosty's face had taken on quite a different expression: one of concern. When 'Will' was complete, Adrian directed Frosty's attention to 'Liam', who he assumed was a child. As in real life, he had been overlooked, he was an after-thought.

'What about him?'

'He's not that much of an angel, you know,' said Frosty, more relaxed now. ' He can be a manipulating little sod.'

'Can't they all,' Adrian agreed.

Frosty began, delicately, to sculpt the shape of the head and to make the child smile.

'He's only a kid, like. It's not his fault he is the way he is.'

The way Frosty was holding this piece was so revealing. He cradled it in the palm of his hand with such a caring gesture.

It reminded Adrian of some delicate man-angel he'd seen in a renaissance painting, holding the baby Jesus.

When he'd finished, he began putting the pieces to one side as if completed.

'You know, there's one piece missing in all this, and that's you. Where do you fit in all this? I want you to try and model a form that shows something of you. Don't try and do everything, just try and capture one aspect of yourself.'

Frosty looked surprised, as if to say 'what's it got to do with me?' He looked at Adrian for a second but then began to model without further comment. He set about it with determination. It was interesting to see that the calm achieved by healing the other three was now being reversed. He started pummelling the clay again. He had gone instantly into reverse. He was undoing what he had so far accomplished. It was quite disturbing to see how much he disliked himself. Adrian decided he needed to give him some direction.

'Hey, let's make your sculpture that of the creator, the artist. This is turning out really well. Artists can play God, you know.'

'I think in my case the Devil would be more appropriate.'

Frosty began to soften with the clay as it absorbed the blows and began to mould himself. A rather small, frail figure, that could hardly stand, began to emerge. It didn't take long. He had given it no care at all. When he put his self-effigy on the table, he had to squash down the feet to get it to stay upright. After a few seconds, it wobbled and collapsed. Unfortunately, this made his head fall off.

'Come on, let's give him a work-out.'

Together they picked him up and began restoring him, adding substance and character to the broken man, until they had something that Frosty recognised as himself and was happy with. To get the head back on securely, they had to attach it further up the skull, so when it eventually stood, its head was slightly raised, as if it were looking to Heaven.

'You know, I don't think I'm that bad a person really,' he said almost absent-mindedly.

'Come! Let's arrange these pieces into a group and take the process a step further. We can create the spaces between them and then fix the figures permanently onto a base. How do you think we should place them?'

He began to move them around as if in a chess game. Will, Sandy, plus her friend, and Liam were arranged in a triangle. Frosty was representing the relationship that lived between them through distance and angle, geometrically .

'I think Will should go closer to Sandy but not near Liam. There's nothing between them at all except Sandy. Then these two should go together but I'll put him over here, more to one side. There! That's about it.'

'Don't forget to put this one in,' Adrian said, pointing to the small, insignificant model of Frosty.

'Don't forget this miscreant?'

But Frosty carefully picked it up and with lots of thought placed it in the middle, between Liam and the others.

'I think that's about right. Though the way he's standing there he seems to be in a trance. He seems to have his head in the clouds, which, thinking about it, isn't far wrong.'

'Yeah. I think it looks good. You've become the lynchpin, standing in the middle of all this. There is one last thing left though that still doesn't work.'

Frosty smiled. Without saying anything, he leaned over and removed a tooth pick he had run through Sandy's head.

Frosty was now almost completely at rest. He smoothed over the blemish left by the pick.

'It really looks excellent now, don't you think? You've made it look just right.'

'I like clay,' he said, standing back and admiring his work. 'It's really strong stuff, you know. It can take all the blows you care to throw at it and still get itself back together again.'

'I suppose so. When hard rocks break they stay broken, don't they?'

Adrian often wondered whether Sandy felt anything when that toothpick was removed from her head... *'Oh, thank God! You know that migraine that I've had for the last three years? It's finally lifting.'*

Voodoo is still practised in Feldon Park as well as Fiji.

# 33 ADE KICKS OFF

*Understanding is born of knowledge, knowledge develops from experience and experience comes from life.*

The *Guinness Book of Records* is full of interesting and useless facts. Insect was reading some of them aloud, interspersed with remarks like 'Fucking Hell!' or 'Jesus!' Nobody was really listening, but the halting monologue created a sort of background ambience that filtered into everyone's consciousness and led them to make their own impossible lists. Adrian was thinking about more realistic and relevant statistics.

Once every three seconds, somewhere in the world a child is born into poverty. Just as every two minutes, someone, somewhere else, is murdered. And similarly, every day, someone in Feldon Park prison 'kicks off'.

Kicking off is the result of a build-up of frustration that eventually has to be released. Every time you attempt to do something and get thwarted (like an A-level) and then don't do anything about it, a little more steam is added to the pressure pot. Eventually, it gets so bad that you can't contain it any more, and then *kapow!* It's all let out at once, in one monumental outburst. All those little niggling problems that never got resolved, all those requests that just got ignored, all those completed forms that 'went missing' - at last they explode, having sat underground fermenting all this while. The volcano gathers force deep in one's guts and once collected, the point of focus is turned to the centre of the head. Here the tension mounts, until there's only one thing left to do... Kick off.

There are many things to get pissed off about in prison, apart from the obvious, and it's down to each individual how he deals with his own personal cocktail of grievances. But one thing is certain, eventually there'll be the need to kick off. It's inevitable. It's just a matter of time. When Adrian first started working at Feldon Park he witnessed Mofty kicking off. It was scary. Mofty asked to go to the library but was told to wait his turn. His request was subsequently forgotten. This resulted in him suddenly punching the door twice, once with each hand for what, at the time, seemed a triviality. He managed to break both his knuckles.

'God! What's up with him? That was so over the top.'

'Wait till it's your turn,' said Jabba. 'Then you'll understand.'

Adrian carried these words around with him, like a kind of predicted threat, for a long time after.

How you kick off is down to who you are. Many of the men vent their anger by trashing their cells, others shout a lot and some, unfortunately, lash out. Then come running the bully boys looking for action: 'Kick off! Let's bend him up...' Strange how so many things in prison reminded Adrian of things that used to happen at his old school.

Adrian, however, when he did eventually kick off, didn't do it in any of the above-mentioned ways. He developed his own personal technique and just moaned incessantly.

* * *

Adrian had once seen a television documentary about gang culture in a South African gaol. The offending inmates made a weapon from a blade melted into a toothbrush. Since then he had often heard mention of such razor/toothbrushes, though he had never actually seen one. This was to Feldon Park's credit, but as a result, Adrian's pencil sharpener often seemed to transform itself into a weapon, depending on who was looking at it. Unfortunately, for drawing tuition, there was no substitute for a pencil sharpener. Adrian had to use them, at least until self-sharpening pencils were invented. (A good question for Mr Smith.) The Art Department, bless 'em, buys in a considerable number of these 'weapons of mass education' every few months. The need for repeated orders is not because so many go missing, or the stockpiling of weapons, but because the quality of the blade is so crap, that in a very short time they start eating the pencils rather than sharpening them. This is so frustrating when all you've got is a few pencils to start with anyway, and they are quickly reduced to nothing, as the sharpener whittles them away, right in front of your eyes. The seeds for Kick Off were long since sown.

One lunch time, Adrian was returning to work with his pet pencil devourer safely in his pocket, when he was stopped by the officer on gate duty, a woman known affectionately as 'the Rottweiler'. She was already straining at the leash, craving blood, and at the height of a searching frenzy. She swooped into action as Adrian approached. He could feel a knot forming just above his left eyebrow.

'Empty your pockets.'

Amidst the elastic bands, eraser, snotty hanky and other assorted pocket rubbish she immediately caught sight of and focussed in on Adrian's offending pet, and informed him that sharpeners were definitely 'not allowed'. Therefore Adrian couldn't take it in - and never should have in the first place. What was he thinking of? Strange, as he'd been issued it by the education department in the first place, and secondly, he'd been keeping one in his pocket for several years up to that moment. Adrian thought he should maybe point this out, but the Rott-weiler just lunged at his throat, as they do, and hung on. It was subsequently confiscated and Adrian was permanently scarred.

When he got to the wing, leaving a trail of psychological blood behind him, Adrian carried on with his drawing lesson. However, it wasn't long before every pencil in his possession was blunt. He thought his little sharpener must be starving. The work in hand, though only about a quarter of the way through, ground to a frustrating halt.

'I'm sorry, guys, I don't have my sharpener this afternoon. It's been arrested. We'll have to do something else. We can't sharpen the pencils any more.'

'*Derrr!*' (This was one of Adrian's favourite words, it expressed so much, so simply. Basically it meant don't be such a dickhead.) 'You can borrow one of ours.'

At which the inmates produced a whole assortment of them. This was the first of many such contradictions that excelled in prisonland and instigated the build-up to kicking off.

Amazing how certain prisoners were apparently deemed safe to possess sharpeners but not Adrian. The psychological puncture marks in his throat began to smart and then fester. He thought he might be coming down with rabies. Those seeds that had been planted were just beginning to germinate.

Another contradiction, and one that Adrian almost took personally, occurred while he was working on the protected block where sex offenders are in the majority.

'You must understand that under no circumstances are you to bring any material on the wing that contains anything that may be considered of a sexual nature...'

Having made his speech (i.e. a sentence without the word fuck in it), the PC05 (important officer person) turned away to do other things. This topic was not open to further discussion. As Adrian didn't immediately get out the officer turned round again. His eyes said it all: 'What - you still here?' Adrian obediently threw away all the explicit porn he was carrying. (Yeah, right.)

What could be interpreted as 'of a sexual nature' varied from day to day and seemed to depend on who was sitting in the office at the time.

Adrian was concerned. Several of his long-term students were now enrolled on the A-level course, and he had resolved that if they were willing to put the effort in, he would do his best to help them at least meet the curriculum requirements. The first module was entitled Portraiture - Exploring the Self, and a long list was given of artists to be studied in depth. It was going to be difficult for them to access this amount of material, so the students, on Adrian's recommendation, all chose Modigliani, whom Adrian, in his innocence, thought pretty non-provocative. As the prison library had no books on Modern Art that did more than briefly refer to this painter, Adrian brought in a fine book of his own on Modigliani for the men to look at. Respecting the rules, he first showed it to the PC05, who looked through it.

'Oh my God! You can't show them this, there's a breast on this page.'

At the bottom of a portrait of a woman was what could only be described as a circle with a dot in the middle of it. Adrian had totally overlooked it as it was so un-sexual, but this was, it appeared, indeed provocative stuff. The book was not to go on the wing. Adrian couldn't bear it: another problem. Rather than hold the students up any more he tore the page out in front of the officer. *Aargh!* His favourite book. The sound of the ripping paper tore his heart. There were already so many restrictions for the students to work against that it seemed unfair to hold them up further because of a circle with a dot in it.

Later he learnt that censorship included all nudity and all children. This entirely wiped out classical art, the Renaissance, the Baroque, Symbolism, Expressionism and a lot of modern art just for starters. What was left was still life and landscapes, Adrian supposed.

When Adrian later found that all prisoners on the wing had access to the tabloid press, all the Sunday papers and even certain 'men's' magazines such as *Maxim,* he was particularly incensed. Such hypocrisy. He supposed it was alright to see nudity in the light of news (though that's a debatable term when applied to such papers), whereas for education...? Adrian was on an internal meltdown programme.

Besides, Adrian wondered, who chose the videos for broadcast on the wing or, more to the point, who gave authority for them to be shown - or did anyone think about it at all? *Essex Boys, Twin Town, The Krays, Trainspotting, Pulp Fiction, Natural Born Killers,* etc. etc... Good character-building stuff, what? Not a patch on a Modigliani breast though.

The final straw came when Adrian introduced calligraphy, another field of art that he supposed was free from any 'sexual allusions'. He selected a poem which he photocopied to give the men to use as a text. It was taken from a book that he'd used extensively in school, written by a professor of education. It was in the section for eight-year-olds and was called *Evening Bloom.* Unfortunately, after all these years, it was only now he realised that he'd totally missed the point, that he'd been teaching suggestive prose that was full of sexual innuendos. It was definitely banned. It went like this:

*Adrian's poem*

*As I wandered half-dreaming*
*Along the lone street*
*A gleam in the hedgerow*
*Appeared me to greet*

*A flower bud swelling*
*Pink petals unfurled*
*glistening with dewdrops*
*Newborn to the world.*

*Open, bright blossom!*
*O beauteous bloom!*
*O heaven-sent wonder!*
*O sweetest perfume!*

*Though your glory soon pales*
*Petals wilt, petals fall*
*Yet red rose hips remain*
*And your beauty recall.*

*Their poem*

*After eight pints of lager*
*Somewhere near Roath Park*
*I spied a red light*
*Heard a voice in the dark*

*Saw a girl, young, pubescent:*
*Her skin soft and pink*
*And she's wet in the loins -*
*Such a babe, don't you think?*

*Throw open your legs -*
*Oh my God! What a sight!*
*And that body - divine!*
*And that smell! Wow!! Alright!*

*Now you've gone on the game*
*So it's off with that dress!*
*Though you've still got your figure*
*You used to weigh less.*

This 'let's make it up as we go along' attitude guaranteed that certain men don't get very far, and showed that education is generally considered something that many people apparently don't deserve. 'Why should they get it free when my wife has to pay for evening classes?' (Yeah, yeah! I met her earlier at college.)

These are the kind of things that would lead Adrian to kick off. The constantly recurring feeling of being on the wrong side of the bars. Of constantly hearing the word 'no'. He was experiencing dinosaur Feldon Park, as a Tyrannosaurus Rex. What was he doing here? Education should definitely not, it seemed, be fun.

Adrian felt something erupt inside his head, and he crushed the paper cup he was drinking from and scalded his leg. It bloody hurt, but now, having kicked off, he felt an overwhelming calm descend upon him.

'God, that feels better!' he said as the boiling tea burnt into his leg. Nothing like a good kick-off to wipe the slate clean again.

# 34 ROWLANDS FINDS GOD, SATAN AND OFFICER BROUGHTON

*Fijian voodoo is a form of shamanism that has ritualistic ceremony at its centre. Many curses and spells involve much chanting, dancing and copious amounts of bodily fluids. Fijians believe these fluids, whether blood, sperm or piss, have within them an extract of the man who produced them. Concoctions made from these carry strong magic.*

Rowlands had always been a pain in the neck, and what's more, he was one of those people in prison that could be quite frightening for no apparent reason. There was something about him that let you know that you shouldn't get too close. We all have our personal space, lines that we don't want others to cross, but Rowlands was always standing on his threshold, sword in hand, waiting for trespassers. He was raw. Even the other inmates gave him a (healthy) wide berth. His criminal record, true or elaborated, was enough to generate respect. His voice let you know if you were approaching 'Out of Bounds'. It had something to do with its tone and volume, and it was wise to listen to this warning and back off. Teaching him was difficult, as communication was always so strained. He was not a great conversationalist and either gave lengthy monologues or sat in silence.

Adrian didn't immediately realise how totally isolated Rowlands was in his restricted box of uncrossable lines. He had hemmed himself in and was unable to move. He lived in a very lonely space twenty-four hours a day. The wing was not a naturally friendly environment. Warmth and friendship were there, but had to be earned and weren't given away freely. Rowlands didn't let anyone close enough to even try, and on top of that he was carrying a lot of unseen, internal baggage. Press the wrong button and a whole blitz of emotions would be launched. The red hot, emotional soup would well up and explode. The loudest eruptions came in the dark of night, when sleep would not come down and he felt particularly low. The red hot soup grumbled deep in his guts, pressing against the wall of his stomach, wanting to spew itself out. It very rarely reached the surface though. Instead it just stayed gagged up and, at most came out as a stifled whimper. Locked in prison, locked in his cell, locked in his own head, Rowlands was desperate for someone to listen to him, to understand, to say, 'There, there - you're OK.' Trouble was, no-one would dare.

Then one long, endless night, when all others slept, something happened, something changed. Rowlands at last found a listening ear that wasn't afraid of him and didn't judge or try to change him either. He first read about this very special friend in a copy of the *Watchtower* that someone had left in the library, and he recognised him almost immediately. It was the same person who lived in his volcanic head and occasionally spoke to him. For the first time he realised that he knew who God was, and what's more, God loved him dearly. The raging fire in his guts which he had mistaken for Hell was nothing other than God's burning love for him. Rowlands was overwhelmed and filled with a warm, happy feeling instead of pain.

When Adrian arrived on the wing, he was immediately aware that something had changed. He soon realised what it was: Rowlands was smiling a lot more than usual. Before he could ask what had happened, the telepathic Star read his mind.

'He's got religion,' he said dismissively. 'It happens occasionally.'

'What?' Adrian asked incredulously, but before he could get an answer, the chosen one was upon him. Interestingly, the other inmates gave him an even wider berth than before, and dispersed before his divine presence. The smile reached Adrian first, followed by the person.

'Hi, Ade! How are you today?'

'Fine. What's happened to you then?'

'You've noticed. That's a good sign.'

'I've noticed that you're smiling a lot and that you're talking to me first thing in the morning. But tell me what's happened? What's brought this about?'

Rowlands gave an even more scary, insipid smile.

'I've found the Lord. Or rather, He has found me. Do you know what I'm talking about? Have you ever heard Him calling to you?'

'Maybe, but I'm not sure we're talking about the same thing,' Adrian said, trying to be as evasive as possible.

'Oh, you would know if He were talking to you. It's unmistakable. He called me last Monday night. I heard my name, turned around and He was standing there. He was wearing white. He just smiled at me and beckoned me over to Him.'

'Could you see him, then?' said Insect, who had crept out of the woodwork with a few others in tow.

'Well, almost. He called me to him and put His arm on my shoulder. I felt this tingling that racked my whole body, and He told me to follow Him.'

'It sounds really dodgy,' said Star with newfound bravery. 'Do you follow anyone who calls you over? It could have been one of the screws or one of the nonces playing a trick.'

'No. When you hear the Lord, you know. It couldn't be anyone else.'

There was a general silence. How could one argue about something that only the enlightened could see.

Inside everyone's head, the same monologue was running simultaneously. 'You can talk to the Lord too, you know. If you like, we can find the Lord together. All you have to do is open up your heart and invite him in.' The men knew what was coming next. They had heard it all before. Rowlands began: 'I can show you if you like...' Immediately, the men, of one accord, turned and began to leave. In the past, no-one would have dared walk out on Rowlands when he was in mid-flow but now, who cared? Rowlands was God's messenger of love, he wouldn't hurt a fly. Yet another barrier had been put up. His wan smile was almost a mockery of the hard man who was there only yesterday. At least he had commanded some sort of respect then. But now that he had surrendered to the Lord and to his own pain, he seemed rather pathetic. Rowlands may have had his new friend inside, but outside he was being shunned by everyone else even more vehemently than before, well nearly everyone.

'Hey Rowlands! If you talk to Jesus, maybe there is something you could do for me. You could ask him to get rid of that Woman in White. She's an absolute pain.'

'Yeah! She'll be coming again soon. I get goose-bumps just thinking about it,' threw in Dexter.

Star nearly choked.

'What you still being bothered by her? I thought she'd long gone!' Star gave a side-ways wink to Adrian, who stared appalled. The biscuit game was either still going on, or Insect and Dexter had really gone over the edge.

'No, she comes as regular as clockwork,' said Insect. 'I've seen her loads of times.'

Rowlands closed his eyes, momentarily, and then agreed to do it. He felt the Lord's power in his veins. His St Paul-like conversion phenomenon wasn't that dissimilar, when viewed from the outside, to the workings of fate that Adrian experienced at the beginning of this story. It was just that in this case, whatever had taken Rowlands over wasn't going to let go again that readily. It had decided to stay there permanently. Rowlands had been squatted. He had opened himself up and this higher (or maybe not) being, had stepped in and was now in control. It was not going to give up the reins that quickly. Rowlands was left a displaced, anaemic soul, wandering aimlessly around like a shadow. Christ died for our sins in the same way that Rowlands died for his, and was now reborn as Mr Smiley. Adrian sat and talked with him more out of pity than anything else. However, his good intentions were immediately worn away. He felt undermined. He had been perceived as 'convertible'. His feelings of duty were rapidly replaced by ones of irritation. One can't imagine anyone ever being brought to spiritual experience by Bible bashing. It usually has the opposite effect.

When the third week of the month approached and the moon began ominously to wax, Rowlands began to talk to the Lord audibly, which was a bit confusing, especially when it was in the presence of the other cons. It had something to do with the Woman in White, who was about to make her presence felt, once again. Rowlands saw her as the antithesis of God and took it upon himself to rid the wing of this demon once and for all.

'Lord, protect my soul from the evil one that stalks the night, neither shall I walk through the valley of death, without your rod and staff to comfort me.'

'How can a rod, or a staff, for that matter, comfort anybody? A rod's not soft or cuddly, unless it's a fluffy rod, maybe. Yeah, it's a fluffy rod,' laughed Star.

'Yeah, and the staff are probably office staff. Please comfort me, officer,' joined in Frosty.

'It's no joke, you know. The Woman in White will be coming tonight, and I'm going to lay her soul to rest.'

'You're in the wrong cell for that. You should be in the one next door.'

Totally ignoring the jibes, Rowlands continued his telephone-like conversation. One wasn't sure who he was talking to - or listening to - any more.

'I needs to exorcise her tonight. Tells me, Lord, how to do it.'

'I saw this film once, I think it was called *Bride of Satan...*' said Insect (Rowlands crossed himself three times) '...and when it came to sending this vampire-thingy-woman back to Hell, they threw a magic concoction of yellow liquid at her that sort of burnt her away, like acid. It was a good film.' Inseot was concentrating, trying hard to remember. 'I think it was piss.'

Not totally convinced that the Lord would miraculously intervene and get rid of the wandering, un-dead biscuit thief, Rowlands decided to cover his options and put an empty bucket from the store cupboard by the toilet. It was just possible that God was in a strop today and 'couldn't be asked'. He requested that some of the men 'miss' when they took a leak. He needed more than he could supply himself with his prostrate problem. As the evening rolled by, the Holy Grail began to take on an ominous, yellow glow. Soon the cauldron of piss was almost brimming over.

'It's funny, when you see that much piss, it looks orange, not yellow. I wonder why. I suppose you just don't normally see that much in one place, do you?'

Frosty raised his head and narrowed his eyes. He knew about these things.

'It's because most of us normal people piss normal yellow pee, but it seems to me that one of us here, someone you probably least suspect, is pissing blood.' Frosty's voice lowered and he looked furtively from side to side. All of a sudden he grabbed hold of Insect's arm. 'One of us is a ...vampire!' He shouted this out so loud that Insect nearly fell of his chair. They all laughed. At least someone had grasped basic colour theory, thought Adrian.

When it was time to return to their cells for the night, Rowlands emptied his pop bottle and filled it with 'the holy orange juice'. He sat on his bed and prepared himself. He poured the piss into a plastic cup and took out his bible and began to read. All around him were boxes of Jaffa Cakes to act as bait. As the night progressed, the waiting became increasingly difficult to bear. What if it didn't work? Up until now, the ghost had always ignored him, being only interested in the Jaffa cakes which he had placed on his bedside table. His reading became louder and louder as his nerves became increasingly shot. The suspense was killing.

'For I am the power and the gory, I mean glory...' he shouted. His voice echoed in a shrill, high-pitched whine along the landings, throughout the wing. The noise was above regulation levels and began irritating people who were trying to sleep. The officer on duty went to investigate. Officer Broughton stood outside the cell door and listened. There always had to be one on every shift. Rowlands was almost hysterical. The tired officer put his key to the door and suddenly opened it. He was immediately met full in the face by a golden shower of unpleasantly-smelling liquid, and a screaming Rowlands.

'Die, die, Fiend of Hell... oh shit!' (Or more exactly, piss.)

For weeks later, whenever Officer Broughton was about to appear, a rancid, ammoniac smell would fill everyone's nostrils, like a premonition. Subsequent comments were not appreciated.

'Feeling pissed off, butt? Or should I say pissed on?'

'Anyway, where you went wrong,' said Insect, 'was when you said *Die, die, die,* you should have said *Live, live, live,* like, cos she's dead already, and so you've probably made it worse, now.'

# 35 STAR'S SINGULAR MEMORY GROOVE THING

*In Fiji all art, apart from the incarcerated portrait of Captain Cook, is symbolic. Nothing is represented as it appears to the eye, everything is reduced to pattern and symbol. To make images of the real world was to freeze it in matter. It was bad magic. If everything was drawn 'naturally' then the real world would cease to exist. It always pains a Fijian to see representational artwork.*

It was nearly six months since Star had won his Koestler award and he was gaining confidence daily. 'Come on!' he'd say, 'Let's get started, we haven't got all day.' But although he had done loads of work, he needed to move forward, he constantly needed challenges to sink his teeth into, or else he would lose his momentum. To show just how confident he had become he would even volunteer to show his work to visitors when they came on the wing. ('Do you like this one? You can have it for fifteen quid.') It was while he was in one of these upbeat moods that Adrian popped him a question.

'Why don't you take an exam? You should pass easy enough.'

This was more than a casual enquiry. The Education Department were serious about GCSEs and wanted to get as many people through as possible. Star had already loads of OCN (Open College Network) certificates, which had helped to build up his confidence, but all these were set and marked internally and were geared so that the student shouldn't fail. Adrian made sure they couldn't bite off more than they could chew. Although Adrian was still reeling at what had happened to Daniel with his A-level, he felt this was the right time for Star.. Adrian was still going to have to be super-vigilant, but surely, this was only a GCSE. The sort of thing his previous, private school pupils went home with sack loads of. Surely he could get Star through just one. Adrian felt, for the first time, that this was the right time, the right level and the right pupil. Star was ready for it. An externally marked paper, a GCSE, would be quite independent and give Star the chance to stand, in the outside world, on his own two feet, rather than under Adrian's. His release date was to be just after the results came out, so that tied in nicely.

After a little pause for thought, he said: 'Yeah, I think I could too.' Then, as an afterthought, 'I had better pass, though!' Already blame culture was kicking in, and guess who was being targeted.

When the paper arrived, they opened the envelope together. The exam was made up of modules. Star immediately looked worried.

'What the fuck's a module?' The language of exams, like the language of tax returns, grant forms or passport applications, was not designed to be easily understood - unlike those nice easy ones for credit facilities. The modules had titles such as:

1) Packaging, safely contained.
2) A sense of place.
3) Memories and reflections, and
4) A study of time.

Star looked briefly from one to the other and then chose to paint a landscape. Adrian pointed out that this wasn't an option.

'Why not? All these ones are crap.'

'You have to choose one of these,' Adrian insisted.

'This ain't going to work, I don't like this shit.'

Making choices was not one of Star's strongest points. Eventually he decided upon 'memories and reflections'. Unfortunately, he did not have much of either, and to prove it, within three minutes had forgotten what he had chosen and reverted to landscapes again. Some things, apparently, were easier to remember.

They sat down together and began to work out a strategy.

'First, let's make a list of everything to do with memories and reflections. What do you think of when you hear the word memories?'

'I think of the time when I was fourteen and I went with my mum and dad to North Wales. We went camping in Snowdonia.'

'That's a memory, but it's not really what we're looking for. We want to think about memories generally.'

'Why not? It's a place I remember. In fact, it's about the only good time I do remember.'

As with all private conversations, Adrian had forgotten that their discussion was being listened to by the entire wing.

'That's just because you don't remember things - you're headshot. It's not because you had such a hard life as you make out, it's because you're a smackhead and don't have a working brain.' Adrian could always rely on Frosty to enrich things. Star and Frosty loved to have a go at each other, as did Frosty with everyone else on the wing whenever the opportunity presented itself. It was probably the most comfortable way for them to relate to each other and remain friends.

Adrian tried to put the conversation back on track. 'That's a nice picture, a camping holiday, but let's try and be less specific. What about memories generally? For example, what about photographs? You could say they're frozen little snippets of the past. Let's write that down. What do you think?'

'But we didn't have a camera then. I don't think we had any photos. But I did have a postcard of Snowdon, but fuck knows where that is.'

'Good, but I didn't literally mean photos of that one holiday, I meant photographs generally. We could explore that direction, if you like. Or postcards, that's another possibility.'

'Well, I kept it as a souvenir, but I think I've lost it.'

'Souvenirs! That's another one. Write it down.'

'No, the post card was the souvenir. We couldn't afford real souvenirs. They're the same thing. Why are we writing these things down, anyway?'

'We're writing a list of things that we associate with memories without being specific. I don't mean that particular post card or souvenir but the whole subject of souvenirs. You could do a project that explores the world of souvenirs. Look, I have a sketch book for you. I want you to start with one of these things we've worked out today and I want you to explore its possibilities. OK?'

Adrian left, still not convinced that Star had understood what it was all about.

When he returned the following week, Adrian was pleased to see that the sketch book had been considerably used, though unfortunately, on inspection, nothing in it was relevant.

Star hadn't grasped the plot. This was going to be an uphill struggle. Inside were four carefully painted watercolours of tents at the foot of Snowdon. Star was trapped in his singular memory. He was also subconsciously determined to do a landscape, no matter what.

'They're very good, but you don't need finished pieces yet. It's far too early for these. We're supposed to be developing ideas. We have to look at all the possibilities and finally choose which direction to go in for our final piece. It would have been better had you drawn lots of different souvenirs for instance.'

Star was looking blankly at Adrian. The fires of pain and blame began to smoulder in his eyes simultaneously. Adrian thought he'd better sidestep.

'They're very good though. We just have to do things in the right order. The finished pictures come at the end of all your research, not the beginning. What they want is to see is how you work things out, how you come to your conclusions. Think of all the things you can take home from a holiday as a souvenir. Use this as your starting point.'

'Well, there's that postcard.'

Star's brain was tightly locked in its memory groove and was not going to be dislodged easily.

'What about sticks of rock, or ashtrays, or key rings - you know, things in a gift shop. Start by making lists, then draw them and try out different things. Just play about with your ideas.'

From his expression he didn't look as if he was in the mood for playing with anything.

He began to draw a pink line that was supposed to represent a stick of rock. He was not looking happy. His whole attitude was of one dejected and fed up.

'This looks crap. Why have I got to do this when my other paintings are already good. This stick of rock has got nothing to do with my holiday on Snowdon. The only rocks there were grey ones.' Then came the inevitable.

'I wish I'd never let you talk me into this piece of shit.'

'You haven't even started yet. You've got to explore the possibilities. Look at how rock is made. Look at its history, look at where it's sold. Look, I've brought you some pictures from magazines. And this is an article about the history of candy sticks...' Star squinted his eyes and stared at the article. A new age of understanding dawned - or did it?

'Oh, I get it,' he said, taking away his book. 'You want me to do something with the stick of rock, like. Not just leave it on the page on its own.'

An inevitable and predictable comment issued from Frosty's mouth about sticks of rock and bottoms that I won't bother writing down. Anyway, this sounded more promising, but Adrian knew better than to count his souvenir chickens before they hatched.

'I could paint this stick of rock sticking out of my rucksack, in front of the tent,' said Star hopefully.

'Yeah! Or you could put a huge stick of fucking rock there, just by the tent, sticking out of the ground, like a tree trunk,' said a more enthusiastic Frosty. Adrian hadn't realised until now how much this was to be a group exercise in many respects.

'It's a start,' he said dejectedly, 'but you must do more research. You need to fill this book up with all sorts of ideas. And don't forget to write on each sketch why it does, or doesn't, work as a picture.'

It was the end of the session. Adrian was not sure whether Star was up to this. As he left the wing, he could hear Frosty giving more animated advice.

'You could paint it as a totem pole, or a tent pole, and have some babe pole-dancing on it, getting it all sticky, like, and then you have to paint this guy licking it all off...'

The automatic door shut behind Adrian and spared him the more graphic details.

When Adrian returned the following week, there was a buzz in the air. It seemed to fill the whole wing. The entire place was full of celebration. Something amazing had happened. There had been a nativity and the angels were in full party mood.

'You should see Star's painting, it's brilliant,' said Frosty as he sauntered over. He swung his arms like a gorilla. He did this when he felt confident. Adrian knew that the entire wing had seen the picture, had judged it and were of one accord. It was brilliant. They had all probably given their two pence worth. Adrian hoped it wasn't the singular memory thing at work again. He went over with Frosty to where Star was sitting grinning at him. Adrian almost couldn't bear the suspense and pressed his anti-blame force-field button. What he was presented with made him gasp. Star had re-painted his holiday in Snowdonia, but unlike the previous pieces, the whole mountain was made of sticky, pink, tooth-decaying rock. It resembled a sugar addict's 'Giant's Causeway' with candy floss sheep stuck to it. Key Rings littered the scree slopes and at the foot of it all were two tents made of postcards - of Snowdonia, of course. It was amazing. Salvador Dali would have been proud.

'Well done! Now this is more like it.'

'Well, I thought I might as well put all my drug experiences to good use, like.'

'Why not, why not indeed.'

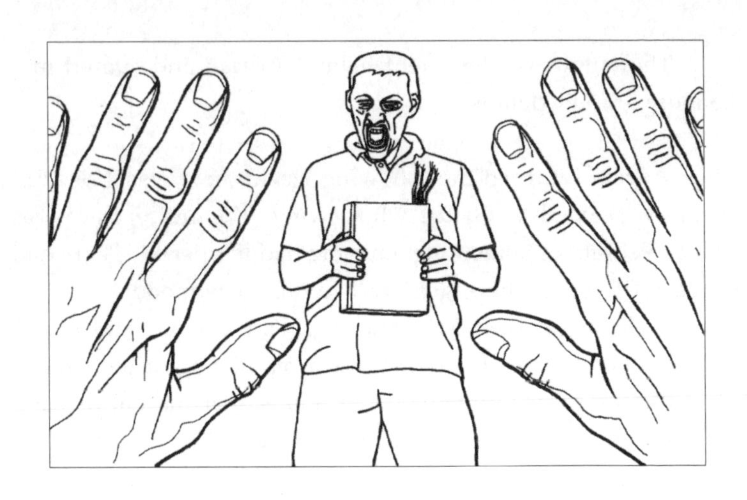

# 36 FROSTY TAKES THINGS INTO HIS OWN HANDS

*A good illusionist can bend reality if his audience is with him. He can then lead them anywhere he chooses. A bad illusionist sets himself apart, walks alone and only fools himself.*

Like Star, Frosty was not good at making decisions. When presented with two options he would always choose the worst, or most inappropriate, and then struggle with the results, making loads of other bad decisions on the way. No wonder he had ended up in the position he was in now. The only certainty he had was that things would go wrong. Could it all have been different if somebody, early on, had taken the time to teach him the basics of decision making? Instead, here he was, aged twenty-four and still always picking the short straw. Making those wrong choices.

When Adrian asked him once what he thought was the worst mistake he'd ever made, he replied that it was being born in the first place. 'I should have stayed in my dad's testicles.'

Interestingly, there was no mention of his mother at all.

Having most of the Angela Neustatter list of seven requirements for a life inside, Frosty differed from the others in that he still thought he could win. Frosty was headshot. His brain was the aftermath of a rave, littered with spent chemicals that occasionally flared up to illuminate the damage. The landscape of his distorted, contorted head contained numerous dark shadows between the sulphurous lights of ecstatic pleasure. Being Frosty was not something to be envied. There were numerous scary things living in those dark, shadowy regions of his brain, and every now and then they would whisper to him. They weren't giving him good advice, they spoke *chemical.*

The shades had been very vocal lately and they were making Frosty more paranoid than usual. They led him to new heights of confusion on one particular afternoon.

'I don't like the way that screw is staring at me. Look! He's doing it again.'

'He's not. He's just checking that the cell doors behind you are all shut. There's no need for you to worry, he's not looking at you.'

'But he's been doing it all morning. I think they've told him to watch me. They're trying to catch me out. They're preparing to get me.'

'I don't think so. I think you've got a touch of the paranoias, and anyway, what are they trying to catch you out for?'

'I don't know. Anything they can, I suppose. They're just on my fucking case, all the time. They won't leave me alone.'

Beads of perspiration were forming on his forehead, and his voice became noticeably shriller.

'Do you need to go to your cell? If you're not feeling yourself...?'

'He's always feeling himself - that's why he's going nuts. He's wanked himself senseless,' said Star, never missing a chance to crank up the irritation factor. 'He's been whittling on all morning. Give us a break, for Christ's sake.' Frosty's anger boiled over. He shouted far louder than he needed to: *'Shut the fuck up Star ! Nobody asked you!'*

It echoed across the wing. The officer on duty got up to see what was happening.

'Oh God! Look! That screw is coming over. See, I told you he was watching me.'

'Is everything alright over here? You look agitated Frosty - anything going on?'

'Yeah! Fine! It's just that I know why you're watching me all the time, so you may as well give up. Cos I won't do anything with you watching me.'

'What the fuck are you talking about? *You've* been staring at *me* all morning. Every time I look up your big ugly eyes are right in my face. Just lay off, will you?' The screw turned and walked away. Frosty stared at the end of his cigarette and then stuck it back in his mouth, sucking in a load of new agitation with each draw.

'I'm going to write out a complaint to the Governor.'

'About what?'

'About how that screw is staring at me all the time. It's actually a form of intimidation.'

'Maybe, but he's not staring at you. Why don't you save yourself a load of hassle?'

'Maybe he just fancies you. Maybe he's eyeing you up for later. Maybe he'll be bringing his mates up to your cell later on,' said Star, stirring with an even longer ladle.

'Shut the fuck up, will you.' This time he spoke a little more quietly.

From the dark corners of Frosty's brain, a fallen angel had stepped out into the phosphorescent light. The sudden glare weighed down on him like a ton of real bricks. His form was stooped and bent. The sudden shine of the chemicals blinded him. He covered his eyes and cast them downwards. The Fallen

Angel spoke, filling the chemical wasteland with his luciferic advice.

*'Don't let them get to you now. The bright gleaming of your chemical self will strengthen and grow and eventually overcome all adversity and your brightness will shine forth and you will fill the world with the light of your own genius.'*

The angel whispered to Frosty as he rolled up more burn and sucked in more death. The fallen angel then began to dance in the swirling nicotine...

*'Yes, bide your time. Your moment will come.'*

'You're right. I don't need to do anything... yet.'

Frosty answered the angel aloud which made Adrian look up. 'Sorry - I didn't catch that...'

'Hey Frosty, just chill out,' said Star. 'You don't want to Syd Barrett, do you?' Even Star realised there was something wrong. There was concern in his voice, his tone was gentler and soft with no trace of the earlier venom.

Frosty loved early Pink Floyd. He regularly saturated his brain with 'Astronome Domine', letting the spacey rhythms temporarily banish the demons. It was his aural medication, and stirred up a nice warm feeling somewhere in his chest. This glow swirled around his heart chakra, sending soothing balm to his barren brainscape. The demons returned to the shadows and all was calm again. Until next time.

Adrian would regularly Floyd out with Frosty and they'd stroll down the 'Arnold Lanes' of 'The Piper at the Gates of Dawn' and worship the ancient 'Relics'. Adrian later thought he should have paid more attention to 'Careful With That Axe Eugene'.

Before Adrian left, he went to speak with Officer Grey and explain how agitated Frosty had been today.

'I know. I noticed. I'll keep an eye on him, though he gets so rat-arsed if I just look at him.'

The demons, were subdued temporarily, whilst on the wing, but re-emerged when Frosty was back in his cell. They started calling to him almost as soon as they heard his door slam shut. As soon as he entered his familiar ten by twelve, the voices started again. They were now certain , he was on his own, so took on an increased urgency.

'Frosty, oh Frosty, are you going to let them squash you? Are you just going to fucking take it?'

The demons knew exactly which words to choose. They knew Frosty well. They'd been there a long time. Their memories stretched back into ancient history. They remembered the divorce, the foster care, the home, the nightly abuse. Chemicals, bring on more chemicals. Get that adrenaline pumping. Frosty was festering. That fucking screw, he embodied everything. He was the beatings, the cruelty, the cock-sucking abuse. He was all the accumulated hurt personified. He had stared at him and he knew.

Officer Grey was semi-dozing in front of the flickering blue screen when the stomach-churning buzzer woke him out of his daze. Cell 79. Frosty. 'What's that bastard want now? Fucking fruitcake.' His companion, Officer Harrington, reluctantly got up and together they trudged their way on to the threes and lifted the flap of Frosty's door. They saw Frosty lying face down on the floor. Thinking the worst, they rushed in and picked him up and asked if he was alright. Frosty was playing dead. He let himself go limp lettuce.

'We need to get some help,' said Officer Grey.

The demons in Frosty's head began shouting louder than they ever had before.

*'Now, now, now.'*

Frosty couldn't think, his head was full of them. He had no choice. He grabbed hold of a box by his bed and shouted: 'This is a bomb. If either of you move it's going off.' He held it against his chest. There were two wires sticking out of it. The demons rolled Frosty's eye-balls wildly around and shouted 'Bravo! Well done! You've shown them a thing or two.' But the officers were not cowering in their boots.

'Don't be a dickhead! That's a shoebox, not a bomb!' Officer Grey stared Frosty in the face with steely determination, but the demented grin plastered across Frosty's face told him not to take anything for granted. Frosty allowed Officer Harrington to go. His grievance was with Grey. Grey knew too much. The demons were ecstatic. They had reclaimed some of their ground.

'This isn't going to get you any sympathy, you know. This is just going to make things a lot more difficult for you.'

Frosty stood firm and refused to move. He remained in his cell with Officer Grey for all of twenty minutes. Just long enough for the 'mufties' to arrive. Frosty was quite relieved when they burst in, as the vigil with Officer Grey was becoming slightly ridiculous, and even he was thinking maybe he shouldn't always listen to the shadows.

The 'mufties' bent him up. They didn't even bother to look in the shoe box. They took Frosty to seg and then, two days later, shipped him out to Albany on the Isle of Wight. The demons didn't say a word when Frosty was apprehended. The dark shadows remained noticeably silent and didn't begin again until he was on his own, sitting in the meat wagon, and then it started all over again.

When Adrian next came in, Frosty had disappeared: he had been ghosted away. Adrian noticed a shoe box sitting in the rubbish bin. Mikey casually walked over to where Adrian was sitting and handed him an envelope.

'It's from the Space Cadet.'

Inside was a letter written in Frosty's recognisable scrawl. It read:

*Dear Ade,*

*The lone dark one has had to take his leave. Will they never leave me in peace with their constant interference? I did listen, and I wish you well. Do write to me, if they let you. Tell Star he never really got to me. It's all a cosmic mind-fuck game that the brain police need to play to justify their existence. You can keep my picture.*

*Your friend,*
*Frosty*

Adrian had forgotten he'd still got Frosty's painting from the last lesson. It was a portrait of a tortured-looking man with rolling eyes. It still sits on the wall of Adrian's study.

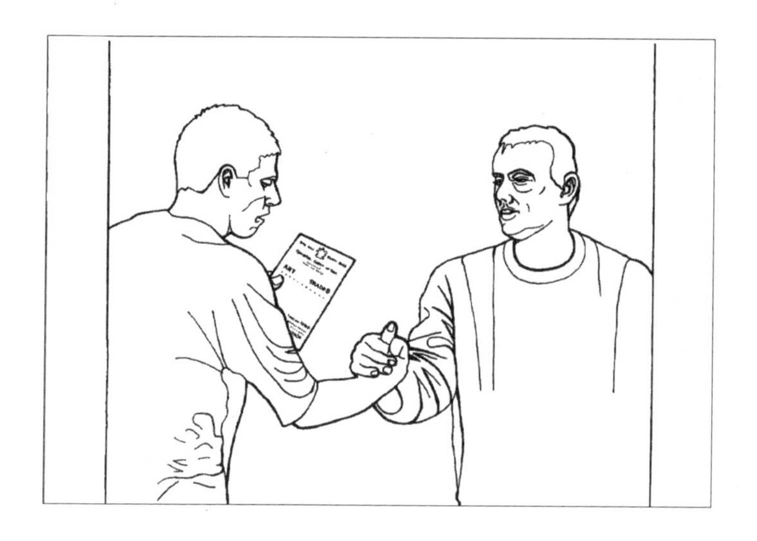

# 37 AT LAST, FIJI

*The chief of Kaduva, one day whilst out walking, saw a young man tottering on the cliff edge as if about to jump. He rapidly approached him and asked him what he was doing. The young man, through tear-filled eyes replied that he wanted to leave, he was going to swim to America. 'Oh!' said the chief,' Good luck, I hear it's a long way though.'*

The day of the GCSE results was getting ever closer. A week later Star would be walking out of here, hopefully armed with his certificate, the passport to his own Fiji. Now that Star was standing on the threshold, Adrian increasingly wondered whether, once out, he could actually cope with paradise, with Fiji. The more Adrian put himself in Star's shoes the more scary the outside world looked from close quarters. The land of opportunity seemed to be inhabited by many flesh–eating monsters, waiting to chew him up and spit him back behind the walls.. Could Fiji actually exist for Star and all those like him?

Was he ever going to be able to find it? Was anybody capable of finding it? The questions were becoming so huge The magic GCSE was looking increasingly feeble. After all, it was only one little GCSE. Was Adrian being overoptimistic or unrealistic, was he putting too much emphasis on this single qualification? The reality of one exam, in the career world, didn't amount to much, especially when accompanied by a history of prison sentences and drug abuse. The gap between the inside and the out appeared as an ever-widening chasm that needed more than one little piece of paper to fly Star across it. Having taught in Feldon Park for what at times felt like a sentence in itself, Adrian was inevitably going to lose some sense of realism. It's so easy to create a make-believe world to help you cope.

The previous weekend, Adrian had been invited to dinner with some old teaching friends of his. It wasn't long before the subject of exams had come up. Not only had several of them pupils taking exams but several had children of their own who were sitting their GCSEs this year. They were discussing their children's chances. It was all about how many A's and A stars they needed. There was no question of getting low grades, let alone failing. Was that possible nowadays? A-levels and degrees were all expected to follow on, with high grades too boot. Adrian was getting to see some of Star's demons close up. He left the party feeling quite despondent.

It only took Adrian to drive to work the next day and pass through those pearly gates, to cross the gaping chasm, to appreciate the GCSE from the other side, from a different perspective. Of course it was a lot, lot more than a little piece of paper, it was so much more. This one exam carried with it everyone's hopes, everyone's aspirations. In fact everything that was ever good about all the inmates throughout the gaol, throughout the world, was pinned on this one exam of Star's. This was *so* important. Yesterdays doubts melted away as Adrian went onto the wing.

Who knows how many times Star had been let down before? But the funny thing was that he seemed remarkably laid back about the future. He was slouched over a cup of coffee. The prospect of his release, let alone of getting his certificate, didn't, outwardly, seem to have any effect on him. It was as if he didn't believe anything was going to happen.

'It's so exciting! I can hardly bear it,' said Adrian, trying to work up some enthusiasm in him.

'I'm not so sure. It's not that brilliant, and I don't think I'm going to pass anyway.' The first monster; self-doubt, raised its head.

'You can never be a hundred per cent sure, but I think you're in with a really good chance. The work you did for your final piece was excellent, and don't forget, when you're out of here, you have a meeting at the Further Education College with the Art Advisor. I've phoned her again, like you asked, and explained to her your situation; she'll advise you what to do next. Don't worry, she's safe.'

'I'm not so sure,' he said a second time. He was beginning to worry Adrian.

'Oh, come on, don't fret. She'll help you get on a course in college. You've got to trust her.' Then it slipped out so naturally: 'Do you want me to come with you?' Adrian said this knowing he was probably going well over the line of duty, but so what, this was important. Star thought for a moment.

'No thanks, I want to go on my own. They'll think I'm pretty flaky if I turn up with you towing along. I will go, it's just I'm not so sure.'

'You've said you're not so sure three times now. The one thing you can be sure about is that you've got nothing to lose and everything to gain by going. She'll only look at your work and help you decide the best way forward.'

Adrian realised afterwards that going along with Star would probably not have been a good idea anyway. It would have taken away any choice in the matter, the choice, maybe, not to go at all. It was, after all, Star's choice.

They had arranged for this meeting to happen sometime after his release. All he had to do was to phone and make an appointment to see her. This had been set up several weeks ago, when it was still far enough away for it to be unreal. Adrian felt that Star probably thought that nothing would come of it anyway; just empty prison talk, all he had to do was just make the motions. 'Yeah, yeah...' The gravity of the proposal was only just dawning on Adrian. Looking through Star's eyes, Adrian could begin to see the monsters emerging. He had to get past them. It would have been easier if they really were flesh and blood with tangible reality. But these monsters went everywhere with him. They were inside his head. They were part of himself. He had to live with them and their consequences. They set a monumental challenge for Star, who had been incarcerated for most of his life in a place where you are told when to eat, when to sleep, when to fart. He had to do something now on his own. He had to take the initiative. This had nothing to do with the standard of his work; this was all about confidence, or the lack of it.. All he had to do, and it was a big 'all', was make an appointment and go and see her.

'If I don't get this certificate then I'm not going.'

'You will get it, I'm sure you will,' Adrian said, trying to sound confident, but the negativity was becoming contagious and he was beginning to think he needed a plan B.

'I'm not so sure...' Star began to say again, then pulled himself up. 'Sorry...'

The last thing Adrian wanted to do was to set Star a challenge that he couldn't achieve. Having got so far in building him up it would be such a shame to see him fall at the end of it all, on his own, on the out. Adrian took him aside.

'You know, it's no big deal if you don't go, but it's a fantastic opportunity if you do. You could start an A level, which means you'll be at college only a few hours a week; so the rest of the time is yours, and you'll be able to use their facilities and get tuition, and...'

Star interrupted him.

'It's not that. I'm scared. I've been thinking about it all week. They're not going to want an ex-con like me.'

'Rubbish! Don't think like that.' But years of being told that you've got no value takes its toll. Star was seeing himself through tabloid eyes. A second monster, low self-esteem, raised its head.

'You'll be doing them a favour. Do you know they actually get paid money to take on people who have been disadvantaged and need extra help. The college makes money in grants to develop their facilities. They will *want* you to start.'

'Are you sure?' Then, on a different tack: 'I wish I didn't have these tatts. They're a real giveaway.'

Fiji was beckoning; Adrian could almost hear the waves gently lapping on the white sand in the slop-slopping of the cleaner's mop as he sloshed his path along the landings, and the tropical winds hissing through the palm trees in the frying of the chips in the wing kitchen. Adrian offered Star a coconut.

'Go on, Star, boy - give it a go. Like I said, if there's anything I can do to help, just ask.'

'Yeah, thanks, but let's just take one day at a time for now, right? I'll do my best, but...'

Each new day brought with it an increased sense of anxiety. Star was enacting, internally, every possible permutation of what could happen. Yet, the biggest, scariest thing of all was the very thing he couldn't imagine; it was the unknown. A huge, black, gaping hole opened up in Star's mind whenever he thought of what lay on the other side of those prison gates. He described it to Adrian one day. It was being like a picture Adrian had once shown him of 'This fucking great mouth thing full of zombies and the like...': The Mouth of Hell by Hieronymous Bosch.

Insect was particularly unhelpful, and seemed to take delight in cutting off any sense of hope that reached out to Star from the Jaws of Freedom or Hell, whichever it was. Whenever Star talked about maybe making a go of it, maybe doing something new, Insect would drag him back to the wing with a short sharp tug on the prison leash.

'You'll be back on the smack in a couple of days, if you last even that long. Don't kid yourself. Am I right or am I right? Don't worry, if you're quick enough we'll keep your cell free for you.'

'Why are you so unkind to Star?' asked Adrian, taking Insect aside, 'Don't you want him to succeed? Don't you want to see him start a new life?'

'Of course I do. I just don't want to see his hopes raised and then dashed again. He's learnt to live with failure and he can cope with being let down. But you're taking all that away. Don't you realise how you're setting him up?'

Adrian looked across the wing at Star, standing by the door, waiting for an officer to let him out. At that moment, he saw someone who had no self-will left. He needed permission to do anything. He appeared more bent and crumpled than Adrian could ever remember seeing him before. At that moment, for him to make that phone call, on his own, seemed even more monumental than before. Adrian left thinking maybe Insect was right and this GCSE was causing Star to stretch himself, maybe, beyond his limits. Where was the aftercare? Did it exist? Adrian went home thinking maybe he'd got it all wrong and had made things worse. Deflated and confused by what he thought should have been a wonderful day, Adrian left the prison.

The next time he came in was the day of the results. Adrian had hardly slept the night before. He felt like the worried parent of a wayward child. The envelope would have been delivered that morning and would be waiting on the office desk. Adrian could hardly bear it.

He rushed in that morning half-expecting HMP Feldon Park to trip him up at every opportunity, but the guardians were sweeping over his head, blinding all the uniformed ones with their angel-dust. He got inside the prison in record time. As he swung open the office door he came face to face with the Envelope. He felt his fingers fumbling as he tried to open it without tearing it. The address on the envelope was to the Education Department, so he had no reservations about reading it first. The certificate was upside down but Adrian could already make out Star's name and could see that next to it was that magic letter.

'B! It's a B! He's passed! Fantastic!' Adrian could hear himself (and the chorus of heaven) shouting.

Adrian wanted to go and tell him immediately. First, though, to add to the suspense and share the grandeur of the moment, he resealed the certificate back into a fresh envelope and wrote Star's name on it so he could enjoy opening it for himself. He then almost ran to the wing. When he got there, there was a delay in letting the men out from their cells. It felt like the Greater Being of Feldon Park had sensed something of import was about to happen and was being deliberately difficult. Eventually, the doors were opened and a very pale, baggy-eyed Star appeared. He obviously hadn't slept all night either. His eyes immediately fixed on the envelope in Adrian's hand, and he walked towards him like a ship homing in on an invisible navigation signal. When he arrived in port he didn't say anything, just took the envelope and opened it with as much dignity as he could muster. He froze and stared at the paper. Eventually he spoke.

'What's this mean?' he asked, irritated. 'What's this B mean?'

'It means you've got it. It stands for bloody brilliant, that's what. It means you've passed big time.' A huge cheer went echoing through the wing, informing all of Star's success. It was as if the very building itself was celebrating. Adrian couldn't have told you, at that time, who was the happiest, Star or he himself. Both of them were ecstatic.

Things quietened down eventually and the following days returned Star to worry mode. A new fear kicked in, raising its head as if it had been hiding behind the certificate all the time and was now exposed. It was something which Star had faced many times before: the going outside. This time though, both of them hoped it would be different because of the GCSE Art certificate, and hopefully the added confidence that came with it.

The exam result had taken a while to sink in, but once it had, everyone on the wing was given the opportunity to partake of Star's incredible wisdom. A detailed account of how such a glowing result was achieved, along with several useful tips to remember, were shared by Professor Star, should anyone consider embarking on a similar course. In this incarcerated world where the ropes were known, Star was able to hold his head up and be someone. Someone of Importance. But the Jaws of Hell awaited and nothing could delay their appetite any longer. Star was on the menu.

By the end of the final day Star was standing tall, and looked more prepared to face the world than the figure Adrian had seen earlier. Star saw Adrian pondering him and came over.

'Well, this is it,' he said, shaking his hand. 'I'll be out before you're in next week.'

'Yep! The rest of your life awaits. Don't forget what I said!'

'Which bit...? Only joking. Thanks. I mean it, I couldn't have done this without you. You believed in me...'

Adrian felt a lump forming in his throat and wanted to hug Star, but he saw all the others watching, so he shook his hand warmly for about ten minutes instead.

'I really do believe in you Star, and I certainly couldn't have done this without you. I don't think you realise how much you've taught me.'

Star looked puzzled.

'Well, let me put it like this: I hope I never see you again.' There was laughter all round.

'Me too. But if I do meet you on the street I'll buy you a drink, and I'll invite you to my first exhibition preview when I'm a famous artist.'

'Yeah! Good luck, butt. Enjoy Fiji.'

'You what? Where's that?'

'Wherever you like, Star, wherever you like.'

# EPILOGUE

I'd been working as an HMP art teacher for nearly three years when I began to write *Bang-up For Men.* Its origins lie rooted in many evenings of story-telling, when I was encouraged by many listeners (and glasses of wine) to take up the pen. For most of us life is a complicated puzzle, which is sometimes so baffling that it's hard to get a clear overview on anything at all, but to people in prison, the world is neatly packaged into two halves: 'inside' and the 'out'. Being a prison teacher, I cross this divide regularly, and can bring out stories firsthand, making my tales real and, therefore, all the more interesting. There are very few people that I've met who do not want to hear them. Most have a voyeuristic fascination for what goes on behind locked cell doors (and for the criminal world generally), hence the many TV shows on the subject which entertain and feed the masses, where 'good', i.e. the audience, is reassured and 'bad', the criminals, get their just desserts. The trouble is, life, as we said earlier, is a little more complicated than that. Television panders more to ratings than realism, packing in a stream of non-stop criminal action that's investigated, fought and finally overcome. Events inside prison are no less dramatic, as I hope this book delivers, but television's neat packages of crime and the law cannot bring a true experience of the long hours of 'bang-up' needed to put the dramas into context. 'Bang-up' is being locked inside a small cell with only yourself - or possibly worse, someone else - to talk to. Living in such an uneventful, introspective environment often leads to things being exaggerated or instigated just to relieve the tedium. None of which fits neatly into a thirty-minute tv slot. It's like trying to compress a whole football match into ten seconds of highlights. It's not the same. Maybe if a 'Big Brother' reality TV show was created, it would come close to the truth. A webcam hidden in a cell - now there's a thought. I once overheard some officers discussing the latest episode of *Bad Girls.* (Get a life, boys!) They were enthralled by it because, I suppose, it was pure fantasy, pure escapism that didn't match their everyday world. The real thing is far more complicated and far more human.

I realise that all the staff I work with are full of anecdotes and tales similar to mine, but after working inside for a while, they dry up as, I suppose, the novelty wears off. To avoid the same thing happening to me, I began putting things down on paper whenever I could, recording events as accurately as possible, as near to the time as possible. On the surface, many of the stories are funny and make people laugh, albeit nervously, but I sincerely hope I have also managed to portray some of the darker, more sinister aspects of prison life, and that serious issues are also recognised.

All my characters, on both sides of the fence, are based on very real people, though their names, and those of places, have been changed. This is to protect their identities and my arse, both of which could be put on the line. Any remaining similarities are coincidental and no offence is intended. Honest! What I haven't changed is the dialogue, with all its wonderful profanities. Prison talk doesn't sound the same sanitised: 'Go away, you're confusing my train of logic' doesn't ring quite the same as 'Fuck off, you're doing my head in.' If it offended, I apologise. (The other reason I left them all in is to do with word count: if I took them all out the book would only be half the length it now is.)

HMP Feldon Park is fictitious, there is no such place. But, having said that, it could be any or all of the prisons in Britain. Inmates move about, they are put wherever there is a space. While every effort is made to keep prisoners in their home region, to enable visits etc., the ever-increasing number of people behind bars often doesn't allow for it, making each prison less regional and more cosmopolitan in its intake.

* * *

I dedicate this book to all the boys I've ever had the pleasure of teaching on the various blocks. You have truly amazed me and often made me laugh (you've also frequently made me cry - seriously). You've listened to me, ignored me, and shocked me. You've taught me things about myself and taken me to all kinds of new levels of frustration and anger as well as human understanding. But the most important thing of all is you've allowed me into your world and given me your trust, for without that, none of this would have happened. Billy Bates (an inmate of consequence) told me about an interview he'd just had, with someone from the psychology department, and how he'd made up *all* the answers, for fun (as one does). I naturally asked if that was true of all the things he'd ever told me too, to which he replied: 'Of course not, dickhead! You're safe.'

I dismiss claims that this may still have also been play-acting, on the grounds that he called me a dickhead which, on reflection, was probably true at the time - after all, it was a stupid question. The whole statement was thus validated, knowing that Billy could only either lie or tell the complete truth.

*Adrian Rudesind*
*Somewhere near Fiji, 2005*

# AFTERWORD

One of the most damaging things we do, as a society, is to dehumanise the people we send to prison. It no doubt makes it easier for those of us outside to stamp around on the moral high ground, condemning offenders as the bottom of the pile, people who only get what they deserve. And one of the most valuable things that a few souls strive to do from different perspectives - sometimes campaigners, sometimes those working with prisoners, sometimes befrienders and occasionally politicians - is to humanise those we lock up. And among those who do this most effectively are writers. Ken Smith with *Inside Time* springs immediately to mind as does Roger Graef with his books and films on young people in the criminal justice system. And now we have Adrian Rudesind adding/ bringing enlightenment, humour and some important understandings with his novel *Bang Up For Men.* Rudesind teaches art to men in prison, and although his book is fiction it is based on characters he has known and for whom he has had varying degrees of affection and antipathy at different times, but always interest and awareness of them as people with histories, lives inside and too often circumstances which many of us would find hard to handle. What Rudesind lets us see is that people in prison are not simply the sum of their crime but people whose act of crime has merited taking them out of society. And he helps us understand that prison is not just the punishment of having liberty taken, but a place where your whole life can seem to fall apart, where emotions run high, the enforced *camaraderie* among prisoners can be very difficult and where the frustrations of being parted from loved ones can drive prisoners into despair and craziness. Through work in the art room, where it is clearly possible to be less formal, more accessible, more one-of-them than in other areas of prison, Rudesind lets us into the way he wins popularity and respect. This is a valuable new addition to the canon of writing about prison life.

Angela Neustatter
Editor, Author and Journalist